HIG
BLI

"Jones is a surgeon throughout the novel, extracting the kernels of relationships, the black holes in his characters' characters and giving even the smallest cameo roles unforgettable, essential quirks (reminiscent of Hitchcock). . . . You really do not know, until the bitter end, whether Jennifer Follett will go home or not. You do not really know, in fact, whether you should leave your house again or not." —*Los Angeles Times Book Review*

"AN INTRIGUINGLY EXECUTED THRILLER . . . carefully constructed prose." —*The Virginia-Pilot*

"Nail-bitingly suspenseful police procedural . . . [A] muscular, Elmore Leonard-esque crime tale of a terrifying abduction . . . relentless, lean-and-mean page-turner plotting and a grimly satisfying ending." —*Kirkus Reviews*

"IF YOU READ NOVELS FOR THE SHEER BEAUTY CREATED FROM A TALENTED WRITER'S MIND'S EYE, THIS IS A MUST. Jones leads us adroitly with his artful prose through the Folletts questioning their parental ineptness, misplaced priorities and desire to take the law into their would-be-vigilante hands as a police investigation plods on." —*Pocono Record*

"AN EDGE-OF-THE-SEAT KIND OF THRILLER—difficult to put down even for a moment because throughout the mystery seems ready to be solved on the next page. Jones develops his characters superbly, then forces readers to accompany them into claustrophobic situations . . . a finely tuned story that takes your breath away." —*Naples Daily News*

Please turn the page for more extraordinary acclaim. . . .

PRAISE FOR MATTHEW F. JONES'S
ACCLAIMED NOVEL,
A SINGLE SHOT

"A BACKWOODS DRAMA THAT IS PART *CRIME AND PUNISHMENT*, PART *DELIVERANCE*, AND ALL WHITE-KNUCKLED SUSPENSE. [*A SINGLE SHOT*] is dripping with the ripe smells of sweat, fear, and death. Like a slug of moonshine, it may not go down easy—but it packs a helluva punch."
—*People*

"A TERRIFIC NOVEL . . . unnervingly vivid . . . [Moon's] anguish and confusion are so precisely drawn, physically, spiritually, emotionally, that his crisis evokes every palm-sweating, heart-stopping, seemingly undo-able mistake you've ever made."
—*Los Angeles Times Book Review*

"ROCK-RIBBED AND POTENT . . . Jones has concocted a literary thriller of sorts, for the requisite mayhem and intrigue are present. But it is a satisfyingly dour and deterministic novel, the doom stacking scene by scene toward a startling, macabre and inevitable result." —*The Washington Post Book World*

"HARROWING. . . . A POWERFUL BLEND OF LOVE AND VIOLENCE, OF THE GROTESQUE AND THE TENDER." —*The New York Times*

"THE ULTIMATE NOIR NIGHTMARE . . . JONES CONVEYS THE CLAUSTROPHOBIC, DEAD-END LIFESTYLE OF THE RURAL POOR WITH A FRIGHTENING INCISIVENESS." —*San Francisco Sunday Examiner & Chronicle*

BLIND PURSUIT

Also by Matthew F. Jones

The Cooter Farm (1991)
The Elements of Hitting (1994)
A Single Shot (1996)

BLIND PURSUIT

Matthew F. Jones

Delta
Trade Paperbacks

A Delta Book
Published by
Dell Publishing
a division of
Bantam Doubleday Dell Publishing Group, Inc.
1540 Broadway
New York, New York 10036

The trademark Delta® is registered in the U.S. Patent and Trademark Office
and in other countries.

ISBN: 0-385-31999-1

Reprinted by arrrangement with Farrar, Straus and Giroux

Manufactured in the United States of America
Published simultaneously in Canada

July 1998

10 9 8 7 6 5 4 3 2 1

BVG

To my best buddy in the whole wide world,
Reuben Isiah Jones, forever and ever

BLIND PURSUIT

TUESDAY

6:25 A.M. His first whiff of the still-dark morning through his bedroom window informed Darren Cay it wasn't a school day, though he didn't share the insight with his parents. Instead, over breakfast, he told them he would ride his bike the six miles to school, as he often did, rather than take the bus.

Ten minutes later, after veering into heavy woods, he followed a narrow path a hundred yards to an upturned stump, and dismounted. He hid his bike in the stump's enshrouding brush, and from beneath it pulled the Sportsman rod and reel he'd secretly bought with money he'd earned selling his catch in town. Carrying the fiberglass pole in one hand and a bag lunch his mother had packed for him to eat at school in the other, he hiked east through the virgin forest.

The air was already heavily warm. A lazy breeze barely moved the white pine branches, tinged red by the recently risen sun. Above Darren, a pair of Cooper's hawks idly circled, and though the needle-floor barely whispered beneath his light footfalls, a solitary, perching crow cawed to warn of his presence. Darren ate one of the apples his mother had packed for him, the Mars bar, then half a sandwich. He stopped to drink from a stream before urinating on its far bank. Twenty minutes more of walking revealed to him through the thinning branches ahead a single-lane artery of the county highway, beyond which, after a half-mile jag through deciduous forest heavily posted against trespassers, lay Follett's pond, with its private stock of lake trout and smallmouth bass.

Darren crouched down in the thick piney brush at the edge of the unpainted pavement, across the road from and a hundred yards right of an asphalt driveway winding two hundred or so feet up to the Follett house, obscured to travelers but for a big bay window in the building's front harshly reflecting the sun. At the drive's bottom, on a metal bench beneath a willow tree, sat the small, blond-headed Follett girl, who rode the same school bus as Darren and whose first name he couldn't remember. Atop her folded legs she held a book bag. Next to her lay a paper lunch sack. So not to be seen by her, Darren decided to wait to cross the sparsely traveled road until after the bus picked her up at, he calculated, any moment.

For three or four minutes no traffic at all appeared. Then, from the direction of town, an approaching car prompted Darren to duck down. When he looked up again, a large black sedan sat beyond the end of the long, snaking drive, around twenty yards past the Follett girl. It slowly backed up and stopped short of the drive, still several feet from the girl. The front passenger door swung open.

The little girl—she was wearing a bright yellow dress—stood up, hesitantly stepped toward the car, then halted. The sedan edged back a few more feet. The girl glanced up at the house. A moment later she ran back to the bench, picked up her lunch sack, slung the book bag over her shoulder, trotted the rest of the way to the idling car, and climbed into the front seat. The door shut. The sedan slowly moved off, away from town. Darren watched it until it disappeared. He got to his feet, glanced both ways down the empty road, sprinted across it, and entered the woods on the far side.

11:45 A.M. The unimpeded midday sun illuminated the playground of the Criley Elementary School, where approximately two hundred children, ages six to eight, in grades one and two, occupied themselves. Many of the children were involved in a tag game called snake, in which the tagged became part of the pursuing line of kids, and the last escapee, the winner. Others used the slides, swings, monkey bars. Some dug in a large sandpit. A few of the more timid clustered around the handful of teachers supervising them. A student in the latter group, Susan Myercamp, a small, wire-thin girl, complained to her teacher, Lisa Clymer, "Jennifer Follett stole my *Stuart Little* book!"

"What a terrible thing to say, Susan. You shouldn't accuse people of doing bad things unless you're sure that they have."

"Well, she did!"

"Why do you think that she did?"

"Yesterday I let her read it, then last night I couldn't find it, so my mother called her house, and her mother said it was in Jennifer's book bag."

"I'm sure she picked it up by mistake. Didn't her mother say Jennifer would return it to you?"

"Today. She promised!"

"Jennifer is absent today, Susan. You know that."

"That's what I mean. It's why she's absent—because she stole my book and doesn't want to give it back!"

"You're trying my patience, Susan. Jennifer has plenty of her own books. Why would she steal one of yours?"

"I don't know. But you ought to call her mother up and find out why she's not here!"

Abruptly turning her back to the child, Lisa Clymer hissed, "Not another word, Susan. Go play. Now!"

The weather felt more like July than mid-April. Across the blue sky, a V of honking geese headed north. The fragrant spring air suggested new beginnings. Lisa Clymer decided that that afternoon she would try on her last year's bathing suit to see how much weight she would need to lose before summer.

12:45 P.M.   A late-model Ford LTD coming down Shipman Hollow Road was forced to stop before a string of two dozen yearling heifers crossing from Ned and Hattie Bolan's barn to the pasture opposite it. The animals were five minutes traversing. His face mostly obscured by dark glasses and the windshield's descended sun visor, the LTD's sole occupant sat behind the wheel listening to the symphony music escaping through his slightly open window into the warm, pollen-rich, manure-pungent air.

Ned Bolan stood twenty-five feet from the Ford, by an iron gate, watching the last cow pass through it. He waved on the vehicle, which he hadn't noticed driving by on its way to the hollow's top. The car moved slowly past the gate. A hand came off the wheel and acknowledged Ned. Ned tipped his hat. Behind the visor, the driver, a businessman type, looked to Ned to be middle-aged. He was wearing a dress shirt but no tie. A briefcase and what looked like a tripod sat on the backseat. Ned guessed the man was a realtor who'd been taking photographs of the unoccupied land above his.

Road dust had dulled the Ford's shiny black color. Before the vehicle had disappeared around the first curve, Ned had turned away from it to close the gate.

3:45 P.M.   From the iron bench, next to a stroller containing Edmund Follett, Jr., Hannah Dray watched the still-warm afternoon sun descending toward the tops of the pine forest across the arterial. Earlier she had seen two deer bound across the road and disappear into the trees. Now she heard a pair of concealed mourning doves cooing in there.

Odd, thought Hannah, a lifelong urbanite until moving to the exurbs not quite four months before, how people adapt to their surroundings and even acquire new interests. Like bird-watching. Not the kind where old folks in knickers and funny hats crouched for hours in camouflaged blinds to spot some rare species. To Hannah, the intrigue lay not in the birds' rarity but in their mirroring—if you studied them long enough—of common human behavior. Except for the most obvious, such as blue jays and cardinals, she couldn't identify them, but was fascinated watching at the feeder outside the Folletts' kitchen window the many varieties bicker, cajole, attack, and manipulate one another.

A quarter mile down the road to Hannah's left, its overhead lights flashing red, a school bus came to a slow stop. Hannah stood up, walked to the road's shoulder, and watched two kids disembark from the bus and quickly vanish up the long driveway leading to the Borden house. The bus's caution lights went off. It started moving again. Shortly after, its horn honking and the heads of several waving, screaming children protruding from its open windows, the bus roared past Hannah and Edmund Jr., not even slowing down.

Hannah frantically gestured with both arms at the departing vehicle, but it was too far by her for those on board to notice, or else they took her hand-flapping as a response to their greeting. She watched until, in a half mile or so, before what she knew was the Ziebarts' drive, its rear stop lights came on. A fluttery, anxious feeling filled Hannah's stomach. She turned away and, wheeling Edmund Jr., started back up the drive to telephone the school.

5:15 P.M. In the conference room of a third-floor office suite in a brownstone on Albany's North Pearl Street, Edmund Follett was presenting to a dozen investors his revised blueprint for a minimall when the intercom buzzed. Angry at being disturbed against his express directions, Edmund at first tried to ignore the sound. He interpreted his audience's mood thus far as reserved optimism, an improvement from six weeks earlier, when most had complained that his original design was too "artsy-fartsy" and "monetarily fat" for the mall's targeted patrons.

The intercom buzzed again.

Smiling, Edmund shrugged apologetically. "Excuse me just one moment, ladies and gentlemen."

He walked over to the wall phone and picked it up. "What is it, Marcia?"

"I'm sorry to bother you, Mr. Follett, but there's a Detective Levy on the line who insists on talking to you. He says it can't wait."

"I don't know any . . . Detective for what agency?"

"The Dane City/County Police Department."

Edmund felt something turn over in his stomach. "What's he . . . ?"

"He won't say."

"All right. I'll take it in my office."

He hung up the phone and turned back to the room. "I'm sorry, folks." He shrugged again. "This shouldn't take me more than a minute. While I'm gone, why don't you"—he jokingly raised his hands as if to ward off their imaginary blows—"think about what you want to inquire or complain about."

Polite laughter.

Thirty seconds later, Edmund, licking his lips, which suddenly felt dry, pressed the lit line on his office phone. "Hello?"

"Mr. Follett?"

"Yes."

"Edmund Follett who lives in Dane?"

"Correct."

"I'm Detective Frank Levy of—"

"My secretary told me."

A brief silence followed during which Edmund was conscious of his own breathing.

"Your daughter, Jennifer, attends the Criley Elementary School here in town, Mr. Follett, is that correct?"

"The second grade. Yes." Edmund swallowed hard once, then again, but failed to remove the impediment in his throat. "Is there a problem, Detective?"

"Probably not, Mr. Follett. The reason I'm calling is your daughter, she didn't show up in school today, and we're wondering if—"

"Didn't what? I don't under . . . What do you mean didn't show up?"

"Her teacher says she wasn't there."

Edmund wiped a drop of perspiration from his brow. "Have you called Hannah Dray—the children's nanny—she must have—Jennifer must have come down with something and Hannah decided to keep her—"

"Ms. Dray's who alerted us, Mr. Follett."

"Alerted you. I see—alerted you, to what?"

"Jennifer didn't come home on the bus this afternoon, so Ms. Dray called the school . . ."

"Some other parent probably—maybe Jennifer visited someone's house, after . . . That's all—a friend's house."

"What they're saying—the school, Mr. Follett—they're telling us she never arrived. Jennifer."

"Not at all?"

"Right. There seem to be some inconsistencies—"

"What does Hannah say?"

"That she sent Jennifer to school this morning."

Edmund wiped harder at his brow. "Well—I don't—have you spoken to Caro—my wife?"

"We thought you might do that, sir."

"Yes. Of course. I'm confused, Detec—you've caught me— caught me off guard . . ."

"You'll be home soon, Mr. Follett? Back in Dane?"

"We'll—yes—I'm in a meet—I'll just pick up Caro . . . You know, an hour and a half—something like—around then . . ."

"Hopefully, she'll have shown up by then, Mr. Follett. She may have just wandered off into the woods. We'll get some volunteers searching in there now."

"Yes. That must—look—we own a pond. I hope . . . ! Jesus!"

"We'll cover the pond. We'll have them look in—around the pond. All right?"

"Okay, good—well."

"We'll talk more when you arrive, Mr. Follett."

"Okay. Yes."

Edmund pushed the phone's reset button, then called his wife.

6:25 P.M. Across from Bob Waite, at the Waite kitchen table, sat Frank Levy and his partner, Mike Abbott, all three men drinking coffee. Pursuant to a prior agreement between the two policemen, Levy led the interview of Waite, a chalk-complexioned, rail-thin, forty-five-year-old with a seven-year-old conviction for check forgery, who'd been driving a school bus, part time, for three years.

"It's happened before, that she hasn't been there at the bottom of the drive, I mean, when you show up?"

"Not often, but, yeah, once in a while. The first coupla times I stopped and honked the horn and the maid or whoever finally came out—you know the house is way up the top the hill there—and she walked halfway down the drive and waved me on, and so, after that—those first few times, if the kid—"

"Jennifer."

"—if she wasn't there, I'd stop for a minute, just to see if she was on her way down, and if she wasn't, I'd take off—I'm on a schedule, you know."

"And that's what you did this morning? Stopped for a minute, then left without blowing your horn or anything?"

"Right, because like I said, the girl—Jennifer—you know, would always be there if she was coming. Christ, I feel awful about this." The room smelled like the chili Frances Waite had burned for dinner and the smoke from her husband's unfiltered Camel cigarettes, which he smoked nonstop, lighting one from the other. "So what do you think—she just wandered off or what?"

Levy disregarded the question. "Why?" he asked Bob Waite.

"Why what?"

"Why do you feel awful about it?"

"Why do I feel awful about it? Why do you think! Jesus, the kid's missing and she rides my bus . . . I'm a parent myself. If a thing like that . . ."

"So what you're saying is you feel awful because she—because a little girl is missing—and not because you maybe feel partially responsible for it?"

"Why would I feel responsible, for Christ sake? I did what I always do. I followed the normal procedure for that house. The kid wasn't there! If anybody ought to feel responsible—why wasn't the maid watching out the window or something?"

"Is that what she normally did?"

"How would I know?"

"I'm just wondering why you said that."

"Only that the kid is eight years old, is all."

"That's not a well-traveled stretch of road, is it?"

"No. It's an artery to Hillside—you know, a handful of rich families living up in the hills."

"How many cars you pass on the artery this morning?"

"I don't know. Half a dozen, maybe less, most of them headed north, toward the interstate."

"Do you remember any specific ones?"

"No. Jesus. Who remembers cars they pass?"

"Let's talk about your normal procedure—it's different, is it, for different houses? Different kids?"

"Sure, like I say, some of 'em—like the Brown kid—you gotta honk the horn and wait 'bout every other morning—which I'm not required to do and really shouldn't do because it slows up my route, like it did this morning—but I know the kid's got it rough at home, his father being dead and his mother being off to work every morning an hour before he has to leave—so I do it, I honk the horn and wait, and in three, four minutes, he doesn't show, then I leave."

"How much later than usual were you this morning?"

"Five, maybe ten minutes."

"And that was all on account of the Brown kid?"

"Mostly."

"Mostly?"

"I got a late start from the garage because halfway there I spilled coffee on my pants and had to come home and change." He flashed what Levy assessed as a nervous smile. Levy finished his coffee. "You can ask my wife."

Ignoring him, Frank Levy placed his empty cup on the table. "How long, exactly, would you say you sat at the bottom of the Folletts' drive before leaving?"

"Around a minute."

"More or less than a minute?"

"I don't know."

"The reason I ask is a couple older kids on the bus said you were there maybe ten, fifteen seconds is all—twenty, tops."

"I don't know, seems like longer—but, like I say, with her, if she's coming, she's there, otherwise—"

"Who else is familiar with the details of your route? Who have you discussed it with?"

"Who have I discussed . . . ?"

"Any particular sleazeballs, Bob, of the sort you've been known, from time to time, to associate with, who maybe were particularly interested in knowing about the daily habits of kids—like Jennifer Follett—living on the Hillside arterial?"

"Hey, wait a minute!"

"I'm sure you wouldn't have initiated such a conversation, but maybe somebody else asked you about it and you, innocently enough, responded in a way—"

"I don't discuss the kids on my route with anybody!" Waite abruptly pushed himself away from the table, causing his chair to screech loudly against the linoleum. "I got one rap, for Christ sake, a seven-year-old misdemeanor—maybe I ought to call myself a lawyer before I answer any—"

"Now, hold on there, Bob." Levy shrugged his thick, muscular shoulders. "Nobody's accusing you of anything." Inwardly castigating himself for pushing the interview too far, he ran a hand back through his unruly hair, which wouldn't stay where he'd combed it. "That's the first thing.

Nobody even remotely suspects you were in any way—intentionally, that is—involved in whatever this might be. Understand?"

Waite, scowling, tilted his chair back onto two legs.

"We aren't even sure if a crime has been committed. Like you say, she might have just walked off, but the thing is, she's eight years old, and whatever happened, well . . ." Levy shook his head.

Mike Abbott sighed and put his cup down. "One thing for certain, Bob," he said, "time is our enemy here, so if—and honest to goodness, Bob, we're not concerned with how you might have been innocently duped into saying something you might not normally have"—he emphasized the words "innocently" and "duped"—"you can recall an individual who might have been particularly interested in the details of your route, it would both help the investigation and make it easier on you because the way it is now, Bob, people in the community—especially those on the school board—are bound to question why, given the age of the girl and the length of that drive, you just drive away after a few seconds with no blast on the horn or anything."

Falling forward in his chair, Bob Waite said, "I followed normal procedure." He grabbed his cigarettes from the table, pulled one out, held it up to the one still burning in his mouth, and lit it. "And nobody, not even my wife, do I discuss the particulars of my route with." Blowing twin lines of smoke out his nose, he crushed the remains of the first cigarette into his coffee cup. "That's the God's honest truth. I wish I could help."

Levy slowly hefted himself up from the table. He was a thick man, of average height, thirty-nine, but with pale, kindly

15

eyes that looked older. "All right, Bob," he said, nodding politely to the bus driver. "If you think of something later, though, don't wait for us to call, right?"

"Absolutely. Look, I really do feel awful about this."

"We all do, Bob, especially the little girl's parents." Levy nodded at Mike Abbott. The lither, younger man stepped sprightly away from the wall and, ahead of his partner, grabbed the handle of the front door, then, slowly turning back toward the kitchen, said, "Boss new Ram 2500 out front, Bob. Four-wheel drive, cruise—yours?"

Waite nodded, exhaling smoke toward the policeman.

"Hummanah, hummanah, Bob."

"The monthly nut's a bear."

"I'll bet." Abbott whistled. "Twenty grand if it's a penny. Well, you only live once, right, Bob?"

Waite scowled.

Abbott opened the door and the two policemen left.

7:40 P.M. In the growing dusk through the woods along both sides of the Hillside arterial, flashlights sporadically turned on, helping their owners, mostly off-duty members of the Dane police and fire departments, comb the pines to the west and the deciduous trees to the east of the road.

One man found a small denim coat that an eight-year-old might wear, but it was mildewy and wet and obviously had been there awhile. The shot carcass of a tagged golden retriever was discovered in a dry creek bed. A bundle of pornographic magazines, probably some kid's stash, was unearthed from a hollowed-out stump. Wendy Best, a small, wiry-strong firefighter, was lowered, wearing a miner's lamp, on a rope into the limestone caves half a mile northeast of Follett's pond. Twenty minutes later, she reemerged holding a knapsack that had been dropped or left in the hole, but it contained only an aged peanut-butter-and-jelly sandwich and a small amount of marijuana.

Found in a clearing on the hillside above the caves were a soiled blanket, several empty beer cans, half a dozen used condoms, and a blue-and-white barrette in which blond hair strands were lodged. The items, though thought to have been left by partying teenagers, were nonetheless transported to the state police barracks for analysis.

At eight-fifteen, the volunteers—mostly parents—met and decided, in lieu of halting the search for the night, to keep looking for two more hours, when, if Jennifer Follett hadn't been found, they would reconvene.

8:40 P.M.   In the center of a sunken living room exhibiting paintings of obscure, mid-level Impressionists and outdated weapons, Edmund and Caroline Follett sat side by side on a white leather couch, facing Detectives Levy and Abbott.

". . . just it's difficult to fathom," repeated Edmund, still wearing over his athletic frame the cotton trousers and sports shirt he'd arrived from Albany in, "that someone didn't—I mean a little girl doesn't simp—someone had to have seen something."

Family heirlooms from Caroline's side, the artwork portrayed motionless yet living objects: dangling fruit, praying men, posed models. The weapons, including a garrote allegedly used by a conquistador ancestor of Edmund's, belonged to him.

"I'm sure," said Levy, from a backless divan, "when word gets around—in tomorrow's paper and—"

"Even," added Abbott, rigidly perching next to him, "on tonight's late edition of the local news."

"—that a person or persons will come forward with relevant information—"

"But the fact that she's—Jennifer's—already been missing over twelve hours!" interjected Caroline. "Really, since seven o'clock this morning!"

"Our hope is, ma'am"—Levy smiled as confidently as he could manage—"your living on such a relatively untraveled stretch of road—homeowners here in the development mostly and a few outsiders using the arterial as a shortcut to or from town or the interstate—"

"Not so few lately." Edmund waved disgustedly.

"—that, as Mr. Follett indicated, information will, eventually, be forthcom—"

"I'm wondering, Detectives"—Edmund abruptly pushed forward, causing his arthritic knee to pop loudly and him to grimace involuntarily—"what, at this point, I mean, based on your experience, do either of you have, at least, a theory as to . . . ?"

In the silence following his dangling question the officers quietly glanced at each other, before Levy, opening his hands to indicate his helplessness, answered, "I can only repeat, Mr. Follett, what I said earlier, that, being perfectly forthright, we're, at the moment, nearly as frustrated and—unfortunately—just as clueless as are the two of you."

"I seriously doubt, Detective, that your frustration remotely approaches our own."

"Of course, you're right, Mr. Follett. I apologize."

Caroline balled up a fist and shoved it against the point of her chin. "This is unacceptable," she said matter-of-factly. "She's only eight years old!"

Edmund reached over and put a hand on her leg. Caroline, gazing straight ahead, ground her jaw into her knuckles. Restlessly clearing his throat, Frank Levy awkwardly stood, tapped his breast pocket, where he'd placed the snapshots of Jennifer given him by Caroline, and said, "We'll get these immediately into the system so that by tomorrow every newspaper and police barracks in the area . . ."

Caroline lowered her head and quietly began to sob. Edmund swiftly got to his feet, glanced at Abbott, who just as quickly rose, then at Levy. Edmund curtly nodded to them both. "Thank you, Officers."

"We'll keep you—"

"Please."

He led them to the outside door. Before allowing them to depart, he indicated with a casual wave the upstairs nursery where Hannah was preparing Edmund Jr. for bed. "I take it, if Jennifer isn't found by tomorrow, you will be speaking again—perhaps in more detail—to Hannah?"

Abbott answered, "I've no doubt of it, Mr. Follett. Is there a particular reason why you think we should?"

Edmund frowned. "Just the obvious one, Detective. My daughter's missing, and Hannah Dray, who's worked for us less than four months, was, apparently, the last person we know of to see her."

9:10 P.M.   Two sets of human footprints—one large, the other small—were found in mud leading to Hansen's swamp, a mile deep in the pines. Three flashlight-wielding police officers—perhaps made overly suspicious by the nature of their mission—followed the tracks to the edge of a poorly constructed wood dock where, guns drawn, they frightened half to death a father and son about to embark, in a rowboat, on a night-fishing excursion. While half-blindly exiting the bog, one officer suffered a severe foot gash when he stepped into an illegally placed muskrat trap. Further searching of the area was adjourned until sunup.

Across the road, over the side of the wooded hill, the hand-held lights lessened in number until, at ten-thirty, the remaining half a dozen converged at a pull-over on the road's shoulder, where a pickup and two cars were parked. The volunteers—four men and two women—tired and perspiring in the evening air, which, though having cooled some since sundown, was no less humid, leaned against their vehicles, drinking iced tea and beer without joy while quietly discussing plans to expand the following day's search.

After they had departed, only the moon, stars, and a few sporadic houselights illuminated the dark Hillside development.

11:50 P.M. ". . . It's only that—Caroline and I—truthfully, Hannah—are dumbfounded that in your care Jennifer could—so—though we don't mean to sound accusatory or make you repeat things—we, her mother and I, simply need to know, Hannah, how this . . ."

Now casually dressed in sweatpants and a Harvard T-shirt, Edmund glanced across the kitchen table at Hannah, whose tear-dry, walnut-brown eyes surveyed her lap where her fingers lay intertwined. Behind and above her a grandfather clock monotonously ticked.

"Admittedly, we were aware—that is, you explained to us how, at that time of the morning, with Edmund Jr. needing to be fed and bathed and the driveway being so long that the practical thing, what made sense under the circumstances, was for Jennifer, alone, to wait—but the point, Hannah, is—I mean we understood that you would—through the front window, at all times, keep an eye on, would watch her until she actually got onto the bus—so I, we, that is, keep coming back to the question of exactly what transpired this morning."

As she had all evening Hannah, not looking at Edmund, answered in a monotone. Her lack of emotion bothered Edmund, as it had Caroline, before, with the aid of two Valium, she had gone into the bedroom to try to rest. Edmund couldn't decide if Hannah's tranquil demeanor indicated her passive uninterest in Jennifer's disappearance or her state of shock over it. "Jennifer was sitting there, on the bench, waiting, then Edmund Jr. started to really wail—he'd just been sort of sniffling before—so I left the kitchen and went into the nursery to give him some formula, and when I came back—five minutes at the most—the bus was just pulling away, so I assumed, naturally, she had gotten on."

"You told the police—earlier, I mean—you said that before you left the window, you saw Jennifer stand up . . ."

"Yes, okay. Maybe I did. I mean, I'm mixed up—but I think, yes—I saw her stand up as if to stretch her legs or look down the road—then Edmund—he started to cry—and when I came back, the bus was leaving, so, yes, that must have been it, Jennifer stood up when she saw it approaching . . ."

"So she was standing up, not sitting down?"

"What?"

"When you left the window, Jennifer had just stood up?"

"I think so. Yes."

"Five minutes, Hannah, is how long you claim you were away from the window. If Jennifer stood up because the bus was coming, it would have arrived at the bottom of the drive sooner than in five minutes. Therefore, it doesn't seem likely, if that was the reason she stood up, the bus would just be pulling away when you came back to the window."

"Maybe that's not why she stood up. Or maybe it was less than five minutes I was away from the window."

"However long it was, Hannah, it was too goddamned long."

"I'm mixed up about the time. All these questions—I thought—I mean, I must've thought anyway—there's so little traffic, on this road . . ."

"That you weren't concerned with how long you were away from the window? That maybe you left it for ten or even fifteen minutes?"

"No. I've told you how it happened. As best I remember." She looked up from her bland cream-colored country-style dress. A pretty girl in her early twenties, she had strawberry-blond hair caught in a ponytail and facial features, Edmund thought for the first time, older-looking than her years, as if those unwavering eyes had seen millenniums. "Are you going to fire me?"

"Whether or not I do is, at the moment, the last thing on my mind, Hannah. I'm only interested in finding my daugh—"

"I wouldn't blame you if you did."

"This isn't about you, Hannah. It's about Jennifer. Aren't you concerned about what's happened?"

"Of course I am. I love Jennifer. If whatever happened to her is partly my fault, I—I am sure . . ." She shook her head as if to clear it. "I mean I have the feeling that—she will show up—healthy . . ."

"What?"

"Anyway, you'll never trust me again."

Edmund was perturbed at how, in Hannah's mind, the focus of the tragedy seemed to be fixed solely on her, as if Jennifer's disappearance was simply the mechanism that triggered her own misfortune. He blamed himself for not having had her more thoroughly investigated before hiring her, but with Mrs. Carrerra, the children's previous nanny, taking sick so suddenly over the Christmas holidays, there hadn't been sufficient time. "You said you noticed maybe half a dozen vehicles pass in the ten or so minutes before you saw the bus leaving?"

"That I recall."

"But none that stopped or even appeared to slow down."

"Of course not. Don't you think if I had, I—"

"I don't know what to think, Hannah . . ." Edmund waved his hand after his trailing words. His veiled accusations suddenly struck him as pointless, as did his worry and frustration that from experience he knew would be alleviated only by action, but that were only intensified by his cluelessness as to what action to take. "You must be very tired."

"No way I could sleep now."

"Why don't you take one of Caroline's Valium and go try."

"Would you rather I pack my things and move to a motel?"

"There's no need to be overly dramatic, Hannah."

She slowly stood up and straightened her dress. Tall and athletic-appearing, she carried much of her height in her legs. "I'm happy to do whatever you and Mrs. Follett think best."

"The point is, Hannah—I, we, Caroline and I, this thing—it's hard to digest . . ." He felt emotion boiling up in him and turned his head away from her.

"The details," he heard her say in the same flat tone. "They're hard to sort out."

He waved her away with his hand. "For all of us, Hannah. I'm sorry if we sound . . . Good night, then."

"If you have other questions—whenever—just knock on my door. I won't be asleep."

"Thank you, Hannah."

With her casual, half-loping stride, she slowly left the room.

3:15 A.M. Edmund sat at the circular oak table in front of the large bay window facing the road. Through the open, screened skylight overhead flowed a temperate, gentle breeze carrying the haunted hoot of a great horned owl. Marred only by a thin covering of mist, the gibbous moon glowed incandescent above the room.

In closed-eyed reflection, Edmund pictured Jennifer, with his assistance, and Caroline looking on, reeling in the first fish she had ever caught—an eight-inch smallmouth bass from their very own pond, which Edmund, flush in his new role as landowner, had stocked to improve the odds. Unlike some seven-year-olds, Jennifer had not been afraid to touch the fish. Pointing to its gills, she had asked, "That's like his nose, right, Daddy?" Her finger gently rubbing its belly, she had assured the fish they wouldn't hurt or eat it.

After removing the hook, Edmund held the bass up between them while Caroline snapped a picture, following which he'd freed the fish, to which the three of them, down on their knees at the water's edge, had waved goodbye. That had been in mid-spring of the previous year, a warm, pollen-rich afternoon, less than a month after they'd moved to Dane.

Winter run-off melodiously overflowing the pond dam provided background music to croaking frogs, blue jays jabbering in the surrounding woods, and the shrieks of fly-searching swallows rifling the air over the water.

Caroline—who had been against the move until Edmund had convincingly pointed out they would be barely an hour's drive from their jobs in downtown Albany, and that, owing to a tax base increasingly augmented by city commuters, the Dane public schools were in the state's top 10 percent—had been pregnant with Edmund Jr. Later, as they had hiked the woods trail back to the house, she had tightly wrapped an arm around Edmund's waist as if to say, "You were right, Edmund, about our needing to get out of the city." And from several yards in front of them, Jennifer had squealed, "Daddy, I love our new home. Can we never, ever move again?"

4:55 A.M.   In the gray, murky light preceding the sun's rising, a horse and rider set out from a small, well-kept stable twelve miles northwest of Dane.

Wearing chaps over pressed jeans, a light sweater, polished riding boots, and a shell cap on his head of slightly graying hair, the rider athletically steered the spirited bay Thoroughbred stallion, forcefully blowing phlegm from its nostrils, through a dew-damp field of timothy and clover above the stable onto a needle-covered path bisecting nearly a thousand acres of woods.

The man greedily inhaled the forest's fresh, piney scent as a potent antidote to the sluggishness he felt in his still-awakening body. With his heels, he gently urged the bay into a brisk trot, causing twin saddlebags, appearing moderately full, to bounce noisily against its flanks. Beneath the canopy of spruce and pine boughs the animal's heavy footfalls incited squirrels to chatter, blue jays to squawk, crows to caw. Disturbed near the end of its nocturnal hunt, a screech owl agitatedly flew from the top of a hemlock tree above which, past the lingering mist, the vanishing moon was a spectral ellipse.

Forty minutes of nimble riding brought horse and rider out of the woods onto a plateau occupied by a natural orchard of crab- and thorn-apple trees, undergrown by clawing nettles, raspberry bushes, and witch hazel. The man's breathing, like the bay's, was intense. His cheeks were flushed. He was fully awake. Half a mile down the hill to his left, at the top of a potholed dirt road winding up through a bowl of gently rising woods and pastureland, lay the former Hanford Dresser farm, now abandoned. In the dull dawn light, the decrepit house and outbuildings, obscured by mist, appeared phantasmal.

The man leaned forward and encouragingly stroked the bay's neck. He pulled its rein to the right. Brusquely kicking the horse, he headed it out of the orchard toward a large stand of sugar maples several hundred yards west of the Dresser place.

5:10 A.M. Edmund opened his eyes to a scuffling noise, spun quickly around, and saw Caroline approaching the kitchen from down the hall, wavering a little on her slippered feet.

He stood up, went to her, lightly grasped her arm.

27

Through pupils moderately dilated by drugs, she desperately queried him for news. He wordlessly shook his head, then walked with her to the table, pulled a chair out for her, pushed it in after she sat. At the refrigerator, he filled two glasses with orange juice, then brought them back to the table.

Caroline sipped at hers, pushed it away. Edmund sat down across from her, reached out, gripped her hand, cold from holding the juice glass. Her damp cotton nightie clung wetly to her armpits and genitals. Her bobbed hair was in sweaty disarray. She had gone to bed without removing her mascara, now smeared across both cheeks.

Edmund drank half his juice. A housefly buzzed around the table before exiting through the open screen door onto the sun porch, from which floated into the house the sweet smell of potted lilies. No wall divided the kitchen from the living room, where Jennifer's pet collie, Garofalo, loudly snored beneath the interminably ticking grandfather clock, which Edmund several times restrained himself from smashing. The smallest sounds magnified silence. The simplest thoughts shattered internal dams holding back whole worlds full. In a tired, Valium-affected drone, Caroline said, "She didn't even have anything to sleep in, Edmund, or her Cabbage Pa . . ."

"We'll just have to hope that . . ."

"And you know how she hates the dark—even in her own room . . ."

"She's not so bad, though—remember?—as right after we mov . . ."

". . . unbearable to imag . . . !"

"Awful . . . !"

". . . how, Edmund, for God's sake . . . ?"

28

". . . hope that some caring person . . ."

". . . she couldn't have simply disap . . . !"

". . . has found her, that's all."

Caroline visibly sagged.

After quickly downing his remaining juice, Edmund abruptly stood up, walked to the window, reached to its left, and switched on the outside light. In its illumination, he could clearly see to the bottom of the drive and even make out, in dark shadows beneath the willow tree, the wrought-iron bench he had bought especially for Jennifer to sit on while waiting for the bus. I will close my eyes, he thought, doing so, then wake from this nightmare, but instead, in his animated consciousness, he encountered Hannah's impassive stare as she rotely responded to his, Caroline's, and the police's queries.

". . . ironic, that we—one of our chief reasons, I mean, for moving to the country, Edmund, was that it would be safer for the childr—"

"This isn't something I decided on alone, Caroline." He nodded at his reflection in the glass, as if to convince himself. "We discussed—"

"I'm not being accusatory, Edmund. It's just now our little girl is—and the world—it suddenly seems precariously large and danger . . ."

Edmund turned from the window.

"We will find her—please, God!—won't we, Edmund?"

"Yes. We will."

Caroline cocked her head at him in a tired way that suggested holding it in an upright position pained her. "I keep thinking if I—if either of us, Edmund—had been here—we certainly would have . . ."

"What are you saying, Caroline—it's our fault that Jen—because neither of us was home?"

"Only that, at the moment, my career seems to me as insignificant as"—she rolled her eyes torpidly toward the skylight—"the faintest of those stars . . ."

8:15 A.M. A dark green unmarked police car, driven by Mike Abbott, hesitated at the bottom of the Borden drive before turning right onto the arterial road and heading slowly away from town. "It's like she went up in a puff of smoke," said Abbott, referring to his and Levy's latest unproductive interview. "Make that invisible smoke, since nobody on the whole goddamn road saw even that much."

"These houses all being set back like castles in the woods," retorted Levy, shoving a piece of Juicy Fruit in his mouth, "unless you were standing on your roof, it'd be hellish hard to see much of anything down here." He wadded up the gum wrapper and stuffed it in the trash bag hanging from his window knob. "And they're so goddamn far apart, with so many trees in between, somebody living in one couldn't have the slightest fucking idea what's going on at his neighbors' or even if he has any." He held the pack out toward Abbott, who waved it away.

"That's the point, isn't it, Frank? I mean, it's what these commuter folks are paying for, right? Privacy."

"Uh-huh."

"Hell, I don't blame 'em. Come out here and get ten acres for what must seem like pocket change to them."

Levy snorted. "Not more than a decade ago, this whole

stretch was nothing but woods with some of the best hunting and fishing in the county. Still is, I guess, only now it's all mostly posted. I pulled many a bass from that pond now belongs to Follett, that he keeps privately stocked so him and his friends can get together weekends and play like Hemingway over there in Spain did."

"It's called capitalism, Frank. If you can afford it, own it. If you can't, be envious."

"I'm just saying, you didn't grow up around here, so you've got no historical perspective, which, in a case like this, might be more relevant than you think. This development, cutting out a big chunk of citizen-accessible land like it did, and raising the taxes of everybody in the community to pay for services for people who are bringing nothing into it, wasn't exactly popular with most of the locals."

"Oh, I get it, Frank—some disgruntled hunter snatched the girl and is holding her until Follett takes the posted signs down from his property. That your theory?"

"Right there suggests why you'll never be a superior investigator, because you think you can delve into the immediate without considering the past, and I'm saying—not always, but sometimes—they're not separate entities but two connected points, on the same line."

Abbott lifted his leg and loudly farted. "Counterpoint to your point," he said, "which I assess as rank noise. This case hasn't got anything to do with history, Frank. It's got to do with an eight-year-old girl who vanished into thin air twenty-five hours ago and at this moment—in the here and now—we're no closer to finding her." He farted again. "And fuck you I'll never be a superior investigator."

"Oh, calm down—you'll be good enough, on account of

you're smart with decent instincts and what's that other thing—dogged—but, I say it again, forget about being Deputy Dawg until you can look at a big pile of dirt and picture what it looked like before a glacier came along and pushed it into a mountain."

"Leaving aside your happy horseshit, dirt-pile philosophy, if you're hypothesizing that Jennifer Follett was snatched—assuming she was, and for whatever reason—by a person intimately familiar with these local byways, perhaps, even, by an inhabitant thereof, it seems, at first blush, plausible, given that the signs discouraging non-local traffic at either end of this arterial suggest it's a cul-de-sac or dead end instead of the through road it actually is, an intentional delusion likely to limit, as it was intended to, excessive traffic and the possibility of an out-of-town pervert venturing onto it."

"But?"

"In its blindered view of the late-twentieth-century criminal industry, your provincial theory doesn't hold water because the snatcher, if there was one, could just as easily have been following directions provided them by a higher-up or an accomplice who is familiar."

Squeezing his eyes to half-shut slits, Levy peered owlishly around the car. "And who might that accomplice be?"

"Up yours, Frank. You know exactly who I'm talking about."

"Humor me."

"Bob Waite, possibly."

"Or?"

"Hannah Banana."

For several minutes they rode in silence down the unlined pavement bisecting woods occupying, on one side, sloping hills ascended every few hundred yards by tongues of asphalt winding through deciduous trees to larger-than-average houses. The structures were competently spaced and concealed to make each, according to the developer's literature, a forest island. On the six-mile stretch connecting the highway loop sat less than two dozen habitations—all uniquely designed—with a similar number slated for across the road where presently there stood mostly new-growth pine fractured by loggers' dirt roads.

"Edmund Follett got to you, did he, Mike?"

"He didn't have anything to do with it. One way or the other, Hannah dropped the ball. There's no way around that."

"Yeah, but dropping it and intentionally drop-kicking it are two different things." The morning was warm, the car's air conditioner broken, and the open windows issued in a stiff, pine-scented wind that mussed Levy's thick hair, prompting him to try to flatten it every few seconds with the palm of one hand. "My guess is, Edmund and Caroline, not wanting to admit it, are feeling more than a little guilty about going off every 5:30 a.m. to their six-figure jobs while leaving their kids to get raised up by a babysitter."

"Having it all, right?"

"Like that, yeah. And how it's easier to blame somebody else, whadya call a whipping boy."

"Whipping girl, there, Frank." Abbott reached up and briskly tugged the white canvas fedora he wore over his prematurely thinning locks, while uncomfortably shifting his marathoner's legs, attached to a mesomorphic torso containing just enough weighty muscle to keep him, no matter how hard he trained, out of many winners' circles, a biological

curse constantly reminding Abbott, with his B.A. in philosophy, of the inequities of heredity. "Whatever else she is, Hannah's all that."

"I'll take your word for it, myself being happily married
and all. Anyway, then there's that whole thing about shooting
the messenger, which was Hannah."

"You got to admit, Frank, for all her looks, Hannah Banana
comes off weird. I get the feeling listening to her somebody
winds her up each morning."

"There's a definite lack of affect all right, but considering
Jennifer disappearing on her watch, and what that might do
to you . . . So what's your theory—Hannah's part of some
sort of extortion conspiracy?"

"I'm just saying, what harm does it do to look into her
background?"

"No harm, except we haven't got the resources for it."
Abbott halted the car at the arterial's north intersection with
the highway. "And another thing—if she was snatched for
money—these people in here got some all right, but not the
real kind, like the millions a kidnapper would be looking for."

"You know this, how?"

"I know the type. Folletts have got curbside appeal—they
look rich and, compared to you and me, are, but what comes
in goes out, and they miss a couple of paychecks and it's
goodbye Hillside and hello Poverty Hill."

"Even if you're right, and I'm not saying you are—for
Christ sake, the guy's an architect and she's into designing
high-priced clothes, not like the rags you wear—the kidnappers might be oblivious."

"Shit-dumb, you mean, and anybody that dumb is too
dumb to pull off a conspiracy like what you're talking about."

"Dumb one way, Frank, doesn't mean dumb every way. Haven't you ever heard of subject dumbness?"

"I know you made that up."

"The great artist, for example, who can't balance his checkbook?"

Levy smirked.

"Or the Wall Street genius who gets bilked by a palm reader?" Abbott turned right onto the two-lane road which from there to Dane proper ran through ten miles of mostly abandoned farmland dotted by clusters of new or partially constructed tract houses and crisscrossed three or four times by single-lane roads winding east or west through the hills.

"Look, Mike, if Follett wants to hire an Albany P.I. to check out Hannah, I wouldn't blame him on account of it'll get done a lot quicker that way and he'll feel like he's doing something and, anyway, what harm does it do? But the sad, awful truth is, most of these disappearances aren't anything about money and of the few that you solve, you usually end up wishing, in their gritty particulars, you hadn't." Heavily sighing, Levy reached up with an index finger and tapped the side of his head. "On the other hand, my friend—Deputy Dawg, all us superior police minds?—we enter every investigation involving a kid too young to have hurt anybody or even pissed them off as if maybe, finally, here's the case whose happy solution will justify our otherwise mind-numbing, humanity-questioning, Maalox-eating, head-butting careers."

10:35 A.M.   Edmund spent half the morning on the phone to his staff, rescheduling meetings, delegating his normal functions to underlings, and explaining he wouldn't be in for at least that day and possibly longer because his daughter had broken both legs in a fall. He hadn't told them the truth because the word "missing" sounded so open-ended and uncertain he couldn't bring himself to utter it, even to himself. Also, he sought to avoid both the inevitable questions for which he had no answers and hearing the well-intended, but vacuous, empathic outpourings of his colleagues.

After faxing to her assistant several pages of instructions along with the same excuse for her absence that Edmund had used for his, Caroline, around ten-thirty, stuck her head in his office to suggest, with practiced casualness, he ought not tie the line up much longer. Continuing his conversation, Edmund blankly stared at her until, in several seconds, she quietly withdrew. Shortly thereafter, having hastily concluded the call, he found her at the kitchen table, working on a pencil sketch of a dress. "I'm sorry," he said. "I wasn't thinking."

She glanced up, the pencil dropping from her hand. "It was Detective Levy who suggested it."

"Of course he—both of you—were—are right."

"I've no idea even what to hope for, Edmund!" She glanced out the window at another gorgeous spring day, enlivened by several species of colorful birds bombarding the feeder and crocuses and early-blooming tulips bordering both sides of the flagstone walkway leading to the drive. Farther and farther from the house, ever deeper in the woods, policemen, now with bloodhounds, were still searching. "Half of me longs for some news—any news. The other half . . ."

Though she looked tired, her gaze was less vacant than it

had been the previous evening. She's rallying, thought Edmund, with a touch of pride.

She picked up the pencil. "Everything squared away at the office?"

"I guess they'll manage all right without me." Bending down and squinting at the design of the strapless, flared-hem minidress she was working on, he dryly remarked, "Interesting."

She released a breathy half-laugh.

"Like less is really more, right?"

"I'm just doodling."

"Is Eddie napping?"

"Hannah took him for a walk in the backpack."

The look he gave her revealed the alarm he suddenly felt.

"He was fussy and didn't want to eat." Edmund abruptly straightened up. "I thought maybe he was coming down with something, but Hannah . . ."

"Where did she take him?"

"To the pond." Caroline flashed a smile that just as quickly faded. "She hoped the motion might help him slee—"

"They took the trail?"

"They ought to be back soon."

Edmund poignantly peered through the window facing the woods. "I spoke again this morning to Detec . . . the younger one—Abbott—on the phone—about what we, uh, last night . . . regarding Hannah?"

Caroline's wordless stare encouraged him to continue.

"To expedite things, he gave me a name—someone in Albany—a private investigator he is apparently acquainted with, who . . ."

"As a routine precaution, you mean?"

"So as to overturn every stone, yes. No matter how small." He pursed his lips. "Abbott—both of them—stressed that they believe her to be in no way involved."

"Well, I'm certainly inclined to agree!" Caroline glanced through the window. "Aren't you?"

At that moment, dressed in lederhosen and with Edmund Jr. sleeping soundly on her back, Hannah stepped from the woods fifty yards from the house. Relief expressed itself on the faces of Edmund and Caroline, though neither acknowledged it, beyond Caroline's commenting, "Though with our being home at present, I suppose there's no need for her to assume so much responsibility for Ed . . ."

"At least she shouldn't disappear alone with him."

"I'll tell her over lunch," agreed Caroline.

Edmund adjusted the empty chairs around the table. Caroline glanced expectantly at him. A decade his junior, she looked even younger than her thirty-four years. In what seemed a sensual dichotomy to Edmund, given the glamorous nature of her profession, her lithe beauty was of the homespun variety. In her pale green eyes, former dancer's body, and soft, full lips existed an allure beyond his ability to verbalize that in ten years of marriage had waxed and waned but never vanished. He leaned forward and kissed the top of her head of natural auburn hair, which smelled vaguely of apples. "It's going to be all right," he whispered.

"Do you really think so, Edmund? Or are you just saying so to placa—"

"I'm saying it because I—we—must believe it. We must!" Then, from behind her, he was hugging her gently heaving chest and feeling her sodden breath maybe mixed with tears, though he couldn't tell for sure, dampen his forearms. A door opened. They heard Hannah step into the mudroom. Caroline quickly ran a hand across her eyes and got up from the table. Hannah could be heard stomping her feet. Caroline cocked her head at the sound. Edmund feared she would ask him something more, but she didn't. He turned away.

"I'm going to go out back," he told her, "and cut up some wood."

In the mudroom, he stopped and held for a moment his sleeping son. "We had a lovely walk," Hannah said in her flat tone, which Edmund, somewhat alarmed, suddenly realized was how she had always sounded. "Edmund Jr., Mr. Follett, was a perfect gentleman. To every bird he waved and cried, 'Bye-bye.' "

11:00 A.M. The bay stallion high-stepped from the woods into the sun-dried pasture leading to the stable; in the paddock a grazing mare lifted its head and whinnied. Fervidly neighing, the stallion fought its bit, was reined in by its rider, then was allowed to traverse the field at an anxious half-trot. Sitting erect on the animal's back, the rider, as if it was instinctual to him, warily glanced fifty yards left of the paddock at a two-story house backing a long sloping drive, occupied at its top by a Jeep station wagon and a Ford sedan.

Before the stable's large front door the rider dismounted, then led the animal inside, stripped off its tackle, filled a pail with warm, soapy water, and, while the unfettered bay obediently stood, thoroughly rubbed down its creamily perspiring muscular torso, first with a washcloth, then with a soft-bristled brush. Afterward he draped the bay in a heavy blanket, secured it with strings beneath the horse's withers and rump, released the animal into its stall, poured oats in its trough and water in its bucket, then opened the rear gate to the paddock, allowing the stallion, if it desired, access to the mare.

After hanging up the tackle, he removed from the saddle-bags, less bulky than when he had ridden out that morning, a Nikon camera, a hand-held light meter, both of which he dangled by leather straps from his neck, and several cartons of exposed film, which he placed in his coat pockets. Perspiring in the rising heat, flushed from his recent exertion, and ravenously hungry, he spryly walked toward the house.

11:40 A.M.   Tired of looking at mug shots of child molesters, some dead, imprisoned, or in new locales, others, who would have to be checked out if they hadn't been already, roaming the local streets, Levy was about to stroll out to the municipal square to pick up a couple of chili dogs from one of the outdoor carts, when the desk sergeant called to say he was sending back two people with information about the Follett case.

A minute later, into his office strutted attorney Harvey Banner, his 125 bustling pounds in a rayon banana suit, followed by a kid of maybe twelve whose dour expression said he'd rather be older, dangling a lunch box from one hand. Banner reached up to his hairless pate, whisked away a cotton cabbie's cap, tossed it on an unoccupied chair, and, in high-pitched staccatos, announced, "Detective Franklin Levy"—he nodded at the kid—"meet Darren Cay."

Levy stood up and the kid stepped forward and shook his hand. "How ya doin', Darren?"

"Okay." Levy thought the kid looked like he was using every ounce of his energy to hold something inside himself.

"You want a Coke or something?"

"That'd be good, yeah."

"Counselor?"

"Diet Sprite, please, Detective."

Levy went out to the machine, got the sodas, and brought them back. Sitting down again, across from the other two, after they'd all had a drink, he smiled and said, "No school for you today, Darren?"

"I left early. When I heard the other kids talking about it."

"About Jennifer Follett?"

"To come to my office," interjected Banner. "Soon's he heard, he did."

Levy frowned uncomprehendingly. "To your office?"

"Darren was compelled by a strong moral and ethical responsibility to come to me, his court-appointed law guardian for a past, minor indiscretion, with information pertinent to that poor child's disappearance, despite that in doing so he was, perhaps, implicating himself in a crime and, at home, jumping into a pot of boiling water."

Levy nodded appreciatively. "We need all the help we can get, Darren. That's for sure."

Darren shuffled his feet. "I just—I never . . ."

"What?"

"I figured it was somebody she knew . . ."

Banner placed a delicate hand on the kid's shoulder. Darren looked glumly at the ceiling. "Detective, we'd like your word that, as much as it's within your power, Darren won't be charged with any crimes he may have committed while witnessing, and shortly thereafter, what he is about to recite to you."

"What category of crimes are we talking about?"

"Specifically, trespassing."

"That it?"

"In the mind of a creative prosecutor, I suppose larceny."

"Of what?"

"Fish. Live fish." Banner precisely tugged at his coat sleeves, a size or two short for him. "Smallmouth bass mostly. And a few lake trout."

"To eat?"

Banner rubbed a hand over the top of his waxed skull. "For others to."

"At a profit to himself?"

"Minuscule, Detective. Minuscule."

Levy frowned. "Okay. My ears are closed to pirated fish."

"Finally, sir, and understand Darren is in no way conditioning his cooperation on this, but if it would be possible for you to refrain from informing the press, or, especially, Darren's parents—"

"My dad'd kick my butt," said Darren.

Levy scowled.

"I don't mean just a little bit."

"It's not a small matter, Detective. Truly." Banner put a hand up to his mouth and ludicrously hissed, "I have pictures of past—ep-i-sodes."

Levy wasn't sure if the boy had heard or not.

"I'll do what I can," he said, "though, as you're aware, Counselor, if Darren's a witness to something material—"

"I'll testify if I have to," blurted out Darren. "I wished I'd a known before—she was a cute kid, quiet as a bug—I didn't even know her name . . .''

Banner held his hand out toward him like a traffic cop. "We ask only, Detective, to the extent it won't hinder your investigation and keeping in mind the potential dire consequences for my client, you do what you can to keep his involvement— hush-hush?"

Levy nodded affirmatively.

To start the kid talking again, Banner, in rapid succession, thrice tapped a minute index finger against his back.

12:35 P.M.   Edmund's hope that physical activity would temporarily take his mind off Jennifer was dashed. With each swing of the ax, his frustration and anger grew. He kept picturing his daughter in different poses—serious, hilarity-choked, proud, as when she had presented him with her first drawing that actually resembled her intention for it, curled feline-like in his lap while he recited a story that, as a child, had been told to him. He hadn't prayed to beget a genius or a great artist. For her, as well as Edmund Jr., he had asked only for good health and happiness. Watching her laugh at anything—the chirping of a bird, the falling snow—was more intoxicating to Edmund than any drug he could take. He'd often wished he could bottle the pure joy he felt in simply watching her, a potion for him to open and consume when the world of adults became too oppressive.

The realization abruptly struck him that the hours he'd actually spent with her had been far fewer than those he'd spent thinking of her while doing other things. He'd not heard her

first word, seen her first step, been with her enough to inter-
pret, as could Hannah and her previous caretakers, the meaning of her sometimes half-garbled words and sentences. He'd
told her "not today" or "maybe later"—always believing it,
too, as if time were a never-depleting asset—how many hundreds of times? Exertive perspiration dampened his clothes
and marred his vision, imbuing the bucolic hillside with an
Impressionist's blur. Occasionally his mind would be jolted,
as if with an electric current, by the inconceivable thought,
no matter how much he tried to push it away, that he would
never see his daughter again or, maybe even worse—he wasn't
sure—see only her small body in a coroner's catacomb.

He chopped for an hour and a half, producing from his
torment a medium-sized pile of jagged-edged, various-shaped
logs, until, from the house, he heard Caroline scream his
name. Edmund dropped the ax, sprinted the fifty feet to the
mudroom, then burst through the front door into the hallway, crashing headlong into Hannah, hurrying in the opposite
direction. In her shock, the caretaker breathily cursed.

"Hann—I'm sor—are you look—for me?"

"Mrs. Follett—she . . ."

"What?" Her expression was harsh or scared, Edmund
couldn't tell which. He stepped toward her. "Where's Caroline, Hannah?"

"Her office phone . . ." She rubbed her jaw where it had
apparently banged into Edmund. "They've called."

"Who've called?"

"About Jennifer."

"My God!" She backed away from his tone, which was
strident. He gripped her shoulders. "What about Jennifer?"

Hannah reached out for the wall. "You know—on the
phone . . ."

Edmund pushed by her, then dashed up the stairs toward Caroline's office. Just as he reached the room's half-open door, he heard the phone replaced in its cradle. He slowly stepped inside.

Caroline turned around. Her lips were slightly parted as if they'd been frozen while forming a word. The fingers of her right hand grasped the air at her side exactly as they had just been grasping the phone.

1:20 P.M. Twelve miles northwest of Dane, in a well-maintained colonial-style house on Hulburt Hill Road, a middle-aged woman wearing a modest but expensive cotton dress, her graying auburn hair in an intricately braided bun atop her head, proceeded down a long maple hallway to a locked, soundproof door, where, after a moment's hesitation, she pushed with one finger the button of an intercom through which she announced, "It's one-twenty, Gerald."

She patiently stood outside the door until, after nearly three minutes, a cultured male voice politely thanked her.

Again activating the machine, the woman inquired somewhat falteringly, "You do remember the Emersons expect us at two-fifteen, don't you, dear?"

Following an interval this time of only a few seconds, the male voice matter-of-factly responded, "I can't just pull prints from a hypo bath, Claire. They'll ruin. To expedite matters, please lay out my tan cords and a polo shirt of any color."

"It's awfully warm for cords, dear," the woman opined into the speaker. "Wouldn't you rather your beige khaki slacks and a cotton shirt?"

"I'd rather my tan cords and a polo shirt of any color," came the courteous but firm reply.

The woman once more depressed the button. "I'll put out your tan corduroys, dear, and a yellow-and-white polo shirt."

"Lovely, Claire. Thank you."

"We really ought to leave in thirty minutes, Gerald."

There was no answer from the man, nor did the woman wait for one.

Shortly after, the man emerged from the darkroom and securely locked it. In the master bedroom suite, he stripped off his riding gear, showered, shaved, and for several seconds viewed his long, fit body in the full-length mirror on the bathroom door. Then, ignoring the clothes his wife had laid out for him, he removed from the closet and put on a pair of beige khaki slacks and a blue button-down cotton shirt.

Five minutes later, carrying a tripod and a Hasselblad camera, he met his wife in the foyer. "Regarding the cords, dear," he said, "you were right."

She lightly kissed both his cheeks. The man opened the outside door and held it as she exited. Grasping one of her arms, he led her down the flagstone walk to a black LTD. At exactly 1:50 by his watch, they started for Dane.

2:15 P.M. Drinking his fifth Coke in two and a half hours, Darren Cay sat at Frank Levy's desk looking at a pamphlet full of colored photographs of automobiles sent up by the evidence department while, immediately to his left, struggling to sit up straight in a plastic, spoon-shaped chair, Harvey Banner, following each nod of his client's head, reached out and primly turned a page of the pamphlet. "It was sort of like that," said Darren, pointing at an Eagle Premier, "but bigger."

"You mean longer?" asked Frank Levy, leaning against the wall behind him.

"Yuh. But wider, too. More like a limousine, you know."

"A limousine. You mean like a limousine that movie stars and like that ride in?"

"Not quite that big maybe, and it didn't have dark glass in the windows. Just that it was black, you know, and fancy."

"One of the Cadillacs maybe?" Levy nodded at Banner. "Show him the Cadillacs again, Harvey."

Banner adroitly shook his head. "He's seen the Cadillacs twice. He says it wasn't a Cadillac."

"A Lincoln Town Car? Has he seen the Lincolns?"

"He's seen the Lincolns."

"What I saw wasn't so much like a box," said Darren.

"It had four doors, though?"

"Yuh, I'm pretty sure."

"Only four?"

"Uh-huh." He nodded his head at Banner and the little lawyer obediently leaned forward and turned the page. "Far as I could tell."

Looking up at the sound of tapping on the glass window of his door, Levy saw Mike Abbott waving at him to come out. "Keep looking, Darren," he said. "I'll be right outside if you spot the one."

"Okay," Darren said earnestly, before quickly adding, "Maybe I could have another Coke?"

"You got it," answered Levy, on his way by the kid encouragingly patting his shoulder, "that is, if I have any change left."

"So long as you're making the trip," interjected Banner,

making no move to reach into his pocket, "perhaps one more Diet Sprite, Detective? This time with a cup, and a little ice, if you please."

Plaintively raising his eyes, Levy wordlessly opened the door and stepped into the hall.

"How's progress?" asked Abbott.

"A black four-door—sort of like a limousine, but not quite that big, but also like an Eagle Premier, though longer and maybe wider." Levy scowled. "Hell, I don't blame the kid for being confused, given how every car manufacturer these days, foreign or domestic, makes about twelve different models of almost the same car that look pretty much like everybody else's twelve."

"Nothing new on the tag?"

Levy shook his head. "Instate, he's sure of that, with maybe a 'D' and a '2,' but without a clue to their order. It's a long shot, but given that Jennifer, according to Darren, stepped into that car without assistance as if she might've known who was inside, the state BCI boys are checking to see how many vehicles registered in the county contain on their plates some combination of the two."

"That ought to limit it to a couple thousand, among them a small Toyota registered to yours truly."

"Yeah, but your little rusted shit pile ain't black and wouldn't be mistaken for a limousine by a blind man. Anyway, I said it was a long shot." He nodded through his office door. "You ever notice the only decent-hearted lawyers are cash-poor? Between the kid and Banner, my pension's going to sodas." He scowled. "So, you ask the Folletts who among their acquaintances drives a black four-door sedan?"

Abbott nodded. "None that immediately came to Caroline's mind, but she was in no condition to think. She said she'd consult with Edmund. I guess I don't have to tell you how the news struck her?"

Levy grimly shook his head.

"I faxed what we've got so far to the FBI in Albany. They're going to computer cross-check it against any cases might sound similar."

"With the number of dirtbags in this world, Mike, who perform similar but different dirtbaggish acts for their own dirtbag reasons, don't hold your breath over their results." Levy stretched and disgustedly exhaled, then yanked at his shirt where it clung, damply, to his broad back of increasingly fat-laced muscle. "The little bit I was home before daylight last night, I spent slouched in a chair next to my daughter's bed, afraid to shut my eyes. How 'bout you?"

"You'll recall I don't have a daughter, Frank. Nor a wife. At the moment I don't even have a significant other." Abbott ran a few steps in place. "I did eight miles through the city at a more than brisk clip."

"At 2 a.m.?"

"It helps me avoid the traffic."

"You've got a mental problem."

"A mutual acquaintance of ours sitting out on his porch at the same ungodly hour yelled to me a similar sentiment."

"You both need therapy."

"Or sleeping pills. My fellow insomniac was Bob Waite."

"No shit. What do you suppose was keeping him up?"

"Same thing as us, maybe, only for different reasons."

"Good nose, wrong scent, Mike. Bob's just a guy some-times gets in pinches and writes bad checks that pinch him even more. Run by there next month and that new truck of his probably will have been repossessed. And another thing, Bob Waite isn't just, to use your phrase, subject dumb. He's allover dumb. A terminal case of dumb. Too dumb to proceed but from the spur of dumbness. Not bad dumb. Just dumb dumb."

Abbott laughed, while trying not to.

"In other words too dumb to act smart even for a second but not too dumb to feel bad about Jennifer Follett—I don't think he was lying about that."

"I'm not questioning the man's honesty, Frank. Only saying he may know more than he thinks he does or wants to, so, even if he is, as you hypothesize, completely, utterly dumb—which, given the many opportunities this world presents a person to be, if only by accident, momentarily smart, strikes me as improbable—he's worth keeping an eye on."

Levy threw his hands up in concession. "As long as you do it at two o'clock in the morning in your running gear, Mike." He turned toward the soda machines. "Babysit my two boys in there while I'm out playing step 'n' fetch it, will ya?"

Reaching for the door handle, Abbott said, "When I'm out there all by myself, Frank—just me and the pavement—I actually believe in miracles, like I might someday even win the Boston Marathon, you know?"

"Yeah, yeah, Mike, only once you've come down from your exercise-induced hormone high, you're still faced with the fact that you're a six-and-a-half-minute miler, tops, destined to always finish in the middle of the pack somewhere."

Levy only had three dimes in his pocket and the dollar bill changer was broken. Nobody upstairs could break his last five. Finally he walked downstairs and robbed the coffee can in personnel of eight quarters. Halfway up the stairs, feeling guilty, he went back and stuffed an IOU into the can. Two minutes later, on his way back into his office with the sodas, he was nearly bowled over by Abbott, Darren Cay, and Harvey Banner, rushing out of it. "Don't you ever just walk, Mike?"

"Get in goddamn gear, Frank!" breathily answered Abbott, hurriedly leading the others, now including Levy, toward the front desk. "Maybe we can still glimpse the son of a bitch!"

"Glimpse who?"

"The car!" said Darren excitedly.

"You mean . . . ?"

"I was looking out your office window and . . . !"

"No fucking way!"

"Oh, indeed, Detective," interjected Banner. "I was standing right next to him when—"

"That sort of shit just doesn't happen!" hollered Levy.

Ten seconds later, the four of them almost simultaneously barreled through the glass doors onto the sidewalk, but, on the street fronting them, saw no sign of a late-model black sedan.

"Who got the goddamn plates!" Levy yelled. "Anybody?"

"NYD 1170," methodically intoned Harvey Banner. "That's what."

5:25 P.M. Even more intolerable, thought Edmund, than total knowledge or the utter lack of it was an obfuscated view. To understand a life issuing partly from your own, and for which you would willingly give up yours, if she was still alive—oh, she must! has to be! otherwise where's the point of anything?—at the mercy of aberrant, obviously heartless beings, and not knowing where or why, was horrific enough, but to imagine those heartless beings as, perhaps, your acquaintances, even friends, was beyond horrific; it was a soul-torturing abomination, nearly insufferable . . . ! Onto the board occupying the table before him he carefully placed the letters "B-a-n-s-h-i."

"There's no such word, Edmund."

"There is. It's like a female spirit or something."

"Perhaps so, but that's not how you spell it."

"Are you officially challenging my version, Caroline?"

"Yes."

He handed her the dictionary. Minutes after she had hung up from Detective Abbott's call, her demeanor had abruptly changed to calm and businesslike. She had insisted they immediately put their heads together and, from among their circle of acquaintances, come up with all who owned or drove a black or dark blue vehicle. The list of twelve—including Edmund's partner and her own sister and brother-in-law in Poughkeepsie—included only three true sedans, the rest compacts, minivans, or station wagons. They had, over three hours before, faxed the names, addresses, and phone numbers to police headquarters and were informed that a detective would shortly get back to them.

Like the imagined sound of cogitation, an electric bread-maker's kneading whir mechanically issued from the far corner of the kitchen, where they sat within reach of the padded stroller in which Edmund Jr. slept. Behind the wheel of her rusted Datsun, on her way to wherever, Hannah presumably listened to the radio, sang, viewed the birthing spring.

Edmund tried to remember the name of the book—something about not talking to strangers—he had so many times read to Jennifer. But had he made clear to her why he was reading it? Or taken the time to explain in language lucid to an eight-year-old that the book's smiling crocodile and gift-bearing fox were metaphors for real-life, human predators whose evil guises might be fronted by demeanors as outwardly pleasant as those of their animal counterparts? Hadn't he tempered his warnings so as not to unduly frighten her? Not to poison with distrust her natural curiosity about the world? But why? Weren't they now—the whole family—suffering beneath proof that the only effective vaccine against evil was paranoia?

"B-a-n-s-h-e-e, Edmund."

"What?"

"It's the only spelling even close to what you put down."

"With two 'e's instead of an 'i'?"

"According to Webster's." Caroline pointed down with her finger at a word in the dictionary. " 'A female spirit in Gaelic folklore believed to presage a death in the family by wail . . .' "

Her hand dropped into her lap. For several seconds their eyes locked, Caroline's intense, wordless stare striking Edmund as the end product of every intimacy and emotion they had ever shared. Oh, please don't ask so much of me! He feared his own eyes would tear. He used what sounded like an engine's low-geared groan beyond the walls as an excuse to turn quickly away. He stood up and hurried to the window. Up the long drive to the house climbed an all-too-familiar, dark green sedan. Behind him came a loud crash.

He wheeled back toward the table, where Caroline had flung the Scrabble board and letters onto the floor. "The police are here," he told her.

Sheepishly smiling, she squatted down and began determinedly picking up the scattered parts of their game.

5:45 P.M.   The black LTD, its female passenger slightly tipsy on complimentary sherry, pulled from a circular drive on Briarcliff Lane, cutting through the heart of Dane's most exclusive residential section. Leaning forward, the man driving shoved a compact disc into the player, the quadraphonic speakers then softly emanating symphony music. The woman remarked, "Pleasant enough, actually."

The man distractedly nodded.

"Will they purchase the whole array, do you think?"

Not replying, the driver electrically lowered his window a crack to lure in the scent of blossoming hyacinths, narcissus, and crab apple. Guiding the car at a snail's pace along the cliff road, he gazed out and down from his side of the vehicle, beyond the steep grass-and-flower-manicured embankment where, in its serpentine course beneath the descending sun, a runoff-pregnant stream glittered like multitudinous camera flashes.

The woman reached in her bag and pulled out a compact. She studied her lips. She put the compact away, and out the opposite window viewed the handful of cliffside estates with their treacherous approaches resulting in breathtaking vistas.

Two miles from the Emerson house, at a four-way stop sign, the LTD turned, instead of right toward downtown Dane, left onto Delaney Boulevard, in the direction of a nonaesthetic strip of minimalls and fast-food restaurants. The woman glanced at the man, but said nothing. Her silent query prompted him to respond, "I need to run some errands." Then, hesitating: "I'll pick you up some sherry."

At the third traffic light, he turned the LTD into the Kmart plaza parking lot, just beginning to fill up at rush hour, late on a weekday afternoon. He parked near the plaza atrium, turned the engine off, wordlessly got out, and entered the store through its glass doors. The woman furtively eyed the car's interior, its rug floor and leather upholstery and seats all appearing spotless, as if they had just been vacuumed, shampooed, and polished. She glanced at the glove box, then quickly away. With fumbling fingers she opened her purse, removed, nipped at, and put away a half-pint bottle of sherry. In the warm, close-to-stifling car, she began to shiver. To combat the condition, she drew in a deep breath, then slowly exhaled.

Carrying a medium-size bag, the man exited Kmart, walked three doors to the left, and entered a liquor store. Less than five minutes later, now carting two bags, he came out. He put the Kmart bag in the LTD's trunk, got back into the car, and mutely passed the smaller bag to the woman.

At six-fifteen, the LTD left the plaza parking lot and headed east on Delaney Boulevard toward its intersection with the county highway.

6:55 P.M.   ". . . odd to me that anyone going to that—anyone planning a thing like this—a cursory investigation would indicate us as unlikely candida—in that our finances, our available assets . . ."

". . . The point, Detectives—what my husband is trying to

say—is that, despite possible appearances to the contrary—our savings—our investmen . . ."

". . . even the equity in our house is minuscule . . . So I just don't see how this can be about mon . . ."

"We're relatively certain that it isn't, Mr. Follett."

"Isn't what?"

"About money."

Edmund and Caroline quickly glanced at each other, then back at Levy, who nervously cleared his throat. "Based on statistics, profiles, etc., gathered by the FBI, who, by the way, are now, as well as the State Police Bureau of Criminal Investigations, at least in a technical aspect, fully assisting us, our belief—I should say best guess—is that Jennifer, that the abduction was carried out for reasons other than, as I say, to obtain a ransom for her re—"

"You're saying some per—" Leaning abruptly forward in his porch chair to stare open-mouthed at Levy, Edmund knocked over his coffee cup. "Goddamn, fucking, goddamn son of a bitch!"

Trying to stem the flow with his hand, he was stopped only by Caroline's firmly grasping his wrist. "I'll get a rag."

Edmund looked at her. "No, I . . . Caroline? Okay."

She stood up and walked stiffly into the house. A moment later, an inside door slammed loudly shut. On the sun porch, the three men gazed out over the valley where orange-hued cirrus clouds, appearing thin as X-ray sheets, radiated the day's last light. Cardinals and grosbeaks chattered above the wind-rustled branches bearing them. "We're saying only, Mr. Follett, that in the majority of kidnappings where the perpetrators seek ransom, a demand for same—or anyway some contact—is effectuated within twenty-four hours of the abdu—"

Edmund reached up and firmly shoved a fist into his own mouth. Levy glanced at Abbott, who, his elbow just then touched by the coffee stream, leapt back from the table, grabbed a handful of napkins, and dabbed at the effluence.

"You mentioned, Detective"—ignoring Abbott's distress, Edmund spoke through his clenched fingers, making it necessary for Levy, in order to hear him, to incline an ear slightly that way—"having obtained some additional information on the, uh—the suspect vehicle, that—something you wanted to question Caroline and me about?"

Levy nodded. "We have a potential identi—a situation that—perhaps your wife should . . . ?"

Edmund dropped his hand. "Yes. She ought to be here."

"Maybe I could . . . ?" Awkwardly standing with the drenched napkins dangling between two fingers, Abbott glanced around for a place to deposit them.

"Just—wherever," intoned Edmund, pushing his empty saucer at Abbott, who, smiling appreciatively, relieved himself of the mess. Edmund glanced through the screen door into the kitchen. "I'm sure she's checking on Edmund Jr.," he assured them. "As you're aware, Hannah has the night—she's out of the house this evening."

"Yes." Abbott retook his seat. "I'm sure that's a delicate situation."

Edmund smiled acidly. "Actually, we've about decided to contact the Albany D.A." He raised his eyes to the policemen. "What do you think of that idea?"

Frowning, the two officers looked at each other, as if each prompting his partner to answer.

"From an investigative point of view, I mean?"

Abbott said, "We've informed the FBI about your P.I.'s discovering that some of her references were bogus."

"Perpetrated frauds, in fact."

Abbott scowled his agreement.

Edmund tartly nodded. "And will they—the FBI . . . ?"

"Of course"—Abbott leaned forward—"but, you know, without another individual to connect her to—"

Levy interjected, "Frankly, with what our witness has told us about the behavior of the suspect vehicle, Mr. Follett—how, as I say, it apparently stopped, backed up, then stopped again, all well beyond the end of the drive, as if eluding a view from the house and in a spot highly unlikely to be seen by anyone from here even watching for it—we have, at this point, little reason to believe that—beyond possible negligence, to a degree, I think, best determined by you and Mrs. Follett—Hannah Dray was, or is, in any way involved in your daughter—in Jennifer's abduction."

A long, wordless minute followed, in which, above the wind, birds, and early evening peepers, a faraway, monotonous dog's bay could he heard. In this din of bestial noises encircling what suddenly felt like his besieged house, Edmund struggled to suppress thoughts of man's depravity—gruesome stories he had read, lurid accounts he had seen, all proof of humanity's shark-feeding appetite for inhuman acts. But not in the civilized world. Not in his world! Not in any world of which his eight-year-old daughter was a part!

Footsteps sounded in the kitchen, then the screen door opened. Before stepping onto the porch, Caroline, holding Edmund Jr., gasped, "I forgot the rag."

Abbott put his hand up. "It's taken care of, Mrs. Follett. Not to worry."

Edmund stood.

"I thought maybe some fresh air," mumbled Caroline,

nodding at Edmund Jr., then carrying him into the room, to the end opposite the table, where the day crib sat.

Edmund joined her there. He gazed down at his sleeping son, safe in a world so circumscribed and tiny there wasn't even room yet for bad dreams, or dreams at all maybe. Caroline gently placed the child in the crib. "This way, if he wakes up . . ."

"Okay, sure." Levy smiled. "We'll just keep our voices low."

Caroline's eyes were bloodshot, as if, thought Edmund, she'd been crying and stanched the flow with tissues. With feigned confidence, he wrapped his arm around her shoulders and walked with her back to the table, while, somewhere far to the west, an unseen helicopter droned.

7:50 P.M. In the sun's gray wake, the state police chopper, before veering north, toward the airport, flew a final pass over the westernmost woods bordering the arterial. Beneath its powerful beam of light, the last searchers, returning to their vehicles physically and mentally exhausted, conversed quietly, or didn't.

A veteran firefighter, who had once pulled three infants—two of them corpses—from a house blaze, in his inarticulate frustration punched a tree and broke his hand. While being herded into their cages, the bloodhounds mewled and continued to sniff. Before departing, several of the volunteers went down on their knees and prayed for Jennifer Follett. Not anxious to return to empty houses, a small group of noncustodial parents arranged to reconvene at a bar.

Over the Hillside development rose a pale gibbous moon and slowly brightening stars. Dark-activated phosphorescent lights illuminated the long, steep drives and wooded yards around the scattered houses nestled deep in the trees. Homeowners who historically hadn't, locked and bolted their doors; those who had, checked them twice as often.

At dinner tables, heads remained bowed longer than they had before the disappearance; silently beseeching lips moved more fervently. Parents not accustomed to seeking their children's conversation and insight did.

7:55 P.M. ". . . the need, then, for you to cooperate, Mr. and Mrs. Follett, in understanding the extreme delicacy of the situation—not only for, perhaps I should say less for, the purpose of safeguarding someone else's interests, but, more important, for protecting your own and Jenni—"

Edmund bobbed forward as if to interrupt Levy, but Abbott cut him off with a raised hand before himself interjecting, "Under normal circumstances, at this point in the investigation, we would not—nor would any police agency—even be sharing with you what we are about to, but given that it appears highly unlikely—based upon what you yourselves have told us about Jennifer—that she would voluntarily climb into a total stranger's car, and that, consistent with the account of our eyewitness, the driver of the suspect vehicle was totally unknown to her, we find ourselves in this abnormal mode whereby—"

"Are you saying that you know who . . . !"

"Absolutely not, ma'am." Levy, raising his voice, briskly

rubbed his cheeks. "Were that the case, the suspect would be in custody at this mom—"

"Suspect, Detective! What suspect?"

Levy turned to Edmund. "I was responding hypothetically to Mrs. Follett's query as to—"

"You don't have a suspect, then?"

"Technically, no."

"What, then, Detective, do you have?"

"We have, sir"—Levy used both his hands, in a calming gesture, to smooth the air between himself and the Folletts—"a possible identification, by the eyewitness we told you about, of the vehicle which he claims he saw your daugh—saw Jennifer—access."

Beneath the table, Caroline tightly grasped Edmund's hand. Edmund took a deep breath, trying to slow his heart rate. "And do you know who that vehicle belongs to?"

"By tracing DMV records, we now know who owns the vehicle our eyewitness ID'ed earlier today, yes."

"Someone lo—a resident of Dane?"

Levy nodded.

Momentarily rendered mute, Edmund questioningly raised his eyes.

"Whether or not it's the vehicle the witness saw yesterday morning," continued Levy, "remains highly problematic—"

"But he, the wit—whoever—they said it was!"

"That's correct, ma'am." Levy politely nodded at Caroline. "But it's a fairly common model that only minutes earlier he was unable to pick out from a photo array, not to mention that of the two numbers he thought he recollected from the suspect vehicle's license plate, only one jibed with those on today's vehicle."

Letting go of Caroline's hand, Edmund queryingly arced his arm. "Have you questioned the vehicle's owner as to his whereabouts yesterday morning, Detective, or conducted a search of his car?"

"Given the dim view today's courts take of ID testimony, coupled with the facts I've just recited and with our witness being only twelve years old and, by his own admission, over one hundred yards from the suspect vehicle when he saw Jennifer enter it, the D.A. is positively convinced that, at the present time, probable cause to obtain a search warrant for the same does not exist."

"Of course," said Abbott, before the silence following Levy's pronouncement became too pregnant, "we can ask the individual in question to talk to us voluntarily, which he may do or not, but, assuming for the moment he is the perpetrator, should we question him without the legal means to search his person, vehicle, or premises for supporting physical proof, we will have, in indicating our interest, given him the opportunity not only to confer with his attorney but to eliminate or destroy possibly incriminating evidence—"

Caroline loudly gasped.

Realizing she had understood his last spoken phrase to include her daughter—alive or dead—Abbott involuntarily reached a hand out to comfort her. "I'm sorry, Mrs. Follett, I only meant to say . . ." Then, aware that to everyone it was clear what he had meant to say, that it needed saying, and that there was no delicate way to say it, he let both his hand and the sentence drop.

Beneath the table, Edmund recaptured Caroline's coldly perspiring fingers. "In determining, then," he heard Levy say, "how vigorously to pursue this line of inquiry, it behooves us to know if the car our witness this afternoon identified is either owned or driven—leaving open, of course, the possibility of multiple individuals—by a person or persons known to your family."

"You want to know if we are acquainted with this—them—whoev . . . ?"

"Particularly, sir, if was—is—your daughter. It would be another reason for us to look hard at the evidence, and certainly germane to the issue of probable cause."

"Tell us who, for God's sake!" urged Caroline, her voice edging toward hysteria. "Were they part of the list we gave you?"

"They weren't, Mrs. Follett. No."

"It's possible we overloo—what make of car, then!"

"What we're stressing here, Mr. and Mrs. Follett," emphasized Abbott, "is that this person or persons—even if you do know them—are not suspects."

"And we require—that is, request—your assurance," continued Levy, "that even were they later to become so, you will not jeopardize the investiga—even, possibly, put your child's life in danger—by doing something . . . inappropriate."

Beyond the screened porch, whirling bats, croaking frogs, an owl hooting at regular intervals as if cued to an internal clock had, without Edmund's even realizing it, supplanted their daylight counterparts. A recollection of Jennifer's fearing nocturnal monsters lurking outside her window after their move to the new house caused him to twitch subconsciously and to worry that his overpowering sense of helplessness would exhibit itself in a series of such spasmodic jerks. Tightly intertwining his and Caroline's fingers, as calmly as he could he said, "My wife and I, Detectives, are not vigilantes, nor, like yourselves, policemen. We are, simply, worried-sick parents, desperately wanting our child home and safe. Now, please, ask us what you need to know!"

8:00 P.M.   At a rectangular oak table beneath a lighted chandelier, over a supper of lamb kebabs and spinach quiche, a man read *Business Week* while opposite him, her fingers rendered spastic from inebriation, his wife struggled to knit a half-completed stream-of-consciousness wall hanging. Twice the man looked up and, seeing her glass empty of sherry, wordlessly filled it.

At eight-ten, a woman came into the room and cleared the dishes. "Very good, Barbara," the man told her, closing his magazine. "How's your family?"

"Everyone's healthy," the woman answered. "That's all you can ask."

"Right you are." The man stood up. "The rest is in our own hands." He lightly took her elbow. "Why don't you leave the dishes and go home to them early this evening."

"That's—"

"Yes, do." The man nodded toward the front hallway. "We'll see you tomorrow night, then, or is tomorrow the day you're to clean?"

The woman nodded.

"At four, then. No earlier, please. You'll disturb my work. And, as usual, only the living quarters."

The woman hastily got into her coat and left. The man entered the kitchen, rinsed the dishes, put them in the electric washer and the leftover food in the refrigerator, then returned to the dining room, where his wife, the long needles lying at her feet, was manually ripping to pieces her artless creation. Gripping her hands, the man softly said, "Take your sherry and go in and lie down, why don't you, Claire. Watch the end of *Wings*."

"Are you going out later, Gerald?" the woman asked shrilly.

"For a short ride, is all—it's such a lovely night."

The woman fixed him with an inscrutable look.

"You needn't bother waiting up."

"What time did you leave the house yesterday morning, Gerald?"

"P.m., dear, not a.m., don't you remember? You were cat-napping in front of *Days of Our Lives* when I kissed you good-bye."

"I keep forgetting things, Gerald. Like last week when I left the French doors open all night and that awful crow got in the house."

The man half smiled.

"Oh, just why the fuck do you even put up with me, I wonder?"

The man dropped her hands and scrupulously wrapped an arm around her shoulders.

"A worn-out old whore who can't cook, clean, is unemployable, and, but for your beneficence, would be penniless"—the woman, now sobbing, downed the remains of her sherry—"a horrible conversationalist, an embarrassing social partner, stupid as a barn door, lacking in humor, vitality, artistic or practical skills, enough juice in my cunt or muscles in my ass, and, worst of all, a hideous mother, disavowed by her own daughter . . ."

The man tenderly stroked her hair.

". . . a nag, a bitch, a drunk, who no one on God's earth but you, Gerald—for which you're either a saint or a lunatic—would ever, in a million years or until hell freezes over, tolerate, let alone protect and attend to my every parasitical whim and nee—"

The man soothingly placed his fingertips against her lips.

"You had your car cleaned today or yesterday, mister!" the woman hissed in a haunted, barely controlled tone. "Inside and out—slick as a whistle!"

The man punctiliously hoisted her to her feet. "You're disassembling again, Claire, on the road to a blackout."

"I'm simply raving, aren't I, Gerald? Tell me!"

"You're exhausted, is all. And a little sherry-drunk," answered the man, half leading, half dragging her down the hallway toward the bedroom. "And in answer to your earlier question, I put up with you in your many faces and moods—and gratefully so—Claire, because, as you perfectly well know, beyond all reason"—he affectingly kissed her forehead—"I love and require each and every one of them."

8:10 P.M. ". . . more acquaintances than friends, Caroline, wouldn't you . . . ?"

"Not close friends anyway. She—back in the fall, remember, Ed—Jennifer's Sunday school teacher and—"

"They were very nice to us—we were just start—new—in the congregation and didn't know anybod—"

"They had us over for dinner once—they own horses—Gerald does—"

"He is—was, anyway—a professional photog—" Edmund abruptly reached into his back pocket and withdrew his wallet, from which he pulled a plastic-enclosed photograph he tossed onto the table. "He took that—when was it, Caroline, a couple months ago?"

"About, yes." Like synchronized puppets, Abbott and Levy bobbed forward and peered at the miniature portrait of the Follett family, with pet dog, posing in front of a fireplace. "Back in mid-February, I think—there's a larger one hanging in the den."

"They came here to take the pic—Jesus." Edmund stared at Levy, now holding the photo in his hand. "Are you saying . . . ?"

Levy, not answering, preferring to study mutely Edmund and Caroline's reaction, handed the picture to Abbott, who, laying it back on the table, asked, "That would be a church in Dane, would it?"

"The, uh, red brick one on the corner of, I think it's Elliewood and Vine . . ."

"Episcopal," said Caroline. "We don't—we stopped going after four or five months—right before Christmas."

"Why is that?"

"Our schedules mostly, and I suppose a feeling, maybe, that we were there for the wrong reasons, Edmund, wouldn't you say . . . ?"

"When we first moved here we thought it would be nice to, you know, be not just bedroom residents but involved in the community, and, particularly in a small area like this and with Jennifer, we thought—we'd heard, anyway—a good way to do that would be to join a church, so, though we're not, either of us, really religious, we tried a couple and this one seemed the most comf—we certainly liked the majority of the congrega—"

"Really, I guess, it came down to our feeling a little hypocritical with the religion part and the church's stance on certain polit—social issues—and deciding to spend what little free time we had doing other—and then we had Jennifer join the Girls Club, where she's been very happy."

"You attended how long?"

"Three or four months, Caroline?"

"More like four or five, starting around the end of summer—then we had to decide whether or not we were ready to make the commitment to actually join—"

"And Jennifer was in Sunday school with Mrs. Sandoval all last fall?"

"Except for a few weeks when we were out of town. Or had other plans, yes."

"How did she, Jennifer, as far as you could tell, feel about . . . ?"

"She liked her. Seemed to. Claire—Mrs. Sand—was a very nice—I can't imagine—really, Detectives, this is ridic—the suggestion that Mr. and Mrs. Sandov—people we met in church!" Caroline precipitately stood up, walked to the window facing the road, and, placing her hands against the screen, scaring from it several clinging moths, stared out. "In this world there are still some things beyond considera . . . !" She worked her splayed fingers in monotonous, winged motions suggesting grounded, tar-soaked birds or, to Levy, a brain wrestling to denude its hitherto civilized version of humanity.

"You mentioned going over there for dinner once," prompted Abbott. "Would that have been recently?"

"In the fall," said Edmund. He rose, strode across the porch, and, heedless of the presence of the two policemen behind them, buried his face in Caroline's hair.

"All four of you went?"

Caroline shivered. Edmund tightly hugged her waist. "That time, yes."

"There was another time?"

"About a month and a half ago."

"For dinner again?"

"No."

"What was it for?"

In a normal voice nonetheless sounding too loud for the small enclosure, Caroline said into the darkness beyond the window, "Ger—Mr. Sandoval, when he took our family portrait, had promised to let Jennifer ride a horse—apparently she had mentioned to Mrs. Sandoval about its being something she had always wanted to do. She—Mrs.—called early in the week to suggest it for Saturday, and at the time it sounded like a nice idea, but then the day came and Edmund had a proposal to finish for Monday—and I wasn't feeling that well." Breaking away from Edmund's grip, she turned around, walked back to the table, and sat down. "It was an unseasonably warm day, though there was snow on the ground." She flicked absently at her hair. "Jennifer had her heart set on it . . ."

"She went without you?"

"It wasn't as if they were strang . . . !"

"I'm just trying to get the facts, Mrs. Follett."

Caroline glumly nodded. Edmund rejoined them at the table. "It sounded, from both accounts, as though they had a pleasant time. Mr. Sandoval called after to suggest he give Jennifer regular lessons, and she was upse—quite angry actually—when we declined."

"A childhood friend of mine," added Caroline, "was badly

injured falling from a horse at summer camp, and we just felt—you know—she's only eight years old . . ."

"Any other reason?"

"No. I don't think so." Edmund frowned at Caroline. "We didn't hear of anything unusual, except . . ."

"Yes?"

"When she was telling us about the day, Jennifer a couple of times referred to Mr. Sandoval as 'Gerald'—I didn't think much of it at the time, but now . . ."

"Did she mention Mrs. Sandoval?"

"I don't remember that she did, other than to say what we already knew, that she—Mrs.—was afraid of horses."

"She doesn't ride?"

"We took it not."

Levy inquired, "The most direct route, Mr. Follett, from here to the Sandovals'?"

"The arterial north," answered Edmund, "then the highway west. They live on Hulburt Hill Road, about three miles up."

"From town, it would be quicker to take the arterial there than the highway loop?"

Edmund nodded.

"To your knowledge, do the Sandovals normally drive that way to and from Dane?"

"I don't know about normally, but occasionally I've seen their—hold on!—they don't own a—Caroline?"

". . . not certain what make of car it is, Detective, but I don't remember it as being black."

"They also possess a late-model Jeep Cherokee," suggested Abbott. "Silver or light gray?"

Edmund frowned his recollection.

"The Ford is relatively new."

Caroline dropped her head.

"The afternoon she went riding," queried Levy, "which of you dropped Jennifer off at the Sandovals'?"

Edmund and Caroline wordlessly stared at each other, then at the two policemen.

"Or did they pick her up?"

"Hannah took her," Edmund quietly answered. "Hannah Dray."

8:55 P.M. In a darkroom smelling strongly of chemicals and faintly of horse sweat, a thin sliver of light, like a phosphorescent tongue, lapped at a wall of full-length portraits, the beam tenderly licking a cheek, a shoulder, a thigh. From near the light's black source issued aroused breathing, loud swallowing, skin rapidly slapping against skin.

With increasing immediacy, the illumination probed, explored, caressed. At the touch of the beam—in the eyes of its holder—body parts, both colored and black-and-white, evolved independently of the larger flesh they inhabited; each ear, finger, nipple, toe, kneecap became a viable, blood-throbbing, communicative entity unto itself.

Like a gently blowing wind, soft symphony music weaved among the harsher sounds, which, less abruptly than regretfully, ended with a prolonged, almost wistful groan.

With a barely discernible click, the light vanished, leaving the room black as the deepest ocean trench.

71

9:10 P.M. ". . . not going to hold you up with a lot of drivel about who our search and seizure laws are designed to protect," intoned County Court Judge Franz Dibble, his deep voice slightly muffled by the bug screen he, Frank Levy, and District Attorney Brad Nesslor sat beneath, "only to say you took the same goddamn constitutional law courses as me, Brad, and you know better than to come here at nine o'clock at night looking for a warrant based on some kid's half-assed identification of a car, make or model unknown to him, that later he swears he sees driving down the street, only with a different license plate number."

On an elliptical man-made lake circled by garishly lit houses, the three men, to escape the onshore noise of Dibble's four children and two beagles, rode atop his idling pontoon boat. "Of the two digits he thought he saw, Judge, a 'D' was part of the LTD's plate, and a 7, especially from a hundred yards, could easily have been mistaken for a 2."

"And a Ford LTD for a Cadillac Eldorado or an Oldsmobile 98 or any other long, black boxy thing. Jesus Christ!" The judge took an angry swallow of canned beer. "On top of which the car's registrants, so far as your search has revealed, haven't got so much as a ticket for jaywalking."

"That covers just the three years they've lived here," interposed Levy. "The FBI's working on tracing their—"

"Then try coming back, Detective, when they've found something makes these people look even a little bit like kidnappers!"

"There may not be time, Jud—"

"You'd be cutting your own prosecutorial throats if I gave you a warrant on what you've got now, and I'd be investigated for judicial incompetence!"

"Your Honor, with all due respect, given the connection between the owners of the car and the victim and that the former are known to regularly—or occasionally anyway—drive the road on which the child lives, probable cause—"

"You don't even have a suspect," interjected Dibble, crushing his empty beer can against his protuberant mid-section. "You've got a car, Brad, if that, and even if it was the same one the kid saw—which I'm far from convinced of—you don't have any idea who was driving it." He glanced disgustedly through the enclosure beyond which fish periodically jumped to snatch at flies. "It's not my job to tell you how to conduct an investigation, but, Christ sake, gentlemen, before you even question the alleged car's owners as to its or their whereabouts yesterday morning, you want me to—what if, let's suppose, it turns out that they and their suspect automobile were the centerpiece in a ten-thousand-vehicle road rally for parents of children killed by drunk drivers!"

"Under the rule of exigent circumstan—"

"Exigent what, Brad?"

"Circumstances, Your Honor." A small, bespectacled man who couldn't remember when he'd last been on the water, Brad Nesslor, suddenly feeling queasy even from the almost nonexistent swell, subconsciously touched his stomach. "The court is given a certain leeway—"

"The only exigent circumstances here, Counselor, are the police and district attorney's office wanting a judge to contribute to their shabby investigation or, by turning down their patently baseless request for a search warrant, to take the media heat for them if and when that poor child shows up dead."

"Our sole concern, Judge," firmly interrupted Levy, placing his hands on the table, "is what these people might possibly do—particularly to the girl, God willing she's still alive—if they get wind of—"

"So you want me to sanction a fishing expedition, the fruits of which any appellate court in the nation would rule inadmissible, almost guaranteeing your alleged suspects—if they're who took the girl—will never get convicted of anything related to it or reveal to you—or, more important, the child's parents—where she or—sad to say, more likely—her body's at?" He inclined his substantial bulk forward, jerked the boat in gear, and angrily headed it toward the dock fronting his house, two football fields away. "I don't mind telling you, gentlemen, I'm plenty pissed at your ass-covering request, and being not just a judge but a concerned parent and citizen of this currently nerve-racked community, I sincerely urge you to put the aforementioned posteriors in gear getting before me a warrant request I'm not shackled by law from granting so that I, in my tripartite role, can breathe a little easier knowing that our county's law enforcement branch is diligently performing its tasks."

10:30 P.M.   In the little free time they had in the evenings, Edmund and Caroline normally preferred reading to watching television, she mostly historical or contemporary fiction detailing familial travails and conquests and he spy or action novels in which an individual or small group battled superior forces, harsh elements, or malevolent organizations, but this night, when the very small, letter-fractured nature of print seemed to their eyes an insurmountable conundrum, they turned on the set and, at opposite ends of the couch, wordlessly sat before its specious din, absorbing none of it.

Like baleful whispering, resisted thoughts tortured Edmund's consciousness, excruciating imaginings of Jennifer at that very moment—where she might be, what she was enduring, how she must be believing her parents had reneged on their promise to protect her from monsters and bogeymen, a recurring vision of her tiny chest barely heaving, then, abruptly, not at all. Dantean in its horror was the mental picture he had of his daughter, ten miles from where he and Caroline sat helplessly worrying: imprisoned, dying, her cries to them falling on the deaf ears of her onetime Sunday school teacher and would-be equestrian instructor.

During a tabloid news show examining modern society's sanctioning of violence, Detective Levy, as he had promised, phoned to give them the results of the district attorney's warrant request and an update on the investigation, a call Edmund fielded and reported on to Caroline, who, resignedly nodding her head as if the outcome complied with her expectations, in a chillingly calm voice inquired, "What now, Edmund?"

"In the morning they'll—the police—question the sus—the Sandovals—as to their—"

"But Detective Abbott was concern—"

"They've no choice now. We can't wait any longer!"

"Why wait at all, then?"

"If the Sand—if they're slee—whatever—they could send the police away and—"

"In the meantime, another night . . . !"

"A policeman is posted out there—on the road, I mean."

"On Hulburt Hill Road?"

"Below the house, you know, concealed from it."

"And what could anyone positioned on Hulburt Hill Road possibly see of those occupying a building set back from it nearly a quarter of a mile?"

Could it really be, Edmund again wondered, that the handsome middle-aged couple who had laughed and commiserated with them over the hardships of leaving the city—no more takeout foreign cuisine or attending the theater or symphony at the drop of a hat—and entering a new community could be so devilishly chameleonic that, until now, neither he nor Caroline had been even minutely suspicious of them? "In the event someone leaves, they can—"

"Leaves?"

"The police, says Levy, can't go on the property."

"Of course not. That would violate the Sandovals' rights!" With exaggerated control, Caroline flicked at her hair. "We wouldn't want to trample on their rights! They're such nice people. And this is America. With the Constitution and all."

But what could possibly have prompted them to it? From what Edmund recalled, they lived comfortably—and anyway, as the police had suggested, ransom-seekers would by now have requested it. A motive other than money was nearly too unimaginable to be considered by him, who had always believed that a truly fiendish or imbalanced mind, though he'd never knowingly encountered either, would, if only in small ways, be discernible to an educated, sound one. "Caroline, we don't ev—"

"I know we don't, Edmund. I'm not stupid! I understand the dilemma! I simply don't give a shit about the Sandovals' rights—or anyone else's! I care only about Jennifer! The rest of the world, for the time being, will have to live with that. I'll return to being a libertarian after she—"

Edmund moved over and tried to put an arm around her, but, abruptly pushing him away, she retreated to the farthest corner of the couch. "This is ridiculous, Edmund! Why don't we just drive over there and—I don't see why we shouldn't?"

"You heard what the police said. They don't think it's a good i—"

"Oh, fuck them, Edmund, what they think—innocent people wouldn't care if we—and guilty ones—"

"We might further endanger Jenni—"

"How much further could she be endangered! For God's sake, Edmund, we don't even have the vaguest idea that she's—or—"

"What choice do we have but to rely on the poli—?"

"The police who, with an eyewitness identification, can't even obtain a search warrant?"

Edmund reached for her again, and she shrunk from his hand as if it were armed with a needle. "We're a great deal to blame for this, Edmund! What kind of parents allow their eight-year-old child to wait alone for a bus or leave her in the care of some—" Swallowing determinedly, she put both hands out to warn off any further attempts to touch her. ". . . no use to cry over spilt milk—okay, I understand—but I will tell you one goddamned thing, Edmund Follett—once Jen—when she's back home with us—we'll have to—yes, we will—all of us—about making changes—commitments to . . ."

Lowering her hands, she allowed herself, finally, to be touched. Edmund kissed her damp cheeks, embraced her, slowly fell back with her on the couch, where they lay statically hugging. "Give it until tomorrow," he whispered. "Till tomorrow, then we'll see . . ."

11:55 P.M. Sitting in the middle of God's country, just him, whatever wild beasts inhabited the woods encircling his pickup truck, classic Led Zeppelin in his ears over regulation-forbidden headphones, Officer David Bink saw the solitary light he had been watching for over two hours in the downstairs of the house several hundred yards up the hill above him suddenly blink off.

"When the levee breaks," Bink melodically whispered to the tune in his head, "got no place to go."

He picked up a paper pad and pen from the seat next to him, glanced at the dashboard clock, and wrote down the time. Three more hours before he would be relieved. He ate his last jelly doughnut and washed it down with his sixth cup of coffee. Five minutes later, his bladder was again ready to burst. After taking off the headphones, he opened the truck door and stepped out into the knee-high weeds occupying the pulloff where, fifteen feet back from Hulburt Hill Road, the pickup was concealed from the sparse traffic—in the time Bink had been there, at most half a dozen cars had passed, all prior to ten-thirty.

Urinating, he counted the stars in the Big Dipper, then watched, just to the left of the handle, in a silent, ten-second free-fall, one of the brightest drop from the sky. The event significantly affected Bink, twenty-four, and vacillating between continuing his police career or quitting to put his energy whole-hog into a slowly, if at all, evolving career as lead

guitarist for a rock band with a résumé of eight to ten mod-
estly received wedding gigs. "Go for the pension," he told
himself, zipping his fly, then glancing up the hill to where a
thin beam of light doggedly bobbed across the frontage of
the house toward where he'd been told the garage and stable
were. It moved in a straight line for maybe sixty seconds,
stopped, shot upward, then disappeared. A moment later, a
larger light came on inside a building that Bink surmised
someone had just entered.

Bink climbed back into the truck. He wrote the time and
what he'd seen on the pad, then, in case a vehicle were suddenly to depart from the house, picked up the radio's hand
mike, cleared it, put it back, assured himself that the pickup's
key was in the ignition, and rolled down the door window.
Flush with the thrill of having reaffirmed his career, he re-
clined and watched.

The building stayed lit close to ten minutes before it
abruptly went dark. Shortly after, from somewhere on the
black hill, above a whippoorwill's tiresome refrain, Bink heard
what sounded, incredibly, like galloping horses' hooves. Half
an hour after logging his impressions, again bored with the
assignment, he put his headphones back on.

THURSDAY

7:30 A.M. "Galloping horses?" mused Levy.

"According to Bink, though he was at the bottom of the hill, so, who knows, maybe it was the natives playing congas in the middle of the night."

"A former farm boy and aspiring rock musician, Bink, it seems to me, Mike, ought to know the difference between the sound of horses' hooves and drumbeats."

"Yourself being a countryite, Frank, with, I take it, some knowledge of equines, let me ask you if they, like bats, can see in the dark?" Abbott slowed the Plymouth to lessen the impact of a pothole on the frost-ruptured road. On another warm morning, though slightly overcast, in the non-air-conditioned interior, the two detectives again conversed over the rush of external air. "I'd not heard they could, though having been raised in the city and never actually on or even much around them, I'm not well versed in horses."

"Nor bats, obviously, or you would know that they, and no animal or man other than maybe Clark Kent when he's wearing a cape, can see in the dark."

"You're saying the winged devils are slandered by the phrase 'blind as them'?"

"Now you've compounded your lack of knowledge." Levy braced himself for another bump. "Seeing in the dark and being blind are the antithesis of each other. It's impossible to do the one, Mike, and be the other."

Abbott raised his eyes at the ceiling.

"Bats, in fact, can't perform the first and are nearly—though not completely—the second," intoned Levy, tightly smiling, "but with their acute sense of hearing they utilize the echoes from their own squeaking to guide them through the night." He pointed to the camouflaged turnoff up ahead where, in a Chevy Cavalier, Bink's relief sat. "Horses, to answer what I surmise as the intent of your query, do not possess that capacity. Nor, clearly, can they see in the dark."

"Galloping by starlight?"

"Possible—even likely if on a route the animal is used to traveling. Horses have excellent memories and well-honed instincts. A couple of times over the same course and they'll know every pothole and low-hanging branch and won't be afraid to run it half-blind."

"You think Gerald is a habitual night rider?"

Levy shrugged. "Anyway, riding after dark sounds like a nice way to unwind. Or maybe he just let the horses out in the paddock to exercise. Or something spooked them."

Abbott put the right blinker on. "Odd that Bink didn't see the flashlight make its way back to the house."

"Not to denigrate Bink's abilities as a stakeout artist, Mike, but what he saw and what occurred where his eyes weren't focused don't necessarily coincide. Or maybe the batteries went dead or whoever found they could see just fine in the moonlight."

Abbott turned onto the long paved drive, bordered on

both sides by middle-aged, evenly spaced, white oak trees, leading up to the Sandovals' house. "Or, like Rip Van Winkle, our rider is sleeping out in the woods somewhere."

"For a married man, not a bad-sounding option some nights."

Abbott scowled.

"The thing to remember, Mike—in our verve to slay the dragon and rescue the princess—is that in this godawful, son-of-a-ballbuster profession, for every mackerel you put on ice, you reel in—or partly do—nine hundred ninety-nine red herrings, which, chances are, is what the Sandovals—like Bob Waite and Hannah Banana no doubt will prove to be—are."

"That's why you tried so hard for a search warrant before we even questioned them and assigned a man to watch their house, right, Frank? And that was before I talked again this morning to Bullet Bob Waite, who recalls on more than a few school mornings seeing on the arterial a Jeep Cherokee identical to that which we're now approaching."

Instead of answering, Levy said, "From what little we know of these people, Mike, they don't come close to the profile of child abductors, kidnappers, or extortionists, so what I can't figure out is why the thought of the next few minutes makes me so nervous over the plight of Jennifer Follett—on the slim chance she's still alive."

"Maybe, like me, you've got less confidence in professional profiles than in the certain recollections of twelve-year-olds."

Levy grunted.

Parking behind the Cherokee and adjacent to the LTD, Abbott, nodding at the two-story, sedately elegant bluestone house, remarked, "Impressive. For a Dane photographer."

Levy opened his door. "Inherited dough," he said, stepping out, "or fruits of a previous career."

7:40 A.M. ". . . what, then? You've had the police following me?"

"Not the police. And no one's been following you, Hannah, just checking into your background and so forth to determine—"

"You hired someone?"

"A private detective."

Hannah's gaze, seeming to penetrate Edmund and Caroline, fixated on the dozens of squabbling songbirds besetting the circular feeder standing several feet beyond the screened window at their backs. "This is about Jennifer, right? You think I'm somehow involved?"

Caroline, feeding a bottle to Edmund Jr., said, "Put yourself, for a minute, in our place, Hannah—our daugh—Jen—disappears in your care and—"

"Now you find out I'm a liar and a fraud," Hannah stated in her flat tone as if announcing dinner.

Edmund, glancing at Caroline, cleared his throat. In the few seconds before he responded, above the birds' clamor sounded only Edmund Jr.'s dogged suckling. "We'd like to know why, to understa—"

"I'd rather you'd just fire me and get it over with."

"I think, Hannah, we're entitled, at the least, to an explana—"

"Entitled? You mean like that would be the fair thing?"

"In that we brought you into our house and trusted you to—"

"Well, trust, that's like fair, and they're both thin air."

"Pardon?"

"You got what you paid for."

"Perhaps."

Just returned from a night in Albany, she sat erect, her hands in her lap, seemingly hypnotized by the flying barrage she faced.

". . . always before been very hap—pleased, Hannah"—as she spoke, Caroline's fingers holding the bottle trembled slightly—"at your relation—how you got on with and cared for the children. We never had any reason to—"

Edmund silently raised a hand to stop her.

"Hannah?"

Her gaze remotely altered to encompass his voice.

"Have you, then, an explanation for not only fabricating your employment background and references but having two individuals personally vouch for you—both with criminal records, no less, and one who—"

"I met in the nuthouse?"

After dropping from Caroline's hand, the plastic bottle loudly hit the floor, rolled across it, and was stopped by Hannah's foot. She deliberately bent down, picked it up, and set it on the table. Edmund Jr. started to wail. Hannah nodded nearly imperceptibly at the feeder. "The small and the weak get just enough to stay that way."

Edmund alarmedly queried her with his eyes.

"The larger birds drive them away." She casually pushed the left side of her long hair back behind an ear. "To get their fill, they'd peck the others to death."

In Caroline's shaking arms, Edmund Jr. screamed more insistently. Seizing the bottle, Hannah stood, prompting Edmund to half rise and Caroline to loudly gasp, strode to the latter, reached down, and abruptly lifted Edmund Jr. from her apparently paralyzed grip, remarking, "I could have been anybody in off the street." She gently placed the nipple in the baby's mouth and him against her chest. "That's how desperate you were to have your childcare problem solved."

"That's enough, Hannah!" Frozen between sitting and standing, Edmund chose the former, collapsing in his chair. "We're not going to sit here listening to you put the blame on us for your deceit!"

Caroline reached up for Edmund Jr., but Hannah easily backed away. "You're just lucky it was me you hired and not some real crazy." In the sudden silence created by the child's halted screams, her words sounded louder than they were spoken.

Taking a deep breath, Caroline got to her feet. Hannah stepped forward and carefully handed her the now placid Edmund Jr. Caroline nodded reactively. "Thank you, Hannah. I sometimes—I get—don't have the patience . . ."

Hannah slowly sat back down. "I do have one."

"What?" inquired Edmund.

"An explanation for lying to you."

7:45 A.M. ". . . if only you'd called first, Detectives . . ."

"As I say, we apologize for that," said Levy, glancing around the mahogany-walled foyer, "but on such a routine matter, and we were driving out past here anyw—when do you think he might be back, ma'am?"

"It's hard to say. He, uh, wanted to unwind after working some . . ."

"He had a shoot this a.m., did he?"

"No. Here at the house—in the darkroom. He often does his developing then—early in the morning."

"He's been out how long?"

"I actually wasn't up."

"I tell you what, ma'am," suggested Abbott, "why don't we talk to you first—that is, if you don't mind—ask you what we have to, and then—it shouldn't take long—maybe he'll—maybe your husband will be back?" He looked openly at Levy, as if the idea had just occurred to him. "What do you think, Frank?"

"I don't know why not, Mike. Might even be quicker." Levy stepped to enter the living room doorway, from which Mrs. Sandoval, firmly planted, didn't move.

". . . actually rather that you wait for Ger . . ." Reaching up, she jerkily tightened the lapels of her housecoat. A tall, handsome woman, she had her hair neatly coiffed in a large braid circling the top of her head. Levy assessed her as fidgety, by nature or circumstances, and her eyes as tired or hungover. "What exactly was it that—did you want to ask us?"

"Truthfully, we're hoping, Mrs. Sandoval, that you and your husband will clear up for us what we feel absolutely certain is a case of mistaken identity." He shrugged. "That way we can get on with following up other—more substantial—leads in the case."

"In what case?"

"The disappearance of Jennifer Follett." Looking directly into Mrs. Sandoval's eyes, Levy watched them momentarily drop, then, as if responding to an internal switch, as quickly rise again, though avoiding his. "I understand you and your husband are on friendly terms with the family?"

She nodded. "Lovely, Christian people—it's—we feel just awful . . ."

"As does the entire community, Mrs. Sandoval, particularly, as you can imagine, Edmund and Caroline Follett. Anyway, I'm sure you've spoken to—lent them your support?"

"I . . ." Her voice slightly cracking, she shook her head. "We've—meant to call or send a card—one doesn't know just what's appropri—do you have any idea what's happened to poor little Jenni . . . ?"

"We're quite certain, ma'am, she was abducted."

Falling back a step, Mrs. Sandoval audibly gasped. "Abduc . . . ?"

Levy thought he heard a noise from the interior of the house. It struck him he was operating under an advantage he was not likely to have again and could soon lose. "As a matter of fact, Mrs. Sandoval, a witness claims to have seen her getting into a black sedan similar—or I should say, identical—to the one you and your husband own." He smiled. "To get it out of the way, then, ma'am—where exactly were the two of you and the car in question early Tuesday morning?"

"What?"

Levy strolled determinedly forward until, stepping aside, she allowed him to enter the living room, a large high-ceilinged space with a fireplace at either end and framed photographs adorning the hardwood walls. After three steps, he slowly turned back around. "Maybe we won't even have to trouble your husband. Were you here at home?"

"Was I . . . ? Yes."

"At which hours?"

"I'm not sure what you—I slept here, Detective."

"Didn't go out at all the previous evening?"

"No."

"What about before noon Tuesday?"

"Not by vehicle. I may have taken a short walk is all."

A large calico cat loped gracefully from behind the couch and wrapped its body around a leg of Mrs. Sandoval, who precipitately reached down and picked it up.

"And your husband?"

She rubbed the purring cat's belly, staring, vacantly, thought Levy, into its eyes.

"Mrs. Sandoval?"

Her gaze responsively lifted.

"Was there any time during the hours I just mentioned that Ger—that your husband—ma'am, took the LTD for a drive?"

She shook her head.

"While you were sleeping or out for your walk, perhaps?"

She placed the cat gently on the floor. "I'm sure he'll tell you he was here all night, Detective. And all morning. Mostly in the darkroom. Working."

"And you can verify that?"

"Haven't I just?"

"And the car wasn't lent to anyone?"

"Not by me." With her leg she firmly pushed the cat away.

"All right to look in the vehicle, ma'am?"

She pursed her lips.

"You know"—Levy shrugged helplessly—"just to satisfy our superiors."

"I really—no, the cars actually are"—her half-smile and regretfully shaking head struck Levy as an appeal for his understanding—"his department—Gerald's—he mostly takes care of that . . ."

She stepped back into the doorway. "If there's nothing else, Detectives, I'll have him phone—"

"Your husband's work, ma'am?" interrupted Abbott.

Standing before one of the fireplaces, he was viewing above it a black-and-white photograph of a preadolescent blond girl, in jeans, black riding boots, and a sleeveless undershirt, leaning almost seductively against a grazing horse's rump. Slowly pivoting her head toward the picture, Mrs. Sandoval nodded.

Abbott smiled his admiration. "Captivating."

"He's especially deft with human subjects."

"Do I notice a resemblance to yourself in this one?"

"Very perceptive, Detective. That little girl is my daughter."

From outside sounded a brusque snort and a horse's hooves sharply clattering on pavement. Followed by Levy and Abbott, Mrs. Sandoval turned, hurried through the foyer and out the front door to the driveway, on which, from the stable at a fast trot, approached a large stallion carrying Gerald Sandoval.

8:00 A.M. ". . . and the letter of reference you gave us on the personal stationery of your then supposed employer, Dr. Mark Howarth . . . ?"

"This guy, David, I met him through his sister at Carter Hospi—she was there with me—I gave him some of my Disability money to make me seem employable . . ."

"I spoke with the doct—a man—at his phone number!" Edmund restrainedly bit his lip. "He was very articu—seemed well informed about your perform—qualifica . . ."

Again pushing at her hair, Hannah nodded, answering, "David's a college graduate. He's real smart."

"But not, I take it, a physician?"

She brusquely shook her head.

"Nor someone who employed you as a nanny?"

"He doesn't have kids," she replied without a detectable trace of irony.

"Only a long prison record for mail fraud and forgery?"

"It's what he does, I guess—to make money."

"Commits impersonations, you mean"—having returned Edmund Jr. to his upstairs crib to rest, Caroline's freed-up hands on the glass tabletop flitted from coffee cup to saucer to baby's rattle to a guidebook on songbirds—"blithely wreaking havoc on and destroying innocent vict—families—lives!"

"David says he can only convince people of what it's most convenient for them to believe."

"What?"

"I don't know him that well. It's what he told me." In fact or Edmund's imagination, Hannah's emotionless cant sounded an increasingly haunted note in the morning-fresh room. "I'm not vindicating it, understand, but what he says is, his gift—that's what he calls it—works only on captive audiences, those desperate to hear what he tells them—dying cancer patients yearning for a cure, old people for salvation, absent parents for—"

"Fuck you, Hannah!" Briskly fanning the guidebook's pages, Caroline intently studied the nanny's face. "And burn in hell for coming into this house and doing what you've done!"

"I didn't do anything but what I was paid for, Mrs. Follett—take care of your kids and love them when you weren't."

"Do you think we would even have considered hiring you had we the slightest idea that—"

"I'm quite positive," plainly interjected Hannah, "you'd have selected an applicant simpler to condone."

Not replying, Caroline stared even more smolderingly. Firmly placing on his wife's wrist a hand she seemed not cognizant of, Edmund to Hannah said, "The other referen—woman—I spoke to over the phone in Schenectady—the one we've learned is—"

"Schizophrenic," Hannah placidly interrupted.

"Your condi—ailment—is similar to hers?"

Hannah's blank stare bespoke Edmund and Caroline's naïveté. "While on her medication, she is—like me—mostly asymptomatic."

"And, like you, a convicted prostitute."

"Certain heads lead the body into dire straits."

"Dire straits?"

"Try getting to Palooka, Kansas, with a Florida road map."

"What?"

Hannah shrugged unapologetically. "A lot of things happened before I was diagnosed."

"And since?"

"The world is calmer. Medicinally peaceful. A windless lake that barely ripples." For the first time Edmund detected a trace of emotion slightly choking her voice. She glanced—embarrassed or ashamed—down at her elegant, sandal-clad feet. "More than anything, I love to hear and feel the warm, gentle wind of children's laughter."

Caroline's loud, tormented sob muted even the birds.

8:30 A.M. ". . . strong, loyal, loving animals," said Gerald Sandoval, the unopened saddlebags hanging from his shoulder as, in the company of the two policemen, he walked back toward the house from the barn where he had just rubbed down, fed, watered, and put out to pasture the stallion, "not, however, near as intelligent as they're given credit for, which, one might argue, also applies to most of mankind—present company excluded, of course."

"Actually, Mr. Sandoval," said Abbott, "I've never heard of anyone giving police, in general, much, if any, credit for smarts."

"Those that don't, Detective, have failed to consider the many manners of intelligence, from the high-cognition, mostly non-utilitarian sort possessed by Mensa members to the less measurable though, for my money at least, far more practical and—to the crooks on the wrong end of it—dangerous intuition owned in large quantities, it seems to me, by every good policeman." He nodded complimentingly at Abbott. "Yes?"

"Maybe by the select few icons—Deputy Dawg, Dick Tracy, et al.—revered by my partner, but, in my view, the large majority of us are dogged plodders, sniffing and following trails until, with a little luck, instead of turning cold, one heats up."

"Less art-inspired as you see it, Detective"—Mr. Sandoval inquiringly waved his long, tapered fingers through the air—"than cobbled together?"

"I liken the job to a game show. On the trail of a porcupine-strangler, I look for people with quills in their hands."

An estimative smile his sole response, Mr. Sandoval dropped his arms and lengthened his already long, powerful stride, necessitating Levy, in order to keep pace with the former and his marathon-running partner on his relatively short thick legs, to break into a half trot and strenuous breathing. He huffed, "You follow a particular route each time out, do you, sir?"

With a backward flick of his head, the photographer indicated befuddlement.

"On the horse, I mean."

Mr. Sandoval neither slowed up nor glanced behind him. "I, as well as my mount, would find that awfully boring, Detective Levy."

"So you ride mostly in which direction?"

"In any direction on God's green earth, sir."

"Do you often sleep in the woods?"

"Do I what?"

"Perhaps I misunderstood—you went out riding early this morning, not last night?"

"Misunderstood whom, Detective?"

"The, uh"—Levy had to stop and catch his breath—"situation."

Sandoval, stride for stride with Abbott, kept walking. "I think you must have."

Abbott asked, "How did Jennifer take to the sport?"

"Totally uncharacteristic of most first-time riders and nearly all children, she was absolutely undaunted by the challenge and, equally amazing, exhibited—I'm not sure how to say it— a rare ability, through her mannerisms and words, to in turn relax the animal, not a small task, given most horses' wariness of being touched or mounted by novices." At the patrol car he stopped and, facing Abbott, while waiting for Levy, stood erect before it, his lean torso, beneath black riding attire, respiring effortlessly. "Had she taken basic equitation classes from me, I'd then have sent her on to someone more experienced in perhaps hunt seat, for which, in my opinion, she possessed—God willing, possesses—abundant natural talent."

"But her parents didn't want her to. Do you know why?"

"Edmund and Caroline, lovely people, raised in the city, share, I suspect, many urbanites' fear—I noticed you yourself, Detective, were more than a little skittish around my big stallion—of large animals and worried about possible injury to Jennifer, who, at any rate, they felt was too young to be so high off the ground."

"You, though, disagreed?"

"Not with their decision, as I'm sure they've told—or will tell—you, but with their viewpoint." From beneath Mr. Sandoval's riding helmet, twin lines of perspiration, the only outward indication that he was exercised, serpentined down his whisker-shadowed cheeks before being absorbed by his collar. "In my experience, at eight—even six or seven—a child's natural sensitivity and vital imagination perfectly complement a horse's even more puerile personality, which, above all, responds favorably to flattery, touching, and the promise of treats."

Still mildly heaving as he joined them, Levy, for not quite tangible reasons related to the previous statement, experienced an inward chill, half doubling him up as if he'd been punched.

"A cold drink, Detective?" Mr. Sandoval unaffectedly inquired. "Or do you simply crave oxygen?"

Abbott reached a hand out toward his partner.

Politely waving them off, Levy, fighting a harsh, momentary sentiment that he was underqualified for the mental rigors of his job, slowly straightened up. "Sugar pain."

"Switching to decaffeinated coffee cured me of a similiar-sounding ailment," volunteered the photographer.

"I take it, then"—Levy smiled weakly—"you have given riding lessons in the past, Mr. Sandoval?"

"Off and on—when a student strikes me as particularly gifted."

"To children mostly?"

"To whoever, of whatever age, shows a unique inclination."

"Here in Dane?"

"No."

"Where you lived previously, then?"

Mr. Sandoval casually nodded.

"And that would be . . . ?"

"In the Midwest."

"Around Topeka, Kansas?"

Mr. Sandoval's eyes questioningly darted at the policeman.

"The Folletts, as well as other members of your congregation, thought they recalled you or Mrs. Sandoval mentioning that area." Levy shrugged indifferently. "Others, including Father Bowker, believed you said the vicinity of Lincoln, Nebraska."

"Bob and Emily Pasternak could've sworn you told them about moving here from a small town—they couldn't remember the name," added Abbott, "in southern Missouri."

Mr. Sandoval laboriously shifted the saddlebags to his opposite shoulder. "During the course of our marriage, gentlemen, we've lived, like many couples"—he rolled his neck as if to loosen it—"in various places for different durations. I hope you've not, with your loaded questions, been sullying our good reputations in the church."

"Experience tells me, Mr. Sandoval, that with your and your wife's cooperation, we can, working together, very soon put this unpleasant business behind you."

"Detective Levy, my wife and I are suffering the same pain as the rest of the community over this tragedy. Every morning and night we beg God to safely return Jennifer to her parents. Tomorrow evening, in conjunction with fellow communicants, we will lead a prayer vigil at our church, which I urge you to accompany your families to." Mr. Sandoval paused, his upper lip quivering. "To be misidentified as—I suppose the word is 'suspects'—in her disappearance is"—he nodded at the house, in the front door of which his wife had suddenly appeared—"unbearably painful, but not half so much as your insinuation that we are somehow attempting to hinder your thus far fruitless investiga—we've answered, I assume consistently, all your inquiries, gentlemen, as to our and our vehicle's whereabouts on the day in question and our relationship with the Folletts, so would it now be too bold of me to suggest that your witness, whoever that might be, is, quite simply, mistaken, or a liar fabricating out of self-interest?"

Abbott nodded encouragingly. "Any idea what that interest might be?"

"Not the slightest, nor even that he or she is actually so motivated, Detective. However, if you were to tell me the individual's name . . ."

"We won't do that, Mr. Sandoval."

"I somehow thought not, Detective—nor would I expect you to—yet my wife and I stand accused by the police of noncooperation."

"Two items"—Levy dramatically held up and wiggled his right index and pinkie fingers—"could alter that perception, the first being your permission for us to conduct a thorough search of the Ford."

Again jerkily shifting the saddlebags, Mr. Sandoval expansively frowned. "At great inconvenience, I'll drive it to your offices tomorrow morning."

"We were hoping to clear the matter up befo—"

"I have two appointments out of town this morning, Detective Levy, and Mrs. Sandoval needs the Cherokee to take her cat to the veterinarian." Lengthily inhaling, he viewed an empty, corpulent cloud before gradually returning his attention to the policemen standing beneath it. "I realize your job is not an easy one, Detectives, and, truly, I applaud your diligence; only please remember this is a small community in which I run a business, on top of which Jennifer's disappearance has me—us—greatly upset, and your showing up here based on some—" The photographer raised his hand as if to interrupt himself. "If it will help, I'll do my best to get the LTD to you late this afternoon."

He turned and started briskly walking toward the house, slowing down only enough to indicate he was listening when Levy called out, "Finally, sir, if you and Mrs. Sandoval would provide us with a list of your previous addresses—say in the last ten ye—"

"Though at a loss to understand your interest in that information, Detective," Sandoval responded over his shoulder, "I assure you that our joint recollections will immediately be applied to assembling it."

10:45 A.M. Edmund imagined hell as less a fiery, barbaric damnation imposing corporeal sufferance than, as was his world of the last two days, a static, outwardly beautiful place where infinitely—in every noise, sight, touch, taste, or feeling—inhabitants were confronted by the earthly pain caused by their neglect of the very lives above all others—even their own—God had entrusted them with to love and protect.

"Give me another chance," he mutely wailed. "One final opportunity not to waste!"

Like derisive laughter, the brusque chatter of squirrels sounded outside the sun porch, which since Jennifer's disappearance had, with the kitchen, living room, and Edmund's office, become most of his universe. "I never saw her have so much fun"—Hannah's account was no less excruciating for him to hear the second time—"she wasn't at all scared. Of course, Mr. Sandoval was always right there . . ."

"Holding the reins, you mean?" inquired Levy.

Her wrinkled, blue-and-white tennis jersey sweat-soaked, Caroline voicelessly stood and entered the house, weariness or something in her shoe slightly hobbling her normally effortless glide.

"At first, yes. Then he got up and sat behind her on the horse and made it trot and gallop around the field. Jennifer loved it. I would have been deathly scared. They're such big animals. And move so fast."

Even Hannah's sometimes delusional mind, Edmund realized, had recognized his and Caroline's desperation to avoid having their lives inconvenienced by their children, who, through their innocent needs and unabashed joy, both drew from and somehow flamed the nanny's drug-diminished life spark, an astounding therapeutic feat which under other circumstances Edmund might have been more amazed than guilt-ridden by.

"Tell me again about the pictures." Placing his hands on his knees, Levy leaned encouragingly toward Hannah. "How many would you say he took of her?"

"It's hard to say because often I was watching Jennifer—patting the horse, feeding it apples, whatever—but a few times, four or five anyway, I saw him doing it—you know, snapping his camera at her, and I would hear the shutter and it sounded sometimes like he was clicking it as fast as he could."

"And what would Jennifer be doing?"

"Things with the horse—like I said—or just whatever. Once, she was leaning over, like with her back to him, picking a flower, and I saw Mr. Sandoval shooting her. Another time she was itching herself." Hannah flicked deliberately at her hair. "Like, you know, kids do—in their butts."

"You didn't think that was unusual?"

"Well, he's a photographer—that's what he does. But I did think he took a lot—of course, I hear they do that, take a lot, and some quite strange—but then, I guess, they only keep the good ones."

"Did he ever ask Jennifer to stand or pose a particular way?"

"Only once. He asked her to lean with her arm up against the rear end of his big horse." Edmund saw Levy suddenly drop his eyes to the floor, then, his face slightly flushed, straighten up and extend his right arm toward the wall.

"Like this?"

"But with the other hand on her hip. And her head sort of cocked." Hannah frowned. "I was afraid the horse might kick her or something—I wouldn't have stood within ten feet of it—but Mr. Sandoval said not to worry, nothing would happen. Then he asked Jennifer if she was all right doing it, and she was.''

"About her—about Jennifer posing that way," Edmund interjected at Levy, "you acted—why did you act like . . . ?''

Levy answered sedately. "On the wall of the Sandovals' living room hangs a photograph of a small child—of Mrs. Sandoval's daughter—standing similarly.''

"No! We were there—I don't remember seeing any pictures of littl—''

Levy almost too casually shrugged. "It may just recently have been hung.''

Edmund coarsely ran a hand back through his hair, sweaty and, since the previous day, in need of washing. "She—Mrs.—never mentioned having a daughter . . .''

Nonresponsively pursing his lips, Levy slowly turned back to Hannah. Edmund gazed at the potted lilies, half to three-quarters open, issuing their sweet, birthing scents, thinking of—and now it seemed so obvious—his eight-year-old child attracted, in a daughterly way, to a grownup, or grownups, who in a single day—or maybe on several Sunday mornings—showered on her more attention than her parents had in months. Despairingly, he recalled that, despite Jennifer's nagging requests, after a string of excuses by himself, they still hadn't repeated their initial fishing outing. "And he never asked for you to pose by yourself or with Jennifer?''

"No.''

"Nor, to your knowledge, took any photographs of you?''

Composedly shaking her head, Hannah, in her unwavering monotone, replied, "My whole life I've been told how pretty and photogenic I am." Again she summarily dealt with her cascading hair. "Though I understand picture takers all have their favorite subjects, so I guessed his were girls littler than me."

Uncomfortably clearing his throat, Levy reached up and adjusted the knot of his sagging tie. "At any time was Jennifer out of your sight?"

"Only when one of us was using the toilet."

"Was she ever alone with Mr. Sandoval?"

"On the horse, that's all."

"With Mrs. Sandoval?"

"In the kitchen, for half an hour or forty-five minutes maybe—she helped her make lunch."

"Did he—or she—mention anything to you about sending copies of the photographs Mr. Sandoval took to Mr. and Mrs.—to Jennifer's parents?"

"Nuh-uh."

Levy glanced at Edmund, who, looking away from the white flowerpots, harshly reflecting the sun, blinked as if coming out of a trance. "On the phone, Gerald told us he'd taken some shots of Jennifer that afternoon, and would let us know when they were developed." He laboriously swallowed, rubbing an eye. "A week or so later, he called to ask if we'd thought more about her taking lessons—as we'd promised to do—and I told him we had but had decided against it, and he—Mr.—suggested, well, anyway, why didn't Caroline and I bring her over an afternoon and he'd show us the pictures, which he thought turned out excellent, and, at the same time, how gentle were the horses and how wonderfully Jennifer got along with them." As if seeking the pots' blinding glare, his eyes moved back to them.

"Did either of them call you again after that?"

"Gerald—two or three times—to schedule a time. Truthfully, Caroline and I were afraid that Jennifer—if she got around the horses—she'd start in again about lessons, but we didn't want to offend the—so finally we set a date for a couple of weekends ago, but something came up and we—Caroline and I—put it off indefinitely."

"And you haven't heard from them since?"

Edmund shook his head.

"The day before Jennifer disa—that afternoon," intoned Hannah. "Monday. Mr. Sandoval called here."

Edmund and Levy wordlessly stared at her.

"I was changing Edmund Jr.'s diaper, so Jennifer"—attempting to concentrate, she closed her eyes—"she'd been home from school maybe an hour—answered in the kitchen."

Edmund fought a compulsion to shrilly shatter the natural sounds of the woods—the chirping and chattering—gnawing at him like constantly dripping water. Levy patiently smiled at Hannah. "How did you know it was Mr. Sandoval?"

"When I came out of the nursery, Jennifer told me."

"Exactly what"—Edmund strained to keep his voice from rising—"did Jennifer tell you, Hannah?"

"That Mr. Sandoval had phoned for you or Mrs. Follett. I assumed she tol—she said she would give you the message herself."

"Had you any idea what he was calling about?" asked Levy.

"I was pretty sure it was about the lessons. Jennifer isn't one to rant and rave, but I knew how upset she was at her parents that they wouldn't let . . ." Opening her eyes, she glanced almost apologetically at Edmund. "I figured it would be best, you know, for me not to get in the middle. So I intentionally didn't ask her about it."

Levy slowly exhaled. "How long did she and Mr. Sandoval speak?"

"I'm not sure. Not more than five minutes, though, since that's the longest I ever am changing a diaper."

11:30 A.M. On the second-story porch outside her sewing room, a woman reclining in a wicker chair sipped sherry from a juice glass while watching, beneath a bald eagle circling the unmowed field of briers and saplings before Hulburt Hill Road, a spring fawn, still with white spots, suckling its grazing mother. Elevated above the woman's waist, around which lay her slip and hitched-up cream-colored frock, her splayed feet rested on the front porch rail, exposing her naked vulva to the sun.

She drank the last contents of her glass, placed it on the rail, and one hand on her genitals. Up from the field floated the essence of daffodils and clover and, from the stables to her left, stallion. Her nipples turned tumescent beneath her bodice. Behind her, the house was a stupendous weight falling. Moisture descended her cheeks.

She idly caressed her mound of soft, sun-warm, graying hair, then, below it, with her middle finger, the tender lips, casually at first, until she had isolated her clitoris, and gradually more intensely to make the pebble-hard protrusion dampen and swell, then, responding to her aroused state, more rapidly, not roughly, though, as if her ministrations were rays of the sun, bringing herself to the pulsating edge of orgasm, when, abruptly, she stopped, lowered her finger an inch, and, with two others, deeply plunged it into her opening, wet and hot as the fiery eye staring into it.

Her silent, climactic screams, deafening to her, were heard by no other creature in that world or, the woman felt certain, any other.

Afterward she withdrew her drenched fingers, rubbed them against her breasts, belly, cheeks, smelled, and sucked them, and inwardly railed, "See how I'm still sopping wet and fertile and my nipples grow hard!"

She mutely sobbed, and her tears to her tasted the same as had her lubrication and the sherry she'd drunk.

11:45 A.M.   ". . . as I'm told was made clear to you during your impromptu visit to them, Gerald and Claire are concerned, like the rest of the populace, in ascertaining the whereabouts of Jennifer—whom they feel a special kinship for—and to that end will offer aid and assistance to the police in whatever ways they are able, though naturally they're upset at being brusquely interrogated by members of this department"—thrusting his thick, prow-shaped head toward Levy and Nesslor, Arnold Bagge aggressively proceeded—"and, through similar grillings of their friends and fellow worshippers, seeing their good names in the community soiled—"

"How many minutes—or was it seconds, Counselor?—did Gerald, the concerned citizen, wait to call you after we left his residence this morning?"

"To consider it suspicious, Detective Levy, that law-abiding subjects of the United States, harrassed by police officers who unexpectedly and without a warrant appear almost prior to the sun on their doorstep, contact their attorney, suggests you ought to review—or, for the first time perhaps, read—the Bill of Rights."

"See—in an investigation, Counselor? Where the law's been broken?—that's how the police go about their work: question people. Follow up leads." As if explaining to a small child or retarded adult, Levy enunciated precisely. "We used to think the bad guys would feel guilty about their indiscretions and, after a while, turn themselves in, then discovered, much to our chagrin, they didn't actually give a shit and we'd have to get off our asses and catch them. What a bummer!"

"And when the real evildoers elude you"—since his long-ago days as a college wrestler, Bagge, maintaining his grappler's orneriness, had to his heavyweight's build only added pounds and whorls of body hair, sprouting even from his ears, nose, and knuckles—"you apparently roust honest, upright citizens for practice!"

From his chair left of Levy's desk, Nesslor thrust a placating hand between the two men. "Your popping in like this uninvited, Arnold, suggests you've come on a mission we're waiting to have revealed."

"Having instructed my clients to respond to no further questions issued outside my presence from this agency, I hereby advise you, Detective, to not again intimidate, annoy, interrogate, or directly contact them." He expansively opened his hands. "Secondly, in that they desire to have this department off their backs and applying its investigative verve to, hopefully, more fruitful pursuits, they will, against my advice, have their vehicle here at four-thirty this afternoon for your technicians' fine-toothed inspection, which I have every confidence will further exonerate them."

"Said vehicle looking, I'm sure, clean as the day it came off the assembly line." Levy bowed his head in mock thanks. "And the list of their previous addresses?"

"That hardly seems relevant to your investigation."

"I'm less surprised than interested that you think so."

"At any rate, it seems to me a privacy issue."

"Not, I would suggest, to people concerned with offering 'aid and assistance.' "

"Put the question to me again once you've gotten back the results of your search." Bagge shrugged accommodatingly. "Now, what can you tell me about other avenues?"

Neither Levy nor Nesslor responded.

"There must be other avenues."

"At the moment," replied Levy, "we're traveling the one we think will take us to our destination."

Bagge stuck a finger in his ear, twirled it around, pulled it out, studied it uncomprehendingly. "This witness, he—it is a he, am I correct?"

Nesslor rocked back in his chair. "Don't run into the door on your way out, Arnold."

"You won't let me question him—even in strictest conf—?"

"We won't let you question her, him, or it under any circumstances you can fantasize," said Levy.

"Should I anticipate . . . ?"

"I would, and then some. Unless your clients are willing to take a polygraph."

"Regarding what?"

"Haven't you spoken to them, Arnold?"

"What do you mean?"

Nesslor frowned. "Gerald phoned her—phoned Jennifer— the afternoon before she disappeared. That's something we'd like to know more about."

"He called to speak to her parents, that's all."

"Only she never told them that."

Bagge probed his other ear. "You know kids."

"And we'd like to see the pictures he took of Jennifer the day she was out there riding. That might be an indication of good faith."

"He doesn't deny taking the pictures. He's proud of the pictures. He tried giving them to her parents."

"Which ones?"

"From that day. Of Jennifer."

"All of them? Sounds like he took hundreds. You don't know. We don't know. He knows, and we'd like to know. And why."

"I don't think the pictures will be a problem. I'll talk to him about getting you the pictures. Honestly, Brad." He looked at Nesslor. "These are good people. They've got nothing to hide."

"When you actually sit down with the two of them," said Levy, "you ought to explain about a snowball rolling downhill, how it gets bigger."

"I'll explain to them about size, how—like evidence—it's in the eye of the beholder."

"My other thought is that maybe the Sandovals aren't such a good duet. Maybe you ought to sit down with only one of them—probably Gerald, since he's the one with the big bucks, the horses, and the camera—and send Claire over to the Public Defender's office."

Bagge, indicating Levy, growled at Nesslor, "For fifteen years this guy, this poet cop, talks in the abstract—never answers a question but with another one or a non sequitur. It wears on you. The job's hard enough. Tell him to speak English, not convoluted horseshit. Everybody here's college-educated."

Nesslor wordlessly shrugged his small shoulders.

"Try this for clarity, Counselor," said Levy. "If the girl—Jennifer—if she's still alive and your clients, or one of them, have anything to say about it—anything at all—as God is my witness, she better the hell stay that way or, to me and the law's wrath, Gerald and Claire might as well be Siamese twins."

12:20 P.M. ". . . really ought to call, I suppose, and fill them in—only they'll just—mine especially and particularly Mother—want to fly here immediately and . . ."

"Really, what can we," agreed Edmund, looking up from the coffee table on which, after he'd taken it from the wall to idly examine it, lay his ancestral garrote, a studded iron collar meant to slowly strangle a neck until it broke, "at this point—better, I think, to wait—to not alarm—until we have information definite to . . ."

". . . same with telling friends or people at work—if you try to explain—impart what little knowledge you have—they—contor . . . act as if she's . . ."

". . . Well, because they love us, is why, and Jennifer—but most people can't, no more than us, handle the thought . . ."

". . . and at the same time we have to—with the investigation, I mean—and remain hopeful, confident . . ."

". . . and informing people—and having them act like that, and hug you and tell you—though they're well intentioned . . . makes it seem worse really than—I believe, honestly—it actually will turn out to be . . ."

"I've been thinking about my self-pitying—at times hysterical—behavior." Briskly standing up from the couch, Caroline smoothed the wrinkles from her slacks. "What's important—what now matters—is that I—we—while under-standing our parental shortcomings and even bearing some responsibility for what's happened, put aside our feelings of self-guilt and misdirected anger until Jennifer, as you said, Edmund, is back home." Almost shyly she reached out and touched his shoulder. "Hannah, poor child, she did not . . . create this."

"No."

"We should, I think, wait to decide about her—how to proceed—until—after."

"Yes."

"And concentrate on—because, though it's hard to believe, a lot of things seem to be pointing at the Sandovals."

Edmund wordlessly twisted the garrote's tightening knob.

"Though, for the most part, the police, I think, seem com-petent and hardworking—their freely living up there and our knowing, or anyway suspecting, makes it frus . . . infuriating—and the law in general—this notion of safeguarding the rights of the innocent by shielding the guilty—and realizing that, even at this moment, Jennifer might . . ." She picked up the nearly full food tray. "Did you get enough soup?"

Edmund nodded.

"There's plenty."

"I've had that. Thanks."

She indicated the garrote. "The boundlessness of man-kind's barbarity as evidenced even in our own keepsakes."

"Barbarity incites barbarity."

Caroline curiously eyed the garrote. "It's horrible."

"Even more so for its methodological simplicity, which in-dicates long and arduous thought preceded its creation."

She abruptly turned away. "I'm going to take a shower."

"And then I will," said Edmund.

"We'll feel better clean," Caroline assured them.

A minute later, she entered the downstairs bathroom. Soon the water began to run. Edmund picked up the phone book. He opened it to the S's. Near his feet, lying in the skylight's eye, Garofalo oozed quiet, potent farts. Edmund, on the portable phone, punched in the number he had looked up. On the sixth ring, a woman answered. Perspiration broke out on Edmund's brow. His eyes watered. His muted voice over and over asked, begged, pathetically mewled to speak to his daughter.

"Hello," repeated Claire Sandoval. "Is anyone there?"

Edmund clicked the reset button.

12:35 P.M. Hanging up to a dial tone, the woman saw the fawn and its mother, in their graceful way, abruptly flee the field over which the eagle circled lower and lower and where, harshly piercing the serenity, a hidden woodchuck whistled. Halfway to the road, a brier thicket trembled as if being shaken, then from out of it loped a large bear, startling the woman into spilling onto her naked abdomen a full glass of sherry, which, like warm, hemorrhaging blood into a surgeon's sponge, was half absorbed by her pubic bush.

The bear tripped and rolled in the heavily foliated field, quickly righted itself, then, furtively glancing around as if for witnesses to its awkwardness, ran across the long drive, disappearing into the adjacent woods. The horses' loud neighing and rapid traversing of the small paddock assured the woman, unaware of previous bear sightings in the area, that she hadn't hallucinated the animal, which, in her drunkenness, she took as a precursor of a tumultuousness soon to befall the hill. With her white panties, she wiped the sherry from her body. She heard the darkroom door behind which her husband had been cloistered for nearly three hours loudly shut downstairs, though she hadn't discerned its opening, then footsteps moving north to south in the first-floor hallway.

Sounding slow and laborious on the hardwood corridor, the walking grew louder as it approached the stairs, then, after passing them, gradually softer until the woman could no longer hear it. A brief interval full of only nature's din preceded a dense reverberating thud beneath and several feet to the left of the porch, as if a heavy object had been dropped on the bluestone floor of the foyer, the bang followed, seconds later, by another.

The woman poured the remaining sherry into the juice glass, set it on the rail, watched a daddy longlegs climb the goblet, awkwardly circle the rim, then oppositely descend, after which the foyer door opened and through it stepped the man, hefting on one shoulder a deep, rectangular wood box, more tall than wide. Appearing to moderately toil beneath his burden, he proceeded straight along the drive to the stable, where he remained long enough only for the woman to secure her dress, rearrange her hair, and feel pooling in her stomach a potentially throat-clogging, coagulant vomit.

Walking sprightly back to the house, the man glanced up, spotted the woman, and acknowledged her with a curt nod. Moments later, he returned to the stable with a second box identical to the first. This time he shut the barn door behind him, not exiting before the woman had adjourned to the upstairs bathroom, where, instead of throwing up, she submerged her torso in a warm bath and, recalling the mother doe's alert instincts, the eagle's circling, the bear's sudden emergence, phoned a friend from church to share her morning's rare sightings.

1:00 P.M.   Less than an hour after relieving Ronald Carrs of stakeout duty, Officer David Bink, numbingly bored, was close to believing he had misinterpreted the message in the previous evening's falling star or, conversely, would act contrary to it because no career path, even that of a busted rock guitarist, could be worse than endlessly sitting in the middle of nowhere, watching a barely visible house, to or from which no one appeared ever to travel, while, prompted by excessive cups of potent coffee, having to periodically venture into fly-infested woods to urinate or, clinging bare-assed to a tree, defecate, as Bink was, with some difficulty attributable to his inactivity and fiber-free diet, when up the hill to his right, from a dense patch of oddly shimmying shadbushes and maple saplings, came a loud thrashing and a brusque or angry snort.

Bink apprehensively glanced at the pickup, forty feet to his left, then down at his lowered trousers and holstered gun, inches above a meager, pellet-hard b.m., and back at the thicket just as it separated to reveal a large, furry head.

"Jesus, God almighty!" yelped Bink, scaring the bear into rising up and bursting from the bushes in a man's lope, a sight prompting the patrolman, without pulling up his pants, to do likewise toward the truck. After falling, he rolled several feet, struggled to his knees, half yanked up his uniform, slapped at his holster and found it empty. Glancing back, he saw his service revolver lying near his turd, sixty feet in front of the hard-charging bear, now galloping on all four legs.

With one hand holding up his belt, Bink again rose and, emitting noises similar to those made by the bear, sprinted for the truck, half-certain he wouldn't make it and wondering if instead he ought—though he didn't quite dare—to turn and, hoping to scare his chaser, wave his arms and yell at it. Still fifteen feet from the pickup and less than half that in front of the bear's harsh breathing and lathery stink, Bink heard the animal's pained or startled yelp, followed by a loud thump, then saw it, slightly to his left, rolling head over heels down the hill.

A minute later, from the safety of the truck, Bink, breathing hard while adjusting his trousers, watched, through shut windows, the spastic bear, whose stumble had perhaps saved Bink a mauling if not his life, sniffing the pickup's tires. The patrolman was oddly calm, surprised only at not being scared shitless, even as the bear put its paws on the passenger door and eyed him through the glass. He understood, first off, that he had been chosen by the God who had tripped up his pursuer to, for good purpose, inhabit the earth far longer than his present age; second, that whether to excel at police work or rock guitar was less the issue than the verve he applied to either or both—for the first time envisioning himself capable of multiple excellence; and, third, that to reveal to anyone the source of his karmic awakening would only diminish its meaning to him.

At the sound of a vehicle descending the Sandoval drive two hundred feet through the trees to their front—a large truck that Bink, otherwise occupied, had not seen or heard ascending—the bear, which Bink surmised might even be God incarnate, abruptly loped off into the heavy woods and vanished as if it had never been. "Thank you," intoned Bink, mystically smiling at the calm woods that had seemingly swallowed the beast.

Then, with renewed vigor for his assignment and suddenly recalling the small girl at its center, he watched the truck come out of the trees at the end of the long drive and turn left onto Hulburt Hill Road. Moments later, as it slowly passed his concealed position, Bink read, in large lettering on the vehicle's side, KATO'S GARBAGE SERVICE. Suddenly struck by a creative thought—an actual investigative insight—Bink flicked on the shortwave radio, picked up the mike, and assertively patched himself through to headquarters.

1:20 P.M. Edmund pictured himself as a train without an engineer programmed for a destination uncertain only to him, fueled, alternately, by hope and fear, the latter paralyzing, a reminder of the grip in which all humankind was squeezed, and the former briefly empowering, like a drug that postulates to those under its sway that individuals control their destinies, that, by one's own forceful action, all may be changed.

From somewhere upstairs, soft, tinkling music reached him in the master bedroom, where, following his shower, dressing in jeans and a T-shirt, he unexpectedly recalled the compelling sense of might and justness he'd earned from his sole injuring punch, at the age of fourteen, to a boy two years older who with a BB gun had shot and made crawl a retarded boy Edmund hardly knew. Despite his parents' ordering him to apologize to the shooter, whose nose he'd broke, Edmund hadn't, and when he wanted to feel good about something, even thirty years later, he thought of how he'd helped the injured boy up and to his home after, and the grateful look on the boy's face.

He followed the music to the second floor and down the hallway to Jennifer's room, where he'd not trodden since her disappearance, hesitated beyond the partially closed door, then, cognizant of his heart's rapid beat, entered to find Hannah and, tight to her bosom, Edmund Jr., casually rocking in the chair fronting his daughter's bureau, on which played the *Lion King* music box he and Caroline had given her that Christmas, both their eyes closed, in sleep or rest, faces placid as only those steeped in childlike innocence or abject consciencelessness can appear. Viewing the pink, flower-print-bordered walls hung with drawings and paintings of posed and active horses whose significance just then occurred to him, Edmund, as if struck by the unblindered knowledge of his own naïveté, loudly gasped and fell to his knees.

"On such a beautiful day, Mr. Follett"—he looked up into Hannah's dispassionate eyes, the rustic brown of leaves unearthed after a winter's thaw—"Edmund Jr. was disdainful of sleep." She spoke in a matter-of-fact whisper. "I thought a familiar scene might . . ."

"What?"

"We used to sit here—and Jennifer on the bed—before Edmund Jr.'s late afternoon nap." She nodded down at the sleeping child. "As you see, he is calmed by music." She smiled serenely. "Sometimes Jennifer would rock him and he would go out"—she soundlessly snapped her fingers—"like that."

Edmund gazed dizzily overhead at a dangling mobile of galloping horses, the animals suddenly seeming to be all around him. "We actually—her mother and I—worried she was a bit young yet to be holding him."

"Oh no. Jennifer is very good with infants."

"Well, she loves them, I know."

Hannah nodded. "And animals. And toys. And most people."

Edmund slowly got to his feet. "She—confided in you, Hannah?"

The nanny slightly shifted her eyes. "We became good friends, I think."

"When did she begin"—Edmund inclined his chin at the walls—"you know, this fixati—about horses?"

"After riding one."

"She was terribly angry at us—Caroline and me?"

"She couldn't understand why you let her go once, then not again."

"We tried to expla—I thought she realiz . . . !"

Hannah wordlessly allowed his emotion to recede.

"And Ger—the Sandovals?"

"What are you asking me?"

Edmund unconsciously stepped toward her. "Did she—I mean what did she . . . ?"

"They were nice to her." Hannah shrugged. "And they have horses." She adjusted Edmund Jr. against the black, heat-absorbing turtleneck over her chest. "That's about what I gathered. Jennifer's only eight, after all."

Edmund reached down, stroked his son's fragile head, then, inexplicably drawn to Hannah's blond hair, moved his hand up and touched it. "Where did you learn so much, Hannah—about children?"

Unperturbed, she gazed up at him. "At sixteen, I inherited my mother's sickness. Before then, when she couldn't—most times—I cared for my younger sister."

Edmund smoothly ran his fingers through the long yellow strands—like rays of light puncturing a dark cloud—wishing her bland demeanor to contain soulful, God-granted wisdom. "Where is your sister now?"

"In heaven for sure."

"And your mother?"

He heard her intricate swallow. "Still living."

"As self-reliantly as you?"

Hannah didn't reply. Edmund lowered his cheek to the top of her head, so softly warm and soothing, desiring to feel from her the same love his children had. "Do you miss her, Hannah—miss Jennifer?"

She gazed down at Edmund Jr.

"Both of us do. Very much."

Suddenly embarrassed, or just uncomfortable, Edmund straightened up.

"She's in my heart, Mr. Follett. And me in hers."

"Thank you, Hannah. Thank you for that."

He turned and hurriedly left the room.

Downstairs, entering his office, he immediately sensed someone else had recently been beyond the door he kept firmly latched. A hint of soap or perfume tinged the air, and it appeared the papers on his desk had been rearranged. Then he noticed the bottom right drawer storing the pistol he'd inherited from his father and, since he possessed no ammunition for it, didn't lock up was ajar. Edmund abruptly remembered he'd not laid eyes on Caroline since his shower. He ran to the desk and yanked open the drawer.

Not in its metal case inside a file folder where he stored it, the weapon lay prominent atop the two, as if someone—Caroline?—wanted to draw his attention to it. Edmund picked up the gun, slipped it into his belt, then quickly departed.

1:50 P.M. On the dirt shoulder at the bottom of Hulburt Hill Road where it connected with the county highway, Abbott, seeing through the windshield the slow, exhaust-spewing approach of Kato's garbage truck, reached through the Plymouth's driver-side window holding a red bubble, which he set flashing on the car's roof. Then he stepped from the car and, as the truck drew closer, waved it to the side of the road.

Almost prior to the vehicle's stopping, its doors opened and the combined six-hundred-fifty-pound Gaberdeen brothers, Harold and Billy, climbed apelike from opposite sides, reunited at the truck's front, and, shoulder to shoulder, advanced in their primordial gaits on Abbott, who though not really concerned by their imposing formation, nonetheless reached into his jacket and unsnapped the holster strap securing his automatic. "This 'bout last week at Feely's?" shouted Billy, at three hundred fifteen pounds the smaller of the two. " 'Cause if is it you ain't heard but one side a things, being that Rhino Clausen to get the war started throwed him a live rat in a beer pitcher not hardly drunk from givin' 'im what all in that place 'd tell ya a Chinaman's chance not bein' bad retributed by some one of us turned out be me!"

Fifty feet away, Abbott flashed a peace sign at the brothers.

"On'y sense to any of it was Rhino's old lady throwed him

out for that Hancock woodcutter, which oughtn't ta been skin off'n nobody but hers and the lumberjack's asses!"

Abbott stopped, assumed a spread-legged stance, and, in an unequivocal gesture, extended his palms toward the oncoming pair, who failed to even slacken their paces.

"Ain't no guddamn need," hollered Harold, "to be redlight and 'barrassin' our asses on the job like this here!"

Abbott abruptly returned a hand to his holster.

"Tol' that skinny cop ta other night I'd come in talk on her!" added Billy. "I ain't jis' had the chance!"

Abbott drew his weapon, aimed it skyward, and fired, prompting the Gaberdeens to simultaneously halt ten feet from him. "I'm not remotely interested in transpirings between you boys, some rat, and Rhino Clausen unless from them he's dead, and even then I'm not much, so shut the hell up, walk back to the refuse cylinder, and start shucking out bags until you come to whichever one or more you picked up at the Sandoval place, and if you don't know or can't remember, open as many as it takes to educate you!"

"Do what?" screamed Harold.

"He means git in there find 'em!" yelled back Billy.

"What hell we s'posed to do with 'em, then?" asked Harold in the same booming voice that Abbott, reholstering his pistol, recalled from their one prior encounter passed for both brothers as normal.

"Load them," he said, "into the Plymouth's trunk."

2:15 P.M.   Unable to find Caroline, though her car was in the driveway, Edmund, imagining a weight hovering over their union threatening to crush the life they'd created and the love with which they'd done so, and with the empty gun still on his person, was on his way outside to look for her when the phone rang. He picked it up in the living room.

Sounding strained and tired, Detective Levy caught him off guard by inquiring if the Sandovals—either one—had ever mentioned to Edmund or Caroline any family members or close friends from their past and, specifically, from where.

"I don't actually recall them discussing their histories, period, though I would surmise they had at least a few intimates, if not relatives, in the Topeka area. Why?"

"We're having difficulty pinpointing exactly where these people came from." Edmund let his silence serve as a prompt to the policeman. "We've heard from their acquaintances in the community various locations—none of them specific— and Gerald and Claire themselves are quite vague. In fact, reticent."

Edmund hesitated, trying to register what he'd just heard. "They've told people places other than Topeka?"

"Several."

"Why would they?"

"We're interested in knowing."

"What's it got to do with Jennifer?"

"Are you familiar with the term 'profiling'?"

"I assume you mean in the sense of a biographical sketch?"

"But more detailed—and scientifically designed to highlight common characteristics of a suspect—"

"Suspect?"

Levy cleared his throat. "We feel comfortable referring to the Sandovals as the only people we're investigating at this point, though of course are a long way from—"

"They took Jen—the bastards!" Edmund forcefully interjected. "Actually did, didn't they?"

"We don't know that, Mr. Follett. We certainly don't."

"You know—feel it, though!—like I do, righ . . . ?"

"And we certainly can't prove it, which is why we need more information."

"You mean to ascertain scientifically if these two are what they obviously would have to be in order to—!"

"The FBI," interposed Levy, "is now working on their histories, but, without a starting point—even assuming the Feds, or we, get court-authorized access to Social Security numbers, IRS records, etc.—it may take them a week or so, maybe longer—and given the current exigent circumstances—you know, with Jennifer being maybe—we don't feel comfortable waiting that long . . ."

Edmund heard a loud racket outside and through the top of the kitchen window saw a bird covey fly up from where, concealed from his recessed position, the feeder stood. "Aren't you people—I mean on television—I understood you were trained to elicit information—to grill suspects until they . . . ?"

"Television suspects—at least so early on—seldom exercise their right to speak only through an attorney."

"They've retained counsel?"

"It doesn't mean we can't or won't question them more, just that when we do we want to have our ducks in order— that is, additional, hard evidence in our pockets, so that—"

"But hiring a lawyer indicates tha—"

"Only that they're worried, as they should be."

"And now they're hiding behind the law?"

"From their viewpoint, exercising their constitutional rights—promulgated by minds supposedly wiser than ours to make what we do more challenging."

"So the police must sit idly by while they go about their—!"

"I assure you, Mr. Follett, we're turning over every stone—including recanvassing the area for other possible witnesses—in an effort to accumulate enough evidence to, very shortly, we hope, obtain a search warrant for the house and grounds—"

"And the car, Detective? What about the goddamn LTD?"

Louder chirping led Edmund to again glance through the window where, just above the level of the sill, in the midst of madly flapping wings, obviously free of its mooring, the circular feeder bobbed. Carrying the portable phone, Edmund rapidly moved that way as Levy provided details on the Sandovals' promised compliance. ". . . obviously they're quite comfortable we won't find anything incriminatory in the vehicle, either because nothing was ever there or because whatever might have been has been thoroughly sanitized . . ."

The latter word, with its unspoken implications, voiced as Edmund entered the kitchen, evoked from him an instinctual groan, prompting Levy, after hesitating, to hastily add, "Given that the Sandovals—and their attorney—were certainly aware that we would, at any rate, very shortly have obtained a search warrant, I think it best, is all, not to get our hopes up—about the LTD, I mean."

Edmund watched Caroline determinedly make her way across the front yard toward the garage, half of the bifurcated pole-feeder dangling from each hand while a flock of small, angry birds hovered like mutant bees above her head. What in the world is she doing? wondered Edmund, envisioning their thoughts as parallel, but unexpressed, their pain individually smoldering. "I'll tell you what I think, Detective," he said aloud. "I think our biggest obstacle in ascertaining what happened to our daughter—and perhaps getting her back alive—is the law!"

"I'm sure it must occasionally seem that way, sir, but when one considers the intent of same, then—"

"Save the civics lesson, Detective. To legal scholars this situation may be a hypothetical. To my wife and me it's a war for our child's life."

"I understand your frustration, Mr. Follett, and believe me, no one in this department remotely approaches this case—especially this case—as a quiz, or even just a job, but we can't simply manufacture eviden . . ."

". . . and I keep thinking how it's said that in love and war everything is fair . . ."

". . . for example, were the tables turned and—"

"Were the tables turned, Detective, and I had nothing to hide, my house, my history, every detail of my and my wife's life would be open to you and the Sandovals in an effort to find their daughter!"

Silence ensued from the other end of the phone. Out the window, Edmund watched Caroline disappear into the garage, leaving the birds to scatter.

"Please think hard on the questions I've posed, Mr. Follett. They could be important. One of us will call you again this evening following—you'll be there?"

"Someone will be," Edmund assured him, before hanging up.

He met Caroline in the mudroom. "Why did you . . . ?" He waved toward where the feeder had stood.

"Their insistent clamoring and fighting . . ." She shrugged sheepishly. "And spilling and doodling all over the lawn . . . !"

Edmund spontaneously reached out and hugged her.

Feeling the gun, she gazed down at his belt, then up again, appearing intrigued, alarmed, or both. "While you were showering, I was—in your office—only looking, Edmund—symbolically, you know—for strength?"

He kissed her.

"Then I prayed. For Jennifer. And us. That was better."

Edmund released her. "Detective Levy called. He had a few questions I wrote down for you to look at. He's very diligent, really—all of them. I just feel, to a certain extent, their hands are tied."

"Where are you going?" asked Caroline.

"Into town. To run some errands."

"You'll be back soon?"

"In an hour or so."

"I'll hold this for you"—she pulled the pistol from his belt and gripped it behind her—"until you are."

3:10 P.M. "Your times descending any, Abbott, or have you pretty much peaked at that middle-aged, dilettante's pace?"

Glancing up from a gravy-soaked paper wad, Abbott forced a smile at Samuel Lumpkin—his fellow member of the Dane Track Club before Abbott decided he'd rather run alone—who trained sporadically, ate voraciously, drank excessively, and, from accounts Abbott had heard, religiously toked marijuana, yet, with all that, could at any distance, on his worst day, kick Abbott's ass on his best. "Coming down little by little, Lumpkin, you know."

Its cement floor garbage-strewn, the station's basement blended the smell of sour milk, rotten vegetables, gone yogurt, alcohol, and, from a pool of viscid white sauce oozing out one of the open plastic bags, an herb scent. Six empty sherry bottles were lined up like duckpins beneath a cheap, wall-hung boom box playing Vivaldi.

"Sure—then, too, you took up the sport late, am I right?" airily intoned the evidence technician, a Gumby type, thought Abbott, half legs, the other half a narrow plank crisscrossed by a dangly twig, and, like a dense Thoroughbred, possessing bright, shallow eyes fronting a pea brain rotely instructing its owner—without clear motive, inner pursuit, or spiritual guidance—to balls-out run. "I'll bet you were a wrestler in high school, yes?"

"No."

"What then, feetball?"

Wearing white smocks and plastic gloves, the two men placed on a metal folding table potential evidentiary material, documenting each item on a yellow pad, upon which thence far appeared:

A Dane First Federal Savings and Loan monthly checking account statement for Gerald and Claire Sandoval

Receipts from The Camera Place for twenty-two dozen 36-shot rolls of 35 mm film

A Dominion Liquor Store receipt for six quart bottles of sherry and one of Old Grand-Dad whiskey

Two 8×11 white envelopes, each exhibiting on their front the handwritten letters WORD

Half of a torn legal-sized manila envelope, with the return address:
Samantha Connor
R.D. 2
Tyler, Oregon 97192

From the Great American Grocery Store a receipt for, among other things, a twenty-four-ounce bottle of apple juice, a small soft-bristled toothbrush, Crest Sparkle toothpaste, and an eighteen-ounce box of Kix cereal

"Bowling," said Abbott.

"Jesus! The fat-ass sport"—Lumpkin tossed a banana peel into the refuse can—"God love you! You're getting the lead out now, though, guy, huh?"

Consoling himself with the information that, unbeknownst to Lumpkin, a uniformed officer one night behind the Victory Store parking lot had jacklighted a car in which the distance star's naked wife was seen astride a seventeen-year-old bag boy, Abbott, grunting his reply, picked up a slightly damp clump of papers and started meticulously separating them, glancing at each before placing it on the table or in the trash, while Lumpkin, becoming increasingly intolerable on the sole subject to which, despite his title and expensive training as an evidence technician, he could rightfully claim a modicum of expertise, bragged how his most recent marathon time qualified him to start in the second row at the same event in Boston. He was, absurdly and with a straight face, proclaiming that he might actually win the race when, Abbott, no longer feigning even remote interest, dislodged from a jam-smeared bread slice a $48.92 Kmart receipt on which, at close inspection, he discerned, among a list of purchases piquing his professional fervor and heartbeat, one that nearly brought the latter to a complete stop.

3:30 P.M.   After entering the living room, the man resolutely walked from window to window, opening each, admitting a warm breeze stinking of pollen and plant-pregnant earth that was momentarily harsh as smelling salts to the woman sitting in a cane-backed chair, facing her daughter's likeness, picturing the child's bud fully flowered, the obverse of her own wilted and decaying shell.

"Before dropping the car at the police station, Claire, I'm meeting with Arnold Bagge." In cotton trousers, loafers, and a casual dress shirt adorned with a thin tie, the man, in his bearing, features, and build, thought the woman, was as handsome as when she had first encountered him, trolling, with his camera, the city streets. "I had hoped you'd accompany me but see now you've reached, a bit early, your normal evening condition."

"You're supposed to protect me, Gerald."

He stopped near her. "Haven't I always, Claire?"

"But those policeme—I don't want to answer any more questions!"

"And you shan't. If an investigative type shows up in my absence take to bed and make like a turtle."

"I'd rather we—can't we just go—somewhere?"

"For what reason?"

"I don't want to be looked at strangely by people. I shall go to church this evening, Gerald, and pray not to be."

"You're too pickled for public consumption. You'll have to conference with Him here at home."

Angrily engaging his confident gaze, the woman, as usual when doing so, experienced a sensation similar to staring into the sun, and quickly turned away. "Well then, make them—Gerald, the police—those dick-sucking fucks—only to leave us alone!"

"Poor Claire! When agitated, you revert to speaking your native gutter English." Inclining, he dryly kissed her cheek. "Unless you know something I don't, Claire, they obviously won't find whatever they are searching for in our car"—feeling clammily cold despite the temperate air, the woman began to shiver—"forcing them to stop persecuting us and to redirect—hopefully, for the sake of poor Jennifer and her distraught parents, with Godspeed—their investigative dog-and-pony show down more fruitful roads. Will that ease your tension?"

The woman nodded, but couldn't stop trembling. The man touched her quivering shoulder, which, by his strength, was miraculously stilled. "How like a small child born to yourself you are, Claire, who couldn't possibly survive under your own mothering. Have you any idea of the tremendous burden I carry, realizing that if death or incapacity befalls me you would be not only penniless but on the streets again or, even more tragically, imprisoned or institutionalized for the rest of your life?"

Wordlessly staring at the image of her daughter's halted growth, the woman envisioned her own eternal soul blackening like the charred cadaver of a burned tree, the earth in which it stood rotting. "Arnold Bagge," concluded her husband, striding toward the foyer, "will give me a ride home."

3:40 P.M. ". . . and you say he left about forty minutes ago?"

Caroline nodded, momentarily forgetting she was on the phone with Abbott.

"Ma'am?"

"Yes. He said he was going to run some errands and would be back in around an hour." In the relative quiet resulting from the front yard's depletion of feeding and squabbling birds, her voice, in the empty kitchen, struck her as unusually loud and strident. "I'm just a bit worried that he wil . . ."

"What, ma'am?"

"Pardon?"

"Worried that what?"

To interrupt the pattern, Caroline cleared her throat. "Excuse me, Detective. I'm sensitive to the pollen."

"It's a particularly bad spring for it."

"Why is it that you phon—what was it you wanted me to discuss with Edmund?"

"Well, maybe it doesn't take discussion." He issued a breathy sound, as if attempting to lighten the mood or not to impute too much importance to the call. "As I think that Detective Levy earlier explained to you, we try, ma'am, during an investigation to gather as much background information as possible about not only suspects and witnesses but, uh, victims, so that—well, in the course of a—we just never know what might be relevant."

"You have some questions about Jennifer?"

"Just a few."

Caroline felt her pulse insistently rapping against her temples. "Have you learn—has something come up?"

"Not of significance, ma'am. Not yet, I'm afraid."

Suddenly bothered by the sharp flower smell assailing the house, Caroline, recalling how she'd earlier been driven to extremes by the birds' maddening din, wondered if tragedy was both fine-tuning her senses and making them more irritable. "To start with, ma'am, I'm wondering"—Abbott politely broke in on her silent musing as if responding to a posed question—"if she—if Jennifer—had—has—for example, a favorite breakfast cereal?"

"Breakfast cereal?"

"Maybe she doesn't even eat cereal?"

Caroline made a strange sound similar to Abbott's earlier airiness. "She eats cereal, Detective—usually Cheerios or Kix. Or the two mixed together. Do you know how to spell Kix?"

"K-i-x."

"Some mornings she eats pancakes. Occasionally French toast. What's going on, Detective?"

Abbott loudly exhaled. "Please understand, ma'am, during every investigation countless leads—most proving to be dead ends—arise that, regardless of their chances of bearing fruit, our job requires us to run down." He hesitated, picturing on the line's other end the strained facial features he had never seen in their natural state, a state he hypothesized as kindly, serene, beautiful. "I promise you, ma'am, from the bottom of my heart, that if—when—we have any concrete information, you will be immediately contacted, then kept abreast of the situation."

A short silence ensued in which Caroline understood that much of life entailed decent people colliding in indecent situations. "I will hold you to that promise, Detective."

"I can only imagine how difficult, Mrs. Follett, this situation must be for you and Mr. Fo—"

Caroline interjected, "Please ask me whatever you need to know, Detective, and I will try not to impede you further."

"Dress size?"

"Pardon?"

"What size dress does your daughter wear?"

Caroline loudly swallowed as if bailing against a rising flood. "A child's eight."

"And shoes?"

"Child's size twelve."

"Is there a beverage she especially cares for?"

"Anything fruity. She doesn't like soda. Nothing with fizz."

"Does she read any particular sort of books?"

"She loves books about animals. All kinds of animals."

Abbott could be heard lightly tapping an object—a pencil or his finger—against the phone's mouthpiece. "Is there a particular toy, ma'am, that Jennifer sleeps with at night? A doll, or a stuffed animal maybe, she's especially close to?"

Battling a surging, emotional wave, Caroline pressed a hand to her chest, squeezed shut her eyes, and gave Abbott the answer he was waiting for.

3:50 P.M. So redirected and potential-filled was his outlook for the future that Bink—becalmed from and at the same time energized by his near-death experience—divided his thus far short life into eras self-labeled PB (Pre Bear), the chaotic, confused, two-and-a-half-decade-long, scared-shitless state he'd miraculously exited less than three hours previously, and the corner-turning AB (After Bear) whereby to Bink—and, he assumed, a handful of others lucky enough to have been afforded a similar view—the world was unmasked as not the hard, unyielding rock face he had so long suspected but a soft, transmogrifying beach ready to be whatever one made of it.

After observing the LTD wind down the drive, turn left on Hulburt Hill Road, and disappear, he logged the occurrence, then radioed word of it to Levy, who, subsequent to rogering the information, gruffly added, "That was damn alert—fine police work—on the garbage truck, Bink. You'll be commended and ought to be hellish proud."

"I'm grateful, sir," came back Bink, in a casual tone befitting his new mind-set, which anticipated he would excel and be recognized for it. "From my vantage point, Detective, the suspect sedan looked to contain only one occupant."

"Mr. or Mrs.?"

"Judging by size, the former, I'd say, but, what with the trees and my distance from the road, that's strictly a professional opinion."

"You mean, guess?"

"Roger."

Levy was heard to clear his throat. "Very good, Bink. Keep up the good work."

"And out," Bink signed off.

Around that hour he had meant to light up a fat marijuana joint brought with him to stave off boredom, but in his new natural state of exhilaration perceiving cultivated hallucinogens less as a path to mental enhancement than as consciousness-muddying, he blithely pulled the bummer from his shirt pocket and tossed it out the truck window. Ten minutes later, while envisioning himself as the first superstar rock guitarist to coincidentally serve, in response to his fellow citizens' strong lobbying, as his hometown's police chief, he saw come up the road from the direction of the highway a dark green car, which, turning onto the Sandoval driveway, revealed itself to Bink as a four-door Volvo with a sole occupant. Once more

Bink documented the activity, radioed headquarters, and reported it.

"Blue-balled son of a bitch, Bink," Levy growled, neglecting to say roger, thanks, good job, or in any way compliment the patrolman. "Bastard, shit, and fuck me!"

"Roger and out," meekly replied Bink.

4:10 P.M. After eight times ringing the front door bell to no response, Edmund sat down on a wrought-iron bench beneath a lamppost fronting the house and, to the bawdy whistling of cowbirds, gazed into the forward field of honeysuckle and berry bushes, hoping that Gerald and Claire were the normal, churchgoing couple they appeared, that Jennifer would be back home when he got there and the preceding forty-eight hours a bad dream, but something in that pastoral setting—its very seclusion, maybe—hinted that beneath its exterior churned a strong turbulence not unrelated to what was within himself.

Recalling that he had somewhere learned that the capacity for violence exists like a dormant gene in all of mankind, he— for the first time consciously—embraced his normalcy, picturing his ancestral garrote, through his own ministrations, slowly tightening around the neck of Gerald Sandoval. He thought about Caroline's twelve hours of labor leading to a life so small it could be palmed in his two hands, yet powerful enough to elicit their tears of not just joy and gratitude but sheer wonderment, like a child's when first witnessing a butterfly's flight or a leaf's slow, graceful fall, and he realized, yes, he would kill—or gradations thereof—to save, protect, or avenge those he loved.

In the paddock serenely grazed the two horses, one big and brown, one smaller and darker, which Jennifer, to her parents' incredulity when later she'd excitedly told them, had ridden solo through the field—after they'd stressed to Gerald that he only lead her about, as at a pony ride—which had helped them decide against his instructing her. Not wanting Jennifer to feel punished for having told them what had occurred—or was it more to avoid conflict with the Sandovals?—they'd outwardly cited her youth as the reason for their decision, causing Jennifer to angrily conclude, opined Hannah, that they'd acted vindictively. Might it also have led her, with the prompting of one or both Sandovals, to defy her parents? Was that how it had happened, wondered Edmund. Had Jennifer happily, and by prearrangement, stepped into a black LTD, believing she was going horseback riding? But where had she been taken in fact? And for what reason?

The possible answers were so painful and mind-boggling that Edmund, to expel them, rose, turned to the house, and clamorously pounded on the foyer door, abruptly ceasing several seconds later at the put-put of a vehicle spewing blue-white exhaust out of a rent muffler as it ascended the driveway behind him. Shortly after, between his Volvo and the Sandovals' Cherokee, parked a rust-and-blue Escort from which climbed a middle-aged woman dressed in a soiled pink sweatsuit and black hightops, with a kerchief embalming her high hair, and lugging a mop and pail. "You comin' or goin'?" she snappishly inquired of Edmund.

"The latter." Edmund strode down the walk toward her. "No one's to home."

"That don't sound right."

"I knocked loud."

"Not so 'nough, maybe."

Edmund followed the woman's glance to the east end of the structure, where, in a small second-story window, a curtain moved, briefly revealing in the square of unadorned glass two eyes that, as soon as they vanished, Edmund would have believed were an illusion but for the shimmering of the red fabric concealing them. "Who's there?" he hissed.

"Mrs."

"How do you know?"

"The LTD's gone and she never drives it." The woman quizzically appraised him. "I'd guess she don't want talk to you. Must be you're another cop."

"What do you know about the police?"

"Couple of youse already sniffin' round my place wantin' to know, with me doing their cooking and cleaning, what dirt I could give 'em on Mr. and Mrs." Shaking her head, she turned her back to the dwelling and sibilated, "The tramplin' uh that poor lady's nerves—all 'cause they happen to own 'em a black car!"

"What else did you tell the po—my colleagues?"

"Only that they's good people, even if Mrs. maybe drinks a little much and Mr. acts some peculiar 'bout his darkroom— not wanting me to clean it or go in there, but then, it's where he does his work and I s'pose there's chemicals and such in it." She picked up her implements. "It's plain stupid thinkin' Mr. and Mrs. 'd be involved in snatchin' a young'un, who, if you ask me, was taken to swap for her rich parents' money before somethin'—I don't know what—must gone ter'ble wrong, leading to that poor child likely lyin' dead somewheres only them's a party to it 'll ever know."

His knees involuntarily buckling, Edmund, reeling as if from a blow, struggled not to fall. Carting her tools, the woman bustled past him toward the foyer door which he heard creakily open before a familiar female voice announced, "Come in, Barbara."

Edmund slowly turned around. He watched the maid disappear into the house, and into the open doorway stepped Claire Sandoval, in a knee-length, strapless dress. "Hello, Edmund. I'm so sorry." Her hair looked freshly braided and cheeks rouged, though she appeared trembly, as if a pebble might crack and break her. "My prayers go out—to all of you . . ."

"What?"

She touched a cheek. "I wish I could say mor . . ."

Edmund strode toward her.

She moved haltingly backward, holding the door's edge in her fingers. "Our—my lawy—says I shouldn'—"

"Your lawyer!"

"It's not been eas—been difficult for us, too . . ."

As if approaching a skittish deer, Edmund took another step. "Claire, help us, plea—!"

"It's a horr—tragic—situat—"

"We're not accusing—saying—but you must know some—"

"It's all a mistake, Edmund. A horrible misunderstanding affecting every—all of u—"

Edmund edged nearer to her. "Do you know—anything—we only—!"

"I've phoned the police, Edmund"—she backed up farther—"informed them you're here—they've instructed me to lock the do—"

"For God sake, Claire, you—I know—have got a child of your own—you can't just—!"

"It's all a misunderstanding—I'm praying for you—!"

Edmund moved powerfully forward, reaching the door just as it slammed. He heard the bolt shut and lock, then, vying with his own breathing, inches from where his ear pressed against the heavy oak slab, Claire's deep, tortured exhalations. Seconds later, her receding footsteps echoed through the house. Edmund returned to the Volvo. Feeling as if he'd been mortally wounded, fed water, and then cast out to die, he slowly drove off.

4:45 P.M. Pressing a finger to his chin, Gerald Sandoval, walking across the police parking garage, informed Levy, "I know Edmund—both of them—must be terribly distraught but, honestly, Detective, that sort of behavior . . . Claire, on the phone, was quite upset."

"The man sounds like a loose cannon," added Arnold Bagge.

Leading the two toward the elevators, Levy assured them, "We'll keep a closer eye on him—and Caroline—from now on. It won't happen again."

Sandoval glanced at Bagge, then at his watch. "How long is whatever you have to ask me this time, Detective, likely to take?"

"That's really up to you and your attorney, Mr. Sandoval. I don't have a lot of questions, but they're interesting ones that seem to me to require some explanation on your part." He pushed the button for the first floor. "The municipality's paying a couple of evidence technicians overtime to finish up with your car before morning. If all goes well, maybe you can drive it home."

"I assume that's a joke," said Bagge.

Levy didn't laugh or even remotely smile.

In the upstairs interrogation room, they sat at a metal table, Sandoval and Bagge facing the one-way mirror, Levy with his back to it. Bagge blustered, "My client is here voluntarily in the hope that by addressing whatever of your queries I deem to be relevant, nonintrusive, and designed not to entrap him, he will persuade you to reroute your investigation in a manner more likely to bring Jennifer home and peace to her loved ones."

"We appreciate his taking the time," Levy dryly replied. "Any objections to my videotaping the session?"

"I don't think that's necessary," said Bagge. "We're just talking."

"Shall I Mirandize your client, Counselor"—Levy pushed a paper sheet across the table—"or does he know how to read?"

Bagge glanced down at the form, with its litany of rights. "Go 'head, John Hancock it," he told Gerald, handing him the paper.

Gerald signed his name, then Bagge his, then Levy.

"Your name is Gerald Sandoval?" asked Levy.

Sandoval nodded.

"That the only name you've ever had, used, been known by, or conducted business under?"

The photographer confirmed so.

"Before moving to Dane, did you and your wife reside in or around Portland, Oregon?"

Interjected Bagge, "We're not here to give you an autobiography."

"You won't permit me to inquire about Portland?"

"Not unless you're a member of that city's police force or investigating a particular incident out there."

Levy looked at Sandoval. "Have you previously been arrested or convicted of a crime?"

Bagge placed a preventive hand on the arm of Gerald, who seemed perturbed—or perhaps embarrassed—by being increasingly muzzled.

"You want to specifically probe my client's whereabouts, Detective, or knowledge of the last three days, do it, otherwi—"

Levy acted as if he hadn't heard. "Are you acquainted with a Samantha Connor?"

Bagge abruptly bobbed forward and hissed something in Gerald's ear. Gerald agitatedly listened, whispered back to him, shook his head.

Continued Levy, "What's the name and address of your most recent employer before yourself?"

Bagge frenetically waved his hands at the air as if chasing away a bad stink. "Any more little-green-men, aliens-living-in-your-toaster sort of theorizing, Detective, and we're home to a premature dinner!"

Hit with the same stomach pain that had felled him earlier before the photographer, Levy grimaced.

Sandoval frowned commiseratingly at him.

Levy ignored the look. "What brand of toothpaste, Mr. Sandoval, do you and your wife use?"

"More horseshit," snapped Bagge.

Levy persisted. "You don't know, Mr. Sandoval, or you have a problem telling me?"

Appearing genuinely confounded, Gerald replied, "Crest, I be—"

"You don't have to—" growled Bagge before Gerald, aiming a sharp look at the attorney, cut him off. "Though my wife normally does the shopping."

"What flavor?"

"Baking soda."

"So that would mean unflavored?"

"That's enough," interposed Bagge, "about fucking toothpaste, unless you want to explain your odd oral fascination."

Levy blandly glanced at the attorney. "May I inquire what he and Mrs. Sandoval regularly eat for breakfast?"

"No, you fucking may not, and the reason is I feel like a blind man stepped in a great big turd smells like entrapment!"

"Gee, I thought we were going to just talk, the three of us—" Levy swallowed hard against another searing abdominal jolt. Sandoval, slowly exhaling, crossed his legs, pulled out an emery board, studiously began filing his nails—"like concerned citizens."

"You want to play Alex Trebek, Detective, first give your questions a basis or a goddamned foundation." Bagge made a swimming motion with his arms. "Even on *Jeopardy!*, for Christ sake, contestants know the area being plumbed!"

Levy reached into a large envelope at his side, pulled out a small paper scrap, and pushed it to Gerald. "That ring any bells?"

Sandoval obediently put away the emery board, picked up the paper, looked at it, then questioningly raised his eyes at Levy.

"It's a Great American Grocery Store receipt, Mr. Sandoval, found in your trash earlier today."

Bagge cholerically banged a fist on the metal.

"Trash, Counselor, which, once removed from his residence by private haulers—able to positively identify same from the bright yellow plastic bags, secured by red strings, containing it—entered the public purview, thence becoming legally subject to our warrantless inspection."

The attorney snakily bobbed his upper torso, a wrestler's slip move.

"Take particular note, Mr. Sandoval"—Levy indicated the receipt—"of items six, eight, and nine—Kix cereal, Crest Sparkle toothpaste, and a small, soft-bristled brush—all purchased the day before yesterday."

"Uh, golly, wowee, Detective"—Bagge leaned over and viewed the receipt—"What's your fucking-a point? The man mixed up with what he brushes his teeth?"

Levy shrugged agreeably. "I guess the Sparkle stuff would be in your medicine cabinet and the Kix in your pantry if we looked, Mr. Sandoval?"

Gerald returned Levy's inquiring stare with one of rapt bewilderment.

Bagge said, "I don't see that it matters if there's a tube of llama shit in his medicine cabinet—"

"Let me tell you what I think, Mr. Sandoval"—Levy reached into the envelope and withdrew another paper—"I think items six, eight, and nine were purchased not for your or your wife's consumption but by one or both of you, like a kid's dress, three pairs of little girls' underwear, a child's size twelve pair of Keds, two Dr. Seuss books, and a Cabbage Patch doll, for"—directly gazing into the photographer's face, across which briefly flitted, like a traversing crow's shadow, a dark, prescient cloud, Levy slapped onto the table the previous day's Kmart receipt—"Jennifer Follett, who, if she was alive yesterday—you malignant son of a bitch—damn well still better be!"

Bagge snatched the receipt, for several seconds gravely studied it, then, strenuously exhaling, dropped it back on the table. Once more he hissed, for a longer duration this time, in Sandoval's ear. His features forming a blank mask, Gerald said aloud, "Yes. No. Not remotely." Bagge looked upset. Addressing Levy, Sandoval tranquilly intoned, "The latter items you mentioned, Detective, were purchased for the annual Episcopal Church and Salvation Army Easter Benefit Drive."

Levy stared incredulously at him.

Gerald uncrossed his legs.

"I'm told by parents of six-to-eight-year-old girls—the group my wife and I this year elected to aid—that they adore soft, cuddly dolls, the imagination of Dr. Seuss, and, like their elders, fashionable attire."

Levy suddenly understood his internal pain was exacerbated by pure evil that, even in the face of maddeningly insufficient evidence, his gut defined as Gerald Sandoval. "When is that event to take place, sir?"

"It's a season of giving, Detective, commemorating the anniversary of Our Lord's Resurrection. Feel free to check with the sponsoring organizations."

"Who, I suppose, will verify receipt of the items?"

"They would had the alms not, unfortunately, been stolen from my car before I had a chance to donate them."

"Perhaps if I were to pick up the phone and dial your wife . . . ?"

"My wife witnessed neither the purchase nor the theft of the items, though I suspect she will later—in the presence of Mr. Bagge—consent to being questioned, when, I'm quite certain, she will recall my relating to her the entire sordid affair."

"Would you, Mr. Sandoval, take a polygraph regarding the matter?"

"Not so long as he's my client," interrupted Bagge. "I've witnessed too many inaccurate results."

Sandoval politely shrugged as if the matter, regrettably, were out of his hands.

Grabbing his briefcase, Bagge hastily rose. "Unless you plan on arresting my client—probable cause for which I submit even Houdini couldn't conjure up—I'd say, Detective, we're about through here."

"Does your wife, Mr. Sandoval, have access to your entire house?"

"Say again, sir?"

"Are there locked areas to which she doesn't possess a key?"

"My darkroom only."

"Then I suggest you hurry home," replied Levy, taking from his pocket and handing to the photographer a copy of the house-and-premises search warrant he had, largely upon the contents of the Sandovals' garbage, obtained less than an hour earlier from Judge Dibble and which Abbott, while Levy occupied Gerald, had taken to serve on Claire. "Otherwise an officer will apply to the door of the aforementioned"—he glanced at his watch—"if one hasn't yet, a sledgehammer."

5:00 P.M. In Claire Sandoval's veneer appeared only slight cracks—a fluttering in one eyelid, sporadic finger trembling, dry lips over which her tongue frequently grazed—as with a listing, habitual drinker's gait she preceded Abbott and six uniforms into the parlor, where he explained that the room-by-room search for Jennifer Follett and other items listed in the warrant—"clothing, jewelry, toys, books, photographs of, writings of, writings to, fingerprints, hair strands, or other physical evidence probative of the subject's presence"—would commence upstairs and move down, concluding, hopefully after Gerald's return to avoid their having to force-fully enter it, in the darkroom.

"Barb—Mrs. Fink—is—was"—Mrs. Sandoval jerkily nod-ded at the maid—"in the middle of cleaning."

Abbott replied, "We'll do our best not to dirty things."

One of the uniforms snickered.

Mrs. Sandoval's face flushed. "We'll eat out, Gerald and I, or just"—she turned too formally to Mrs. Fink—"snack lightly this evening, Barbara."

"I'm to go?"

"I think—yes."

Mrs. Fink glanced at Abbott. "Want I should come back tomorrow?"

Abbott didn't answer.

"Usual time, Barbara"—Mrs. Sandoval headed her toward the foyer—"please? For dinner."

Abbott deployed his men.

"If you would kindly avoid moving from room to room," he told Mrs. Sandoval when she returned, "or rearranging things, while we're working."

"It's all a mistake," she matter-of-factly stated.

As casually as he could, Abbott glanced at her. "What is, ma'am?"

"Everything after the first one."

"Which one was that, ma'am—or when?"

She considered him with a mixture of hope and fear, thought Abbott, as if he were a stranger who had stopped to help her on the road.

"Do you want to talk about them, Mrs. Sandoval—your mistakes?"

Suddenly she looked the part of the powerless waif who, convinced that she deserved no better, might compliantly be cowed or beaten. "You're not to question me, Detective. I have a lawyer."

"Maybe not the right one."

"Pardon?"

"Possibly you ought to have your own."

"One for us each? Like lollipops?"

"That might be in your best interest."

Her lower lip began to tremble. Abbott whiffed the sherry on her breath. Moved by her fragility, he felt weak—maybe even duped. He was reminded of the aging but still stately-appearing house in his childhood neighborhood that one day, from latent termite infestation, simply collapsed. "We—the law, ma'am—aren't interested in punishing people for making mistakes . . ."

"It's been my experience, Detective"—Mrs. Sandoval's look abruptly transformed to alluring, as if she might seduce him—"that a person's mistakes are like dropped money for the rest of the world to pounce on." She wheeled away from him, toward the stairs. "When you're through destroying the contents of my house, you'll find me on the sewing room porch absorbing the sun's dying heat."

5:30 P.M.   Edmund's wanderings through the county's hollows and backroads brought him to an intersection with County Route 8, at which an opposite-arrowed sign indicated Dane was twenty miles one way and, four miles the other, Edmund's choice, Cardiff Village, where one winter's night Caroline, Edmund, one of his partners, and the latter's then significant other gluttonously ate and drank at a quaint inn facing a gun and ammo shop with a flashing likeness of a large antlered deer high-stepping across its roof, a promotion they all found riotously funny and, given the nearness of Christmas, too ironic.

Driving through a state-protected pine forest, issuing, with the first warm air, potent-smelling sap that mingled with the sweeter essence of lemon verbena growing wild at its edge, Edmund suddenly recalled the smell of Jennifer's hair on a day she had decorated it with dozens of multicolored flowers to look like—who? He couldn't remember who. A character idolized in her small world, but in his given neither time nor imagination to exist. He remembered complimenting her on the floral design, then cautioning her not to drop petals on the rug. He found himself crying. Ridiculous, but real as his living nightmare. Tears streamed down his cheeks. His rage demanded to know how anyone could intentionally steal from a child—but exactly what all had been stolen from his daughter—innocence? laughter? calm sleep? sleep, period? a future?—he neither knew nor dared guess.

The bulbs illuminating the deer's antlers and legs were dead or had been smashed, so that from a distance its remaining torso resembled—and would even more after dark, Edmund guessed—a map of Italy. The large red-faced man behind the counter found it odd that Edmund couldn't recall what type or model of gun he possessed. Edmund explained the pistol was a gift he'd never fired and its name a number.

The man pointed into a glass case at a Colt, 9 mm.

"Mine's not that big," said Edmund.

"Then it wouldn't be a forty-five."

Edmund shrugged. "I guess it wouldn't be."

The man showed him a smaller gun.

"That's pretty close"—Edmund indicated the weapon's midsection—"only with a round spinner here."

The man pulled from the case a weapon that looked, but for its silver varnish, identical to Edmund's.

Edmund nodded his head. "I'd like a box of shells to fit that."

The man had Edmund write in a notebook his driver's license number, address, and signature, then handed him his ammunition in a paper bag. "You ever fired a handgun of any sort whatsoever, friend?"

"A BB pistol when I was a kid."

The man directed him to a pistol range he could practice on and told him that, if he didn't have one already, he'd need a license for the .38, which was the weapon he owned, and really ought to take a gun-safety class. Edmund wordlessly nodded his appreciation, picked up the bag, and left.

The man called after him, "Have fun, friend."

6:00 P.M. A sour chemical stench permeated the airless soundproof rooms, the larger of which, past the work area, contained a couch against a plastered wall, numerously adorned, like one of those it right-angled, with black-and-white and colored prints of horses, some with riders of all ages and either sex, what looked like homeless or destitute women and adolescents, wandering, talking, clustered in doorways and bus stations, and extreme close-ups of, it took Abbott several seconds to comprehend, sectioned human anatomies—eyes, teeth, buttocks, tongues, a scraped knee, a nipple in yellow light evoking images of the moon through a telescope, a large toe half-buried in a substance resembling Cream of Wheat, a hairless pudendum, which might have been a desert opened by an earthquake, a belly button hauntingly suggesting, in its angled starkness, a mass grave waiting to be filled. "Jesus!" breathed the uniform with Abbott.

On a stand behind the couch, a slide projector faced the opposite wall, taken up by a white screen. "Check what's hanging up and anything in the drawers," commanded Abbott, his eyes darting around the windowless area, "for photographs that might be of the Follett girl."

The uniform waved at the body parts. "How do we know these aren't?"

Abbott didn't answer. Something aside from the visible and chilling obviousness in that scene troubled him. He couldn't put his finger on what.

He walked back into the darkroom, where from a clothesline above a two-basin sink in the middle of a long counter hung developed film of families, two of whom, including that of the Dane real estate magnate Wendell Emerson, Abbott, on close examination, recognized. Stacks of wedding prints lay between sheets of blotter paper, next to an enlarger on a shelf opposite the sink; of the deep metal drawers beneath it, one held developing chemicals, another packets of printing paper, the third files of slides and negatives, which Abbott directed a uniform to mark and put in an evidence bag. A montage of rural and urban citizenry, including stereotypical fat cops, captured naturally, but in a way, thought Abbott, to make them appear boorish and trivial in their day-to-day activities, decorated the back of the foot-thick solid oak door.

What need, Abbott wondered, for a slab so thick? Especially when a thirty-foot corridor segregated the area from the living quarters. And why secure a space inside a house with three interior locks, including two operated by keys? To keep people out—or in?

He got down on his knees and tapped the floor through the rug. Solid. Concrete. No basement beneath this part of the house. Abbott's heart raced. His temples pounded. What was it about the place that struck him, among its paranoid oddities and frightening quirks, as out of sync with the whole?

"I found her!"

Abbott jerked his head at a uniform scanning a photo album, pulled with several others from one of the room's three file cabinets. "She's here!"

"Who?"

"The litt—the Follett girl!"

"Give me that," said Abbott.

He sat down on the floor with the album. She occupied four or five pages. Altogether maybe two dozen shots, any one enough to break the hearts of the parents who had lost her: flinging a rock at an unseen target; laughingly kissing the nose of the same horse that had terrified Abbott the previous morning; sitting, unafraid, on the mare; with, as Hannah had described, her fingers in her butt, the visible result, though, more endearing than lewd. Bending over. Making a sad face. Running. Blond hair flying. Blue eyes flashing. Like who?

The girl over the mantel. Mrs. Sandoval's daughter. And there she was—Jennifer—standing the same way. A hand to the horse's rump. Another on her own.

A certain voice kept repeating in Abbott's head, "As sure as blood is to life is evil to the Sandovals . . ."

But nowhere—not from the entire search or from the suspicions sanctioning it—existed a single scrap of evidence to damn the couple who sat in their kitchen, sipping tea.

Thought Abbott, Levy's right. No more am I a top-flight detective than I am a world-class marathoner. Against deviant brilliance—God's gifts amorally practiced—my plodding can't compete. "Check every inch of the goddamn floor," he directed his officers, "for a trapdoor, anything hollow!"

Fifteen minutes later they had found no such places.

In the large room, Abbott faced the one wall lacking photographs or a screen. Like the others, it had responded to his pounding with a solid thud. But why—particularly given Gerald's high regard for his own artistic brilliance—did it lack his imprint? Then what had been gnawing at him struck Abbott: the incongruity of nothingness in a space otherwise so full.

He took out his pocket flash, approached the wall, and closely examined it. Every six inches or so on the white backing appeared tiny smudges. Like fingerprints but squarer. More defined.

Marks left by something recently removed.

Yes, but what?

Tape.

Looking more closely, Abbott saw between the smudges rectangular strips of paint shining slightly brighter than the rest.

Wall hangings.

More photographs, probably.

In anticipation, no doubt, of the current search, someone, guessed Abbott, had recently removed from the wall dozens and dozens of them, the subject matter of which he dared not even speculate on.

6:45 P.M.   Not hungry enough or in the mood for a sit-down dinner, Edmund and Caroline, with Edmund Jr. propped in his booster seat between them on the living room couch, ate pasta with jarred sauce in front of the six-thirty television news.

A federal building in the Southwest had been blown up by terrorists. Among the victims were several infants attending daycare. Pictures of the dead and dying and their grieving and distraught relatives recalled for Edmund and Caroline the size of the world's suffering in which theirs was but a tiny drop.

"How could most of us and those who do such things," sobbed Caroline, "be members of the same species?"

Edmund had no answer for her.

He turned the channel to a sitcom featuring an obese, rib-ald, talentless woman. The two of them actually laughed occasionally. Now I know, thought Edmund, why, in its pain, much of the modern world has soured on more artful, thought-provoking entertainment.

"What did you do with my pistol?" he asked Caroline, having previously determined that she hadn't returned it to his desk drawer.

"I was frightened seeing you hold it, Edmund"—she looked at him tenderly—"as I was earlier, doing so myself."

"Have you hidden it from me, then?"

She shook her head. "You can have it if you really want—only it should be understood betw—I want us to discuss what you might do with it first."

He watched Edmund Jr. throw his empty juice cup on the floor. "I bought ammunition for it."

Caroline wordlessly bent down and retrieved the cup.

"In Cardiff Village, at that tacky place, remember?—across from—with the deer on its roof?"

"How did you even know what kind?"

"I described the gun, and the clerk—he was just what you would expect—was able to help me."

Picking up a napkin, Caroline wiped Edmund Jr.'s face and hands. She cooed at him, but couldn't divert his attention from the television set he was rarely allowed to watch. "Do you know how to use it?"

"It couldn't be that difficult."

She removed Edmund Jr. from his seat, held him against her chest. Still he wouldn't turn his eyes from the television. Caroline strode to the set and switched it off. Edmund Jr. started to cry. Caroline gently patted his back. "We ought to be clear on exactly what you—we—would hope to accomp—because the issue, Edmund, in my mind—it's not—reveng . . ."

"Clearly not."

"Because that's not a worthwhi—a positive pursuit . . ."

". . . only interested in, however possible—practically speaking—finding Jen—to bring her home."

"I'll put Edmund Jr. down," said Caroline, heading toward the stairs.

In the nursery, she rocked the child until he fell asleep, then laid him in his crib before tiptoeing across the hall to Hannah's room.

In sweatpants and a T-shirt, Hannah sat cross-legged on her bed, scribbling in a small notebook; to Caroline's request that she keep an ear out for Edmund Jr. she obediently nodded. Striving to lessen the tension between them, Caroline politely inquired what Hannah was writing. "Words," the nanny replied, "coming into my head."

Caroline waited to hear if the words composed a poem, a journal, or a story and, if so, about what, but Hannah mutely closed the notebook and tossed it behind her. Suppressing a strong urge to walk over and read what was there, Caroline hurriedly reentered the hallway.

At the bathroom sink, she filled a pitcher, then watered the plants in her office, and in Jennifer's room. She ruffled the covers on her daughter's bed, making it look slept in, rearranged the stuffed animals on their shelves, picked up some clothes from the floor, and, before returning downstairs, carefully remade the bed.

7:10 P.M. ". . . number one, there is no Gerald Sandoval assigned the Social Security number with which your boy opened his account at the Dane First Federal Savings and Loan and, number two, the Samantha Connor in Tyler, Oregon, you inquired about is a sixty-eight-year-old widow with one son, Radford, born forty-four years ago and, according to the Tyler County Department of Vital Statistics, for the last three and a half, deceased."

As he listened over his office speaker phone, Levy's sudden

inclining elicited a loud creak he hoped was from his chair rather than his spine. "Dead how?"

"His cabin cruiser exploded," blandly replied the FBI agent.

"And the exact cause of death?" asked Abbott.

"Maybe I didn't make myself clear, Detectives—his craft blew up with him on it."

"But from a crushed skull or . . . ?"

"Per the brief coroner's report attached to the death certificate, which is faxing to you as we speak, the mishap occurred in over two hundred feet of water when a fifty-gallon gas tank went boom."

Levy snapped, "Are you saying there was no body?"

"From accounts of witnesses who, prior to the explosion, watched the boat depart with Mr. and Mrs. Connor aboard, and the police determining that a malfunction fouled the fuel line, both victims were declared presumed dead due to an accidental explosion."

"Radford had a wife?"

"Margot. Maiden name Bailey. Two years younger than him. Born in L.A."

"I don't suppose her Social Security number matches Claire Sandoval's?"

"No, but Claire Sandoval's doesn't match Claire Sandoval. In other words—so says the Social Security Administration—she doesn't exist either."

"Are the victims physically described?" inquired Abbott.

"I thought I just explained how they weren't available for that."

Abbott silently elevated his middle fingers at the phone.

"What else?" queried Levy.

"Nothing else, Detective. I received less than four hours ago the scant information attached to your requests. Searches require starting points, which in law enforcement means a legitimate Social Security number or, absent that, a suspect's employment record or, at a minimum, prior addresses, not to mention I can't, absent a warrant, blithely access bank accounts and personnel files, leaving me dependent on public records—like death certificates—and the kindness of concerned and informed citizens, a rarer combination than you apparently have been led to believe."

"What have you got on Samantha Connor?"

"Her birth date."

"Will the Bureau have someone question her?"

"That's someone else's call. I operate a computer, is all."

"With a little more digging you might even have ascertained if these people possessed, perchance, a good reason to fake being blown up!"

"And if it turns out that Samantha Connor is the mother of Gerald Sandoval, aka Radford Connor, who actually isn't dead and for some reason is a fugitive from justice—along with thousands of others this office can't keep track of—exactly what, Detective, would that have to do with your abduction case?"

"Son of a bitch if I know, Agent, but my interest is piqued!" Levy fell back in his seat, holding his stomach. Abbott anxiously raised his eyes. Jerking forward again, Levy brusquely inquired, "Falsifying Social Security numbers? Isn't that a federal crime?"

"And if you can prove in an investigation that will take longer than most involving murder that the offense was employed to commit a more serious one, such as welfare or tax fraud, the guilty party might even receive more than the customary stiff fine or a night or two in jail, which, in any case, wouldn't help you find your missing girl—if she's still alive— and might even—depending upon where she's at—further endanger her."

"Thanks much, Agent."

"Tomorrow, after spending a few hours with my family and putting in for the comp time I earned tonight, maybe I'll speak to my superior about freeing up an agent to nose around out in Tyler—one who's just sitting around on tax- payers' money with nothing better to do than make inquiries about a couple deceased for three and a half years."

Levy's hanging up was followed by thirty seconds of un- comfortable silence before he glumly intoned, "Somebody ought to send him a snapshot of the kid."

"And the thousand or so others he's searching for without leaving his office." Abbott scowled. "The guy bleeds micro- chips, Frank. Probably got his soul on hard drive."

Levy nodded at the preliminary lab report on his desk stat- ing that no blood or tissue had been found in the LTD and only scant fibers, all so far appearing to have come from the Sandovals' clothing. "Whoever these snakes are, and wherever from, Mike, they've learned to slither without moving the grass."

"On the other hand, Gerald doesn't mind showing us how twisted he is—or else he can't quite keep a lid on it." Abbott broodingly frowned. "He'd clearly anticipated our search and could have concealed from us his entire perverted, though perfectly legal, exhibition, instead of only the part of it he must have deemed would have tied him to Jennifer or gotten him arrested, which—given what he didn't—I don't even want to think about. It's like he's tweaking us, Frank."

"Or himself."

"Sort of gives off vibes like he thinks he's God, doesn't he?"

"Maybe that's because he's died and been resurrected."

"That was Jesus."

"Whichever. I suspect most onetime corpses tend toward biographical reticence."

"And I'd bet almost anything Claire's sherry bottles hold an antidote to past life experiences." Abbott held his thumb and forefinger less than an inch apart. "She was that close to expounding on them for me."

"However Gerald—or both of them—get their kicks, Mike, I'd guess is somehow enhanced by capturing them in perpetuity, and what I know about pedophiles—if that's what they are—they're incurable and their collected evidence of their obsessions is as sacred to them as Bibles to Baptists, which is to say that somewhere the son of a bitch has theirs stashed."

"Even money"—Abbott tiredly stretched his legs, which, even more than rest, craved exercise—"wherever they are, they're a perfect fit for the blank spaces on his empty darkroom wall, only we looked everyplace out there but through the horseshit in the barn."

Levy abruptly got to his feet. "I'm going to go home, wolf down dinner, drink a bottle of Pepto-Bismol, make a few long-distance calls, and"—he grabbed his coat—"indulge my wife in one of her favorite hobbies."

"Which is?"

"Studying, for the purpose of trying to get me to hike it, this region's topography."

"Lucky you. That leaves me the task of updating the Folletts while trying to keep them from doing what I'd be sorely tempted to were I in their shoes."

7:30 P.M.   Caroline found Edmund reclining on his back, his eyes closed, in the middle of their bed. She quietly removed his shoes, then her own, lay down next to him, and listened to his steady, deep breathing, understanding from their decade of familiarity he was not asleep and praying he wouldn't talk to or look at her. She placed a hand on his head, gently rubbed, then kneaded his neck muscles, taut as the guy wire she imagined extending the canyon of grief between them.

She unbuttoned his shirt, ran a hand over his belly and chest, palpated his nipples until they stood erect as small soldiers, kissed and lightly teethed them. Sensing rather than seeing his eyes open, she reached up with two fingers, tenderly closed them, then unfastened his trousers, deftly lowered them to his knees, and stroked the coarse wool shrouding his semi-erection that in response to her attentiveness but against the blackness in his emotional center strained to reach its full size.

Edmund groaned.

Dangling her head over his groin, her hair swirling around it, Caroline rubbed and passionately blew on his testicles, which, with their life-forming liquid, swelled and grew huge. She took him into her mouth. Licked and sucked him. Felt him momentarily break through the darkness. Plunged him as deep into her as she could without choking, imagining his penis a magic wand plumbing to momentarily dissipate her grief. When she felt his buttocks tighten and in his penis the final surge preceding his orgasm, she abruptly released him and, hoping she'd not done so too late, lay back on the bed.

Edmund hurriedly rolled onto her, pulled up her dress, yanked aside her briefs. He opened his eyes. "I—"

"Shhhh . . . !" she said.

She guided him into her.

No comfort like that from a warm, intimately known body. No strength like that garnered from flesh acquainted with one's own. "Don't thrust," she commanded, halting him between her warm walls, "or even move. Just lie inside me until—"

But it was for naught. Edmund's penis spontaneously erupted with his great shudder and seconds later, in spasms of relief, so did Caroline.

8:30 P.M.   Samantha Connor was not listed in Directory Assistance for Tyler, a seaside town north of Portland, inhabited, according to Levy's AAA TourBook, by around six thousand people of mostly Scandinavian descent.

A woman answering the phone at the police department said Chief Hammrick Bobb was trout-fishing until early that evening. Levy inquired if, in the meantime, she might help him obtain, for official police business, an unlisted phone number in the township. She harangued him for enticing her to break the law and insisted he repeat his credentials for her to give to Chief Bobb. Levy hung up thinking how the worst tragedies in one locale don't even wobble the world's wheel.

He put to bed his daughter, who requested to be told a real-life police drama but, seeking a reprieve from authenticity, Levy instead read her a story about a lost aardvark befriended by a whale, a plot, given the former's inability to swim and the latter's lack of legs, she found not credible. Before he'd completed the tale, he fell asleep prior to or after his daughter, and was startled awake by the falling book landing on his groin.

Downstairs, on the kitchen table, his wife had already spread a tax map of the southern part of Dane County and around a small, mostly wooded area three-quarters up and north of Hulburt Hill Road drawn a circle in red pencil from which straight lines extended several miles toward each compass point. "Near as I can make out from surveys several years old, the Sandovals live here." She placed an index finger on the circle. "North, through maybe a thousand wooded acres belonging to the Uppsala Hunters' Club, is Limekiln Road. South, after descending the Sandovals' drive—"

"Never mind south." Levy placed a cup of luscious-smelling coffee in front of her. "It's too much in the open and from Bink's position, a couple hundred feet from the drive and much less than that from the road, he would have heard the horse more distinctly and might even—assuming his vision wasn't chemically fogged—have seen it cross into, then ascend, the field opposite him."

Renee loosely wrapped her free arm around his thigh. Levy tapped the hunters' club acreage. "Is there a road or a path of some kind wide enough for a horse, in semi-darkness, to travel on through here?"

"Not according to the map. It's all brush and thick woods."

"Can it be accessed from Limekiln Road?"

"Only directly through the backyard of"—she squinted at the map's small print—"Elijah and Betty Broe."

"An unlikely route, but we'll check it out." Levy kissed the top of his wife's bobbed hair, kept short to minimize her time fussing with it. "What's east?"

"Abandoned pastureland and reborn forest that in places"—she showed him with the pencil's tip—"doubles as deep backyards for four Hulburt Hill residences, the most easterly of which—three miles from the Sandovals'—fronts Route Nine."

Levy sat down next to Renee. "Assuming Jennifer's alive—or was for a while—where in there would he hide her?"

"An abandoned woodshed or barn, maybe?"

"On property that's otherwise occupied, how could he be sure someone wouldn't show up or that a dog wouldn't come sniffing around?"

"Maybe he's got an accomplice?"

Levy firmly shook his head. "Excepting whatever weird relationship he's got with Claire, Gerald's a loner as sure as the Pope's Catholic. He thinks he's too smart for the rest of the world." He drank from a bottle of Pepto-Bismol, then reached for Renee's coffee, which she quickly pushed beyond his grasp. "Plus he trusts no one. Not even his own lawyer, who I could tell during our interview he'd been less than forthcoming with." From a jar in the center of the table he grabbed a handful of peanuts and rolled them like dice in his palm. "We'll question the people up there again, see if they remember something they didn't before, but . . ." As he aimed the peanuts for his mouth, Renee snatched them from his hand and put them back in the jar.

"You want to know what's west, Levy?"

Levy raised his eyes to her. She pointed at the map. "A small section of the hunters' club ends at the border of a five-thousand-acre state-owned preserve, where, you may remember, on a day before children and your bad belly, atop a patch of soft grass, beneath a canopy of chirping birds, and next to a gently tinkling waterfall, we ate pastrami sandwiches for lunch and each other for dessert."

Levy deadpanned. "In this lifetime?"

She smiled and passed him a spoon. "Have a yogurt or something soft, Levy."

"As I remember, clear-cut trails, if a little narrow, run through there."

"For hikers who hardly ever show. A lonelier place you couldn't find."

"What's on the far side of it?"

Renee took the pencil and drew a more or less straight line through the preserve, then bent forward and squinted. "It bounds a four-hundred-acre farm owned by a—it looks like, Hanford—Dresser. Only from the tax designation, the place is abandoned."

Levy sat up straighter. "What road is that on?"

Renee again scrunched up her eyes. "Ship . . . Shipman Hollow Road. At the very top. No neighbors for miles."

Levy grabbed the map from her. "What's the distance from the Sandovals' to there—as the crow flies?"

"You mean as the horse gallops?"

"Whatever."

"Seven, maybe eight, miles."

8:40 P.M. ". . . all of which is to say, Mrs. and Mr. Follett, that though we don't yet have evidence to make an arrest, we now have good grounds to believe that, first and foremost—for reasons of which you're aware—Jennifer may still be alive; second, partly because of those reasons, we're nearly certain that her kidnappers are the Sandovals; and third, as the result of, as I've alluded to, further leads we're now confidently pursuing, we hope we're much closer to being able to prove it . . ."

" 'Hope,' Detective?"

Abbott glanced at Edmund, behind whom, where the garrote had previously been displayed between a long-barreled musket and World War I bayonet, the wall, remarked Abbott's attentive eye, was blank. "My daughter's life rests on the police department's *hope* of being able to prove what is obvious—even to one as untrained as myself—in the demeanor, actions, and noncooperation of the psychopaths who stole her?"

"Unfortunately, Mr. Follett, those observances are only cursorily, if at all, probative in a court of law."

Edmund disgustedly averted his eyes.

"We're not criticizing your efforts and honestly believe— both of us"—from the sunken couch, Caroline, whose manner that evening struck Abbott as oddly, perhaps even disturbingly, calm, half nodded at him—"you're doing your best, only with the situation being"—having brought them up to speed, discreetly omitting only the subject matter of Gerald's darkroom hangings, Abbott worried that he might have ignited within the Folletts an already smoldering, as proved by Edmund's earlier confronting of Claire, instinctual passion—"and, as parents—not being one yourself, Detective, perhaps you can't understand our responsibil—pledge— to protect and ensure our children's safety within the bounds of our—not society's or someone else's—moral code—"

Confident that she'd communicated their point, Edmund cut her off by placing a hand on her thigh. "Only just— please—bear in mind, Detec . . . Mike"—between a thumb and forefinger, Edmund severely pinched his nose where it separated his eyes—"that hours, even minutes, may be murd—killing our daughter."

He got up and left the room.

Caroline reached out and, in a bolstering gesture, patted Abbott's arm. Abbott understood that they viewed him as a dedicated clue man, young and naïve to the passions inherent in those who had borne offspring. He told Caroline that the policeman who'd driven him to the house and was stationed at the bottom of their drive would remain there until he was relieved by another. As if to acknowledge his thoroughness, Caroline, at the door, squeezed his wrist. Abbott wrote down and handed her his home phone number. He instructed her to use it if before morning a question or problem arose she wasn't comfortable discussing with his replacement on the night shift.

From the Plymouth's trunk he pulled the gym bag holding his running gear, then, to the stupefaction of patrolman Wallace Flabbe—with his distended belly and larded buttocks, rightly named—changed into his shorts and Nikes in the backseat. Flabbe amazedly remarked it was seven, maybe eight, miles to Dane. "If anyone leaves"—Abbott nodded at the house—"call me immediately or, if you can't reach me, Frank Levy, and if you can't him, Harold Stein at headquarters. Then follow whoever it is." Leaning against the side of the car, he slowly stretched his calf muscles. "And don't, for God sake, Flabbe, wrinkle my clothes or spill on them coffee or any of that garbage you constantly feed on."

9:00 P.M. For several minutes the man stood stock-still in the quiet blackness, only his nostrils moving to detect the lingering stench of sweat, bargain cologne, garlicky burps, and fast-food farts from the puckered assholes of uniformed morons who in their tramping, poking, and peering had—blindly missing the point—fouled the temple of the pure. The sole sanctuary of honesty.

In a self-imposed, suffocating realm, his hunger had so long remained imprisoned that when released it had, like a starved alligator at the sight of a tender-aged swimmer, fed impetuously.

Snapping before stalking. In broad daylight, no less!

He longed for a judgment-free verbal palliative but knew it would require his driving to a public phone booth, and he suspected the police were somehow monitoring his vehicular comings and goings.

Idiot!

His emotions ran a gauntlet of self-loathing, outward anger, panic, stark fear. Less the contaminated air than the realization that the world he had meticulously remade had been violated and once more was in danger of being exposed frustrated his attempts to attain his required state of absolute concentration. He kept thinking of the imperviousness of the police. And of his now concealed art without which his isolation, rather than surpassing all heavenly descriptions, was as insipid as most of life.

And of his current project.

How it would have to be hurriedly concluded. Or terminated.

No! No! No!

Yes! Yes! Yes!

Well, I won't!

Of course you will! Do it tonight!

I've not gone to so much trouble to . . . !

He stopped sniffing the air, reached up, and slapped himself.

The intercom buzzed.

The man waited several seconds for it to buzz again. Then once more. He took a deep breath, blew it out, and evenly responded, "What is it, Claire?"

"I'm anxious, dear. And terribly frightened."

"The latter emotion is the product of the former, Claire. And there's no need for either."

"I'm afraid of being gawked at and thought badly of."

"By whom?"

"Like before."

"Before doesn't exist, Claire. That's something you've dreamed. And I'm here to protect you."

"Forever?"

"Always."

"Stay in tonight, Gerald? And make love to your little girl?"

The man didn't respond.

"You'd have to be gentle, though, because I—earlier in the bathroom—shaved her. Then applied baby lotion. But it still hurts her some, Gerald."

The man felt a pounding in his temples.

"Will you not go out, dear? Please? For her?"

"We'll see, Claire. I have a little work to do. Then we'll see."

9:15 P.M.   A quiet house. A ticking clock. A desk light shining on incongruences: a loaded weapon, an instrument of torture, a picture album recording moments made more memorable from the viewer's fear that backward glances are all that will be left to him.

A telephone off the hook.

A father seeing his daughter's eyes. Clear-water blue. Unmarred by sights too hard to look at and, even more, to comprehend. Radiating awed innocence, wonder, joy, naïve sensuality. Laughing, pouting, smiling, curious eyes. Still-evolving eyes.

An imagined set of dead, benumbed eyes stealing and trying to suck from these vibrant eyes their nerve-tingling wonderment at even the simplest of sights.

A pain like drowning in that thrashing heightens it and yelling can't save you.

Rational reasoning followed by irrational scheming.

Guilt. Hope. Frustration. One's own impotence against evil. One's character turned inside out. A pacifist contemplating barbarous acts. Torture inflicted to bring about a right result.

Minutes, seconds wasting.

Fear of aggressions backfiring.

Hamstrung by a nonviolent nature. Sickened both by recognition of this and by a strong desire to be the opposite.

Reasoned but skewed logic once more prevailing. Appealing via the Devil to humanity's basic goodness.

Seven little bleeps like audible finger marks in drying clay.

Two rings. An answer.

A recorded voice announcing, "The number you have dialed is no longer listed in this area code."

9:30 P.M.   After slogging through sugar pains on joints stiff from inactivity, Abbott, halfway toward Dane, fell into a comfortable pace at which he soon attained the mental equivalent of a drinker's buzz-on, thereafter convincing himself capable of feats—a sub-two-and-a-half-hour marathon and single-handedly bringing the Jennifer Follett case to a happy conclusion—beyond his God-given abilities.

From the woods bordering the lightly traveled highway, trees creaked and owls hooted as Abbott's footfalls echoed in the warm air. Infrequently passing headlights illuminated him in his endorphin intoxication, in which, bathed in a pleasurable sweat, he viewed talent, like wealth, to be relative, and he, on that lonely road, a rich man.

The illusion ended halfway through his shower when from the station Harold Stein phoned to inform him that a Chief Hammrick Bobb from Tyler, Oregon, had, after failing to reach Levy at home, tried him there. "Claims he was returning a call Levy made sound important, then the mother-in-law says he's on a date."

"Whose mother-in-law, Stein?"

"Frank's."

"How'd Frank's mother-in-law and Chief Bobb end up conversing?"

"She's there watching Frank's kid."

"Frank's out?"

"Says Chief Bobb, who got it from the mother-in-l—"

"What's Chief Bobb's number?"

Stein gave it to him.

Still wrapped in a towel, Abbott reached Chief Bobb at home. As if challenging a weak hypothesis, Bobb queried, "It's past nine-thirty there?"

Abbott assured him so.

"That always gets me. The time difference—why that should be."

"It has to do with the earth's rotation—how the sun hits different spots at diff—"

"Yeah, yeah, yeah—still, I'm intrigued by it."

Abbott politely cleared his throat.

"Your partner's message said he was wanting news on Radford Connor, and the best is he's been fish bait three-plus years now."

"We understand a casket wasn't necessary?"

"Whenever I eat seafood I worry I ingested part of him, but so far haven't died or got ptomaine poisoning, so I'm hoping maybe he got shipped out in a can of tuna."

"Not a highly-thought-of past resident of your burg?"

"He had—and still has—his share of local supporters who remember him pumping plenty of money into this community, though, except to visit his mother, he didn't come here much after he was a kid."

"But you aren't one of them?"

"What?"

"Radford's supporters?"

"My opinion: he was like an apple looks good on the outside but past the skin is rotten to the core." The ensuing gulping sound led Abbott to believe Bobb was imbibing. "But you'd be better off—if you haven't already—asking about him to the folks down around Portland, where he had his allotted fifteen minutes."

"Tell me about her."

"Who?"

"Samantha Connor."

"A type, you know: longtime widow to a millionaire she married with next to nothing left on his odometer—socialite, horsewoman, patr—"

"She's an equestrian?"

"Owner and rider. Even now, at past sixty."

"What about Radford?"

"Before my time, he was some kind of junior national champion until his title got stripped in a scandal that got covered up, but based upon the later events down in Portland, where among some people—the same sort, I'd guess, that ooh and aah at fags wearing dog collars and at artifacts bottled in piss—he was known as an 'ar-tiste,' I could make a pretty good guess at its alleged content."

Abbott ran several fingers through his hair, looked at them, and was distressed by the speed at which he was falling victim to his father's male-pattern-baldness genes. "What sort of artist?"

"A picture taker nobody'd mistake for Norman Rockwell." Abbott felt his pulse quicken as if he were out on the road again. "From what I understand, his favorite theme was desperation and his subject little street kids, a combination enough of these artsy farts admired to arrange for a public exhibit of his work, which, according to his enemies and advocates alike, led to the onset of the investigation."

To fill his suddenly emptied lungs Abbott removed the phone from his ear and half bent over.

"More than a few later red-faced local art critics, in maybe one of the world's bigger ironies, gave his work high praise for its 'gritty realism.' "

"Investigation of what?" Abbott watched drops of perspiration fall from his still-damp hair into his lap.

"You don't know?"

"How would I?"

"From the message your partner left I had the impression he'd called because someone there—another one, that is—familiar with the case thought they'd spotted him."

"You're saying it's not the first time?"

"You know how it is when the infamous dead—or even locally semi-infamous—don't leave a body to stick in the ground—the Elvis Presley thing." Bobb gulped again. "But I think it's more likely, given the rumored evidence against the two of them, Radford rigged it for them to go out in a blaze of glory looking like martyrs to his supporters—the loudest being his rich mommy on whose trust fund he lived—claiming he was only being persecuted for his artistic views."

Abbott envisioned all his ever-felt or imagined pain squeezing into the tight ball his heart had become.

"If this is all news to you, Detective, what's the purpose of your call?"

Instead of answering, Abbott inquired, "You're saying the Connors were on trial at the time of the explosion?"

"That, my friend, you would have read about. Though unless it was all hype—which, as I say, some people claim—the D.A. supposedly was all set to seek indictments."

"For what?"

"Give me your fax number," replied Bobb. "It'll be easier."

9:45 P.M. Guiding her minivan back onto Shipman Hollow Road from the driveway of the Arthur and Mildred Quinn residence—whose inhabitants couldn't, for Levy, recall recently seeing in the vicinity a black LTD, silver Jeep Cherokee, a man resembling Gerald Sandoval, or an unfamiliar little blond girl—Renee, indicating the map atop her husband's legs, studiously informed him, "Assuming neither place has been vacated in the last year and a half, we've got, according to my calculations, two strikes left between here and the top."

"Only one of which," replied Levy, wanly frowning, "appears to sit close enough to the road for anyone in or at it to have an unobstructed view of the traffic."

"For argument's sake"—Renee assumed the prosecutorial tone to which Levy, over fifteen years, had grown accustomed to responding—"suppose Gerald, or maybe Radford, has, or had, Jennifer at the Dresser place and, on more than one occasion, has returned there on horseback through the woods, why wouldn't he have brought her there the same way, instead of up this road by car?"

"With the caveat that the entire theory is, to say the least, speculative, I'm hypothesizing he would have deemed it more likely that someone would spot him with Jennifer—who, remember, at least to begin with, was sitting next to him in the front seat—if he drove her directly to his house up Hulburt Hill Road, which is not only farther down the highway from the arterial but more densely populated and traveled on than this one, on which we've already spoken to a majority of the populace." Once in the hollow, Levy recalled having been there before to mediate a dispute over possession of a satellite dish, flattened, as he'd arrived, by an estranged husband's bulldozer. "Not to mention that our thorough search of the Sandovals' premises yielded not a single hair strand or fingerprint belonging to Jennifer, nor any of the children's clothes, toys, food, or toothpaste that Gerald—I'd bet my pension on—bought for her, strongly suggesting to myself, and Mike Abbott, that she was never there."

"You left out, I'd guess, the best reason, Levy."

"Turn up here," said Levy, indicating a house to his right in which a single light dimly burned. Renee downshifted, then flicked on the blinker. "What did I leave out?"

"He didn't bring her home because he didn't want his wife to know what he'd done."

"Who?"

"Gerald."

"She knows. Goddamn right she knows! It's all over her!"

"Strongly suspects, definitely. Maybe even, in a way she refuses to acknowledge, for sure realizes. But I'll bet my anticipated inheritance, dear—as I don't have a pension—that Claire hasn't laid eyes on the child since the day Jennifer was up there with the babysitter."

"How can you be so sure?"

"No woman, especially a mother, would be an active part of whatever he's into!" She turned into the drive.

"You're saying women are less prone than men to commit evil?"

"Only that male to female evilness is the hand that inflicts pain to the eyes that turn away from it."

She parked the car to the sound of a barking dog and mooing cows. "It's ten o'clock at night, Levy"—Levy opened his door—"and these people are farmers who get up with the sun and probably haven't received a visitor past 8 p.m. this decade."

"So?"

The house's front door creaked open, revealing the dual barrels of a low-gauge shotgun.

"We're the police, folks!" Levy loudly announced.

Following what sounded like a rifle bolt slamming shut, a male voice called, "In a goddamn Mitsubishi Colt?"

"It's my wife's car!"

"And this gun aimed at your head is empty!"

Renee hissed, "Authenticate yourself, Levy. Jesus!"

Levy resoundingly identified himself. "May I come up and show you my credentials, sir?"

The voice responded that would be acceptable only if he did so slowly, with his hands seeking the stars.

Shortly after, a middle-aged, small, knobby-muscled man in faded red longjohns closely examined Levy's badge in the doorway light, telling him, "Sneakin' up to a sleepin' house, D'tective, ind'cates you's severely addled or possessin' a dire reason." He lowered the rifle. "Which is it?"

"I pray God, sir, the latter." Levy pulled from his shirt pocket, then handed to the man, a police photograph. "You're the owner of these premises?"

"Since the day my momma died," answered Ned Bolan, prefatory to gazing down at the snapshot of the Sandovals' black LTD. "But I'd a told ya that o'er ta phone."

10:00 P.M. Like the swishing made by a snake slithering through the grass, the man's labored breathing announced his entrance into the shadowy room, where, three-quarters shrouded by the bed's covers, the little girl sat sucking a peppermint lollipop to give her courage and a sweet taste. "I'm scared," she said in a barely audible whisper.

"Say again?"

"Frightened"—she panted—"that you might. . . ."

"Louder."

"I've never . . ."

The man impatiently put a finger to his lips. "That's enough."

The girl clamped her teeth around the candy.

The man slowly unbuckled his pants, dropped them to his ankles, stepped free of them. The sharp, startled intake of the girl's breath angered him as would a misplayed chord. Her forceful head-wagging, as if against invisible bonds, sending her tightly twined braids slapping against her face, struck him as all wrong. "Stop that!" he commanded.

She stared wide-eyed at him.

"Move into the light." He nodded behind and slightly left of her at the open venetian blind, issuing in, from the clear night sky, the room's only illumination. The girl slid sideways on her rump before the window. The man walked over and sat on the side of the bed nearest her. He flicked his eyes at the sheet. "Pull it down."

The girl timidly lowered the sheet from where it rested beneath her chin to her knees, exposing a half-length, baggy undershirt several sizes too big, belly of baby fat, lint-filled navel, pliable abdomen, glabrous thighs, and, tucked between them, a pink skin crease, hairless and smooth as the head of a baton. "It's a trick," snapped the man.

"You can touch it," breathed the little girl.

"It doesn't smell right," said the man.

"Are you afraid, too?"

The man labored to enter her world.

"Gently," whispered the little girl, "like you would a kitty."

He moved a finger to within two inches of her opening, then quickly jerked his hand away as if from a flame.

The girl physically balked.

The man glared at her. Thoughts of being exposed as a deformed ugly bug seared his brain. "Take off my underwear?" he suggested in a small, embarrassed voice.

The little girl reached down and tugged at his briefs, while the man lifted slightly from the bed until the underpants were around his knees. He removed them, then, sheepishly, dropped them on the floor.

He was soft. Had not progressed at all. Was like a torpid smoke cloud sitting above a razed sanctuary.

"Your peter's not so very big," whispered the little girl, rolling the lollipop into one cheek.

The man reddened. He seemed cowed by the remark.

"Shut your eyes," ordered the little girl, "while I play with it."

The man did as she'd told him. In the darkness created by or indigenous to him he felt ashamed that he should have to suffer such indignities, though he understood himself to be the world and all other earthly inhabitants as existing solely for or to aid in his evolvement. Recent events saddened him most in that they reminded him that he, and thus the universe, would someday die. With what then would he educate and amuse himself? His body began to gently tremble. "Touch her, Word. Go ahead," his mother's voice sounded in the darkness, while the little girl firmly stroked him. "Reach out and lay a hand between her legs."

The man petulantly shook his head like a disobeying child.

"You know you want to."

"No."

Claire remembered how he used to pay her to do this schizophrenic thing, as much as a thousand dollars a session. She'd done a lot more degrading things, for much less money, with individuals far more difficult to tolerate. In her world he had been strange only in that afterward, instead of self-consciously hurrying to leave, he would want to stay and talk or take Claire—and later, after Claire had introduced him to her daughter, the two of them—to dinner or a play. He had struck Claire as more normal than most men she encountered, a kindly, rich suitor who had, she thought, understood her desire to live well and to shield her child from her means of doing so. Impossible, she thought, to reenact how one gets sucked into the maelstrom of a lunatic whose godless eye is that of one's only intimate.

10:25 P.M.   Sporting a full beard and collar-length hair in a neat ponytail over husky shoulders, Radford Connor, in the faxed black-and-white photographs, appeared the counterculture artist he was described to be in the accompanying article, and Margot, stylishly thin with bobbed blond hair, the high-priced Portland call girl, albeit aging, she reportedly had been when she met and married him. Even to Abbott, predisposed to believe they would resemble the Sandovals, they didn't.

Attuned as he was, with his running and strict diet, to corporality, the incongruity mentally threw him. In viewing pictures of the couple side by side with their Dane reincarnations, he was awed at how they had been able, like certain lizards, to completely alter their outward manifestations. For Radford and Margot had to be Gerald and Claire.

Didn't they?

The Oregon couple looked to be the approximate height of their Dane counterparts, and Radford's being a photographer and amateur equestrian, together with the nature of the investigation swirling around the pair at the time of their alleged deaths, made it seem virtually impossible that Abbott was looking at more than two people.

Still, the sensation was akin to gazing at the moon while being promised it was the sun. They were outwardly that different. And Abbott, a physiognomist, was unable to divine in the blurred features of Radford and Margot the abstract characteristics which, in his mind, would, as unequivocally as their matching fingerprints, label them Gerald and Claire.

A spark of hope that the first couple weren't the second briefly flickered in the mind of Abbott, whose thinking since his conversation with Chief Bobb had sharply altered, and steadily more so while reading the faxed articles. He found himself praying for an implausible coincidence. Against all odds he hoped the Sandovals were exactly who and what they appeared to the Dane community to be, even while he knew that improbability would mean he and Levy had been dead wrong in their instincts and would put the Jennifer Follett investigation back at square one. Above all, while studying the Portland accounts, he inwardly invoked that Jennifer not be—or have been for even a second—in the custody of Radford and Margot Connor. Then he came across Samantha's maiden name, Wordsworth, the first four letters of which, according to the article, formed the mother's nickname for her son.

Recalling the handwritten WORD printed on two otherwise blank envelopes in the Sandovals' trash, Abbott felt his heart rushing to exit through his throat as if to glimpse the sometimes horrific world it labored in.

His mind's eye detected faults, cracks, gaping fissures in the legal foundation on which he had elected to build a career. He envisioned compassion thwarted by justice; practicality swallowed by theory.

He saw the Portland case file arriving with fingerprints to match those which a judge might eventually compel from the Sandovals; then confusion, over a period of days—maybe weeks—ensuing. Never having been formally charged in Oregon and being legally dead, the Connors, as far as Abbott had ascertained, were not named on any outstanding warrants. The FBI, hopefully before the couple vanished again, might arrest them for faking their deaths or falsifying their Social Security numbers, giving the Portland authorities a chance to reconsider their charges. No matter what, Dane County would be crawling with zealous investigators who in their eagerness to apprehend two infamous fugitives would reduce little Jennifer Follett to a footnote and, by panicking or too quickly taking into custody her kidnappers, decrease from slim to none the chances she would be found alive.

Abbott envisioned Gerald's photographs of Jennifer, her innocent, trusting face appearing thrilled to be the focus of someone's attention, and heard Claire's chilling declaration: "It's all a mistake . . . everything after the first one."

He painfully reread a portion of the article:

. . . police theorize that before being killed, dismembered, and buried in plastic bags in three landfills surrounding the city, the five victims, all preadolescent girls between the ages of seven and ten, hailing from distressed sections of the city, were held captive and tortured, their bodies mutilated with surgical precision, in a secluded cabin located in woods east of Portland near where the artist and his wife own a vacation home . . . Authorities are investigating the possibility that a sixth victim may be Selena Volk, Margot Connor's nine-year-old daughter and, like two of the latest victims—whose pictures were recently spotted by their relatives in a public exhibit of Mr. Connor's work—a probable model for the photographer, who was reported by the couple to have disappeared eight years ago from a theme park she and her stepfather were visiting . . .

Abbott abruptly stood, rushed into the precinct bathroom, and vomited into a urinal.

Back at his desk, he again tried and failed to reach Levy.

He thought of the unorthodox routes to greatness followed by some of history's superb distance runners: Zola Budd training barefoot in the South African hinterland; Kip Keino racing goats in the Kenyan savanna; Bill Rodgers consuming a strict pre-race diet of pizza. Runners by nature were non-conformists, individualists to whom rules and established patterns were as irrelevant as reality to abstractionists.

After hurriedly faxing Hammrick Bobb's information to FBI headquarters in Albany, he shoved the articles into his top desk drawer, grabbed his car keys, and left.

11:00 P.M. Edmund woke from a nightmare, less horrific for its specific content, which he couldn't precisely recall, than for its essence, which held mankind, severally and as a group, blameless for the world's travails in that lives were preprogrammed for goodness, badness, or mediocrity, which no amount of earthly effort could alter.

Terrible because if evil were simply a gene, what sense in teaching a child right from wrong?

Awful in that where would be the point in expressing love or hate when the object of same was as directed in his or her behavior as a computer?

Horrible as directionless anger.

Unthinkable as experiencing the worst sort of soul-wrenching pain without having a hope of undoing it.

Intolerable as having no higher power to appeal to.

He heard music and voices outside his office, stood, walked to the door, and lightly pulled it open. Caroline and Hannah sat on the rug around the small circular glass table fronting the living room couch. The stereo was softly playing. "I think I'd like to pray," Edmund told them from the doorway.

They turned and looked at him.

"We're playing Parcheesi," said Caroline.

Edmund shrugged helplessly. "You told me earlier—in the mudroom—that you . . ."

"I did."

"How did you?"

Caroline raised her eyes to him. "Why don't you come over here, and join us."

"If I thought it would do any good—or even not any harm—I'd take the gun and—"

"But it likely wouldn't, and it might—do harm, that is."

Edmund walked over and knelt down between them at the table. He clasped his hands, then looked at Caroline and Hannah, who did likewise. "I'm not sure how . . . I haven't in a long . . ." Edmund frowned. "Even in church I just mostly listened . . ."

"Just speak the words that come into your head, Mr. Follett," suggested Hannah. "Eloquence isn't what's judged. Sometimes you're talked back to, but even when you're not, you're always heard." She matter-of-factly flicked her hair out of her eyes. "That's what I believe."

Caroline placed her hands on his. Then Hannah did.

The three of them bowed their heads and closed their eyes. In a clear voice, Edmund said, "Dear God, please . . ."

11:10 P.M.   Under the star-and-moon-breached nearly cloudless sky, Renee, driving without headlights to the hollow's top, queried, "You're sure this isn't a *mano a mano* thing, Levy, between you and an arrogant, highly intelligent, and likely dangerous psychopath?"

"I'm applying my best professional judgment," snapped Levy, banging the flashlight he'd pulled from the glove box against his hip to make it work. "It would be close to daylight by the time we got a search team up here, and if the house turns out to be empty, as is likely, I'd look pretty incompetent, as well as foolish, to a squad of pissed-off policemen, and if it isn't, a lot of time would have been wasted during which God knows what might be happening to Jennifer, He willing she's still breathing."

"And if Gerald's up there?" Renee asked more softly.

"If I see even a sign of him, which I doubt," answered Levy, strongly suspecting that if he found anyone at the abandoned farm that long after the kidnapping, it wouldn't be someone alive, "I'll come back down and have you drive me to Bolan's to phone for backup."

In the harsh beam, Renee glanced at his grave face, too

coarsely lined for its age, and eyes deepened and slightly sad not so much from their having witnessed more or greater pain than others but from an inability to forget even the least of it.

"And what if you step in a hole and break your ankle or something, leaving you lying up there and me sitting down here without even a shortwave radio or a walkie-talkie?"

Levy wordlessly switched off the light and shoved it into his belt.

"All's I'm saying, Levy, is let me go with you up to where we can see if the place is occupied." Levy pulled out his revolver, assured himself it was loaded, then returned it to his shoulder holster. "On the off chance it appears to be, I'll go call for help, while you keep it under surveillance."

Running a hand over his roughened cheeks, which, even with his twice-daily shaves, remained stubbled enough to noisily scratch his palm, Levy sighed, mutely acknowledging his wife's usual prudent logic, just as her closed-lipped, matter-of-fact frown complimented him for listening to it.

She parked the minivan where the road ended in an elliptical turnaround before a stand of middle-aged Scotch pines through which an eroded dirt drive, interlarded by knee-high weeds and exposed rocks, wound up to the Dresser place, invisible past the trees. Rife with the odor of pine pitch, the warm air entering the car's open windows carried a din of crickets and, from water noisily flowing someplace to the east, frogs and peepers, occasionally interrupted by unseen animals rustling the brush. Levy laid a hand on Renee's knee.

"If Gerald's stallion is tethered near the house, you come back here, drive down the road, and call Mike Abbott, or if he still can't be found"—over Ned Bolan's phone, Harold

Stein had earlier informed Levy, who'd failed to reach Abbott at home, that he'd just missed him at headquarters—"Detective Harold Stein, whom I've informed of our location and intent."

Renee solemnly nodded.

"Tell whichever to stealthily accompany two officers up here, then direct all three—or, if necessary, guide them—to my position."

Renee grasped and squeezed his hand. Levy understood she was, at that moment, thinking not just of Jennifer but of Trish, their own daughter, and how anyone's good fortune was only a matter of luck and circumstances. She intricately interwove their fingers. Across the moon's face, thin cirrus clouds blew like hair strands. A coyote monotonously yapped in the woods somewhere to their left, a lonely, haunting sound causing Levy to subconsciously shake his head as if in mournful reverie. Suddenly he realized his thoughts of Jennifer vacillated between hoping to find her alive and hoping to find her mercifully dead. He turned toward Renee and believed he read in her eyes the same horrible dichotomy. He started to speak, but she cut him off by impulsively bobbing forward to smartly kiss him.

"As the expert hiker among us, go 'head, lead the way," directed Levy.

Renee instructively pointed to their feet. "Just put yours where I do mine."

They simultaneously stepped from the van, gingerly shut the doors, then started single file up the drive, Levy frequently stumbling on concealed rocks even as Renee demonstrated how not to.

11:20 P.M. The woman's regurgitating, long-repressed self-enmity tasted of every man's semen fouling her body since before she was half-grown.

Their talk. Their lies. Their doggish whimpers. Their sad-eyed beseeching of her to make them soar beyond their posturing, impotent, inwardly terrified little selves.

Finally she hated herself for having opened her orifices to it. For so tightly closing her eyes. For blindly embracing the Devil, instead of her earthly lot. For naïvely exposing to Satan her child, more beautiful, she remembered, than in any of his proper photographs of her in which she—not her inwardly regressing daughter, whose symptoms, so much like her own, she had never recognized—took so much pride. To believe he had done to her as the police later claimed he did to others would have been for the woman to believe she herself had. Easier to accept his saying her only baby was kidnapped by strangers or had run away from her. And easier for her to understand. For she was whatever he made her feel. Disgusting. Beautiful. Vampish. Compelling. Ugly as the vilest garbage-crawling bug. Then he'd reach down and pluck her from the refuse. And demand that she become her daughter. Or his mother. And who was she? Without him, dirt to be trod on. He'd even taught her how to speak and dress appropriately.

And she worshipped him. Thanked God for him. Enjoyed holding his hand in church. But who was she?

A small twist of her mind, as to a camera's focus, and what looked like titillation was abruptly revealed to be abomination; soul-inspired art, an incubus's wet dream; a caress, torture; love, a disease; the purveyor of hope, Satan himself.

He lay on his stomach on the bed, slowly returning from

the infant's guilt-ridden world the woman had sent him to and from which she understood he brought back his inspiration to befoul this one.

She rolled away from him.

The man stiffly rose. His back to her, he mechanically began to dress. He put on his underwear. Then his socks. The woman's sudden, clear-minded sobriety was killing her. "I thought you were going to stay in with me tonight, Radford."

The man wordlessly glanced around as if for a third person in the room.

"Radford?"

Refusing to answer, the man stepped into his pants.

"Gerald?"

"I'll be back shortly, Claire."

The woman's thinking was that if she could save one innocent life, maybe she could her soul. "Don't do it."

The man deliberately looked at her. Would God damn a near-blind woman, she wondered, for not helping the children she'd failed to see? "Enough, Radford. No more."

The eyes that had robbed her of her volition and of His everlasting light sought to eviscerate her. "Are you speaking to me, Claire?"

"It has to stop! All of it, Radford! Don't you see?"

The man brushed a piece of lint from his stomach.

"Just leave her where—we'll go—disap—start over, like before!"

The man reached down and adroitly pulled up his pants. "I can't, for the life of me, Claire, understand your soft-brained babbling."

"How long did you keep Selena prisoner before you . . . !"

The woman put a hand to her mouth, horrified at the deeply imprisoned truth it had released. Every night for a full week after her daughter had disappeared, the man had left from their summer house, as he had recently from their home, on one of his moonlight-to-dawn rides. Eternally damn your silent, scared self! the woman inwardly screeched. She heard the firm snap of her husband's pants.

"It pains me to have to remind you, Margot, that Selena was lost to us both"—he truculently sat down on one edge of the mattress and reached for his shoes. The woman groped beneath her side of the bed for the carving knife she had earlier planted there—"and not just to you, whose histrionics so cowed and frightened the poor child."

Gripping the knife's ivory handle, the woman, by its smoothness, was reminded of the effortless flow of words which for over a decade the man had used as a subtle drug to alter her instincts, deaden her emotions, obliterate her free will. Her thinking, clearer than it had been in years, was to plunge the blade into the man's neck so as to blood-starve that virtue-devouring brain. Hoisting her arms above her head, she rose to her knees behind him, striving to utter some damning epithet, but managing, as she drove her hands down, only a lung-depleting grunt.

The man spun deftly toward her.

Easily parrying her weak thrust, he grabbed the weapon from her, tossed it onto the rug, and, using his knees to pin her supine to the mattress, seized and unbendingly applied a pillow to her face.

MIDNIGHT Above patrolman Fred Crowley's upturned countenance, which had popped up from the stakeout car's steering wheel at the unannounced arrival of his superior's green Plymouth at the woods site, Abbott pointedly sniffed the reek of beer. "I had to transport a drunk to county lockup this afternoon," Crowley sheepishly volunteered. "Can't get rid of the stench."

Abbott's flashlight beam divulged no evidence of the beverage in the patrolman's vehicle, only assorted fast-food cartons, multitudinous vacant and full Ring-Ding boxes, and, half-visible beneath the driver's seat, a *Penthouse*. "You're clear, are you, Patrolman, on your mission?"

Crowley stared quizzically at him.

"That feasting on junk food, pornography, and, while snoozing with your head on the wheel, your fantasies of either aren't a part of it?"

The patrolman's crimson face acknowledged the clarification.

Abbott questioningly nodded up the hill at the half-lighted house.

"No comings or goings," asserted Crowley, his left foot surreptitiously working to totally obscure the publication, "in the two hours I've been here."

"What about at the stable?"

"No, sir. The house is all that's been lit."

"About flashlights traversing the grounds"—Abbott thrust his chin at the receding magazine—"you're not in a position to say for sure?"

The patrolman meekly replied, "I've not noticed any."

Suppressing a desire to further upbraid the derelict officer, Abbott said, "I'm going to approach the premises."

Crowley gazed vacantly at him. "At this hour, Detective?"

"On foot, Patrolman." Abbott held up his flashlight. "Through the woods."

"You mean under cover, sir?"

Abbott nodded. "On the sly, yes."

"I understood we weren't to enter onto the property, sir." The patrolman appeared embarrassed. "I mean, without a warrant."

"Around an hour ago I received information, Patrolman, indicating that unless exigent actions are taken, the alleged kidnap victim, if she's still alive, won't be much longer." Abbott leaned intimately toward the open window in which Fred Crowley's face registered the weight of the former's words. "A warrant won't help the situation. A covert operation is called for."

Crowley gravely cleared his throat. "What would you like for me to do, sir?"

"Slightly add to your customary ineptness."

"What?"

"Don't log in or radio to headquarters my presence or our conversation. Not now. Not later. I was never here. If you see my flashlight in the woods, ignore it. Pretend it's a firefly."

"Are you saying the little girl is somewhere up there, sir?"

"The more I tell you, Crowley, the more delicate your position becomes." Abbott, dressed in a dark sweatsuit and his Nikes, confidently clapped a hand on the patrolman's shoulder. "What you, as a pension-seeking public servant, need to be clear on is that you're in a noble and legal alliance here and can only be reprimanded or, God forbid, fired if you do any of what I told you not to do." Removing his hand, Abbott backed up to leave.

The patrolman self-consciously frowned. "What about your car, sir?"

"Till I return, keep your eye on it."

Crowley made a sort of helpless gesture. "And your own out for bears, Detective."

Abbott viewed him curiously.

"Rumor has it one chased and close to killed David Bink this afternoon."

Abbott non-responsively turned and plunged into the thick brush from which the animal had earlier emerged, though shortly the ground cover thinned out, improving his footing, as he entered a forest of aged spruce and hemlock, barely penetrated by the moon's light, forcing him to rely for illumination entirely on his weak-batteried flashlight. With an urbanite's fear of the dark woods, he flinched at every noise. Bouncing tree limbs appeared to him as monstrous arms; flying bats, their thrown punches. Shadows, whose sources Abbott preferred not to guess at, gyrated in the flashlight's beam. The warm air was muggy. His legs still burned from his recent run. In minutes he was perspiring heavily.

At the hill's top, the canopy, comprising there mostly oak, ash, and red maple, in emerging bud, allowed in more of the sky's light. Abbott spotted to the west, barely visible through the foliage, the lights from the Sandoval house. After cutting toward them through a stand of close-to-mature Christmas trees, he came to the edge of a former pasture gone to briers, saplings, and berry bushes, two hundred yards below the premises. He switched off his flashlight, let his eyes adjust to the sky's beggarly glow, then, at a half-lope, started across the field toward the darkened stable.

A minute later, glancing up while crossing the driveway, he panicked at not seeing the LTD, until he recalled it was still at the precinct. The Cherokee was parked near the house, both floors of which were sporadically lit. As Abbott traversed the opposite field, a light blinked off on the building's ground level, behind and to the left of the living room, where he remembered the master bedroom to be. A small room adjoining it went black just as he reached the road side of the stable, after which his view of the dwelling was blocked.

Laboriously breathing, Abbott leaned against the stable, listening to the horses shifting in their stalls and to a big ventilation fan blowing out from the rafters above him and a propped-open window level with his head. He sat down to prepare mentally for the most important race he might ever run and to ask God for the opportunity to do so.

FRIDAY

12:30 A.M.   Some men live for their work. Others for love. Or to create their art. This man, though, didn't live at all except to nurture his overpowering compulsion to feed a hunger he had consciously teased over the past three days to make it ravenous. All his thoughts, rational and irrational, pursued satiation, an attainment beyond worldly description, after which was nothing. Were the state a smell, it would have knocked him unconscious for days; were it a shout, it would have rendered him instantly deaf. Doses of it had to be measured and carefully spaced. When not actively pursuing it, the man was cogitating, scheming, dreaming about how to.

He scoffed at the tedium of living endured by the mass of humanity, who hypocritically championed the quest for perfection while applauding its ultimate accomplishment only within guidelines acceptable to them. Why was it that those least informed about a subject presumed to be its standard-bearers? For art, desire, love, all borderless passions narrowly defined by the world's least-ardent minds? For evil, which most of mankind, with its black-and-white conceptions, would impute to him? And for compassion, which the moralistic vanguard would deem him bereft of, though, upon pulling the pillow away from the slack white face of the sole person next to his mother who had witnessed more than his outward manifestations and still embraced him, he had cried.

Feeling the woman's pulse yet weakly fluttering in her wrist, he had felt his sadness deepen with the knowledge that their union was forever tainted by her having broken their unspoken bond not to openly avow simple facts too horrific for her to live with and for him too exhilarating to blunt by sharing. Though she had correctly perceived that in frankly acknowledging their secret she had condemned one of them to die. And the man planned on living forever. Profoundly sighing, he carefully repositioned the pillow on his wife's face and this time pressed until her body went limp and her bladder released its wet load.

He pulled the covers up to her chin as if she were sleeping, then lightly kissed her cheek. He spent fifteen minutes packing two suitcases with clothes and his important papers. Afterward he turned off the bedroom light, and that in the adjoining bathroom. Entering the hallway a moment later, he was still misty-eyed. Their marriage had lasted more than a decade, a challenge in the best of circumstances. Some of the good times came back to him: those fantastical trances, which, even in her advancing age and sagging corpulence, the woman had been able to induce and prolong in him.

By the time he had reached the darkroom door, however, she was already buried in his mind, which once more was totally focused on sating his voracious appetite.

12:45 A.M. Exiting from a broken window in the top floor of the blackened, sagging structure, a screeching dark shape, flapping giant wings, led Renee to jerkily clutch at Levy and him to recall how predators lurked in the most placid of settings in order to swoop down and surprise their small, defenseless victims. Instantly his stomach began to hurt.

"Vacated by man anyway, if not by nature," Renee fervently panted, loosening her grip on him, where they crouched behind a Juneberry thicket fifty feet before the quiet house with adjoining barn, which looked to Levy fragile enough to blink into falling.

A patch of slightly denser clouds had rolled in to half cover the moon, and the pine trees were thick at their backs, though except for several foliated white birches, the space between them and the house was clear above the patches of briers and heavy brush. Bats flew out of and into cracks in the building's rafters and the top of the listing chimney, which suggested a shot man frozen in mid-tumble. Levy reached down and roughly kneaded his side, prompting Renee to pass him a Pepto-Bismol bottle she'd produced from somewhere.

Levy opened and gulped down half the antacid, then, grimacing, handed it back to Renee, prior to snatching and popping into his mouth several Juneberries in an attempt to eradicate its vile taste.

"Those'll only worsen your distress," Renee hissed.

"That strikes me as an impossibility," answered Levy, nonetheless surreptitiously turning his head and, as he stood, spitting out the unripened fruit he hadn't swallowed.

Renee rose in a three-quarters crouch next to him, holding a second flashlight she'd pulled from her belt. Levy firmly gripped her wrist. "You understand she may be in there, Renee"—he forced her to look at him—"though maybe not alive?"

Renee sedately nodded.

"Or she might be badly hurt or"—Renee slightly lowered her head but Levy, increasing the pressure on her arm, made her raise it again—"cut up or mutilat—"

Renee pulled free of him. "The point of my accompanying you, Levy, is my having been a nurse for eight years, remember?"

"And my point is that one thing isn't like the other."

Renee angrily flicked on her light. "If it was possibly Trish in there, do you think you'd be able to keep me out here by alluding to my basic squeamishness?"

Shaking his head no, Levy swiped at the knees of his jeans where they'd indented the soil. "Only please understand this isn't one of your ball-busting hikes, Renee, followed by a picnic. If I give you an order in there—never mind goddamn what—don't argue, or ask why, just do it?"

"I promise, dear." On her muscular short legs, she started determinedly across the field in front of him.

1:05 A.M. Hearing what sounded like a door opening at the house, Abbott made his way to the stable's corner, peeked around it, and saw, in the light falling through the gaping foyer entrance, a tall figure resembling Gerald—though Abbott was too far away to be sure—carrying two suitcases toward the Cherokee.

Abbott's suddenly elevated pulse flushed his face with warm blood as, from the stallion's stall, a loud neigh mocked him like derisive laughter for his thwarted plan. The horse and its master must already have been out and back unseen by the smut-perusing Crowley, thought Abbott, which, with Gerald then packing to leave, suggested to the detective that they had paid a final visit to the photographer's haunt and that if Jennifer Follett was ever to be found it would be in small pieces.

Abbott shoved a fist in his mouth and bit down until his knuckles bled. He found himself trying to recall why he had forgone a Ph.D. program in philosophy to become a small-city policeman and concluded it must have been for the same mysterious and masochistic reasons he persisted in habitually running when he possessed little natural aptitude for it. He inwardly assailed a world that rewarded sheer talent of whatever kind, and regardless of the character of the one blessed by it, more than tenacity, hard work, and the old-fashioned desire to live justly.

He watched the figure stand the bags by the Jeep's rear end, open it, insert the luggage, then shut the back door, knowing that, despite what he'd learned from Hammrick Bobb, without positive proof that Gerald and Claire were Radford and Margot Connor, which proof he didn't have and—no matter how expeditiously the FBI, Portland police, and a local judge acted on his information—wouldn't for a number of days, he was legally powerless to prevent their departing Hulburt Hill Road, Dane, or the state. Apprehending them unlawfully might vitiate, even destroy, the kidnapping case being built against them; though not doing so, feared Abbott, would result in their once more vanishing like blown smoke.

Stupefied, he watched the figure start from the Cherokee

back to the house, then, halfway there, suddenly veer left up the drive, directly toward the stable against whose side Abbott abruptly pancaked himself. Footsteps smartly clicked against the asphalt, above their creator's airy whistling of "Little Red Rooster," a tune which, in this setting, turned Abbott stone cold. Then both noises stopped and Abbott heard the big rollway door at the stable's front slide up and, a moment later, through the window just right of him, saw a thin beam of light hit, then circle, the structure's inner walls. One of the horses garrulously snorted. The flash blinked off. It was instantly replaced by an interior ceiling light.

Abbott edged closer to the window.

Steps sounded on the concrete floor inside. Then a noise suggesting an iron latch being opened. A frenzied whinny. Shod hooves pawing at the concrete. A cultured male voice softly speaking words indecipherable to Abbott. The hooves clomping across the floor toward him at the same time that the animal's large shadow slowly emerged on the strip of lighted grass outside the window. The voice firmly barking, "Stop!," occasioning Abbott to jump reactively backward and the shadow to freeze in the puddle of light, where it gently swayed from side to side like a rolling ship.

"Now stay!"

The man walked again, deeper into the building. Another door opened. An object of some kind clattered onto the floor. What might have been a knee joint cracked. A brusque fart sounded, then a mumbled obscenity. The footsteps returned. A horse tiredly neighed. What Abbott took for shovel thrusts coincident to someone's labored breathing prompted him to cautiously reapproach the window. He peered through it.

The big stallion stood facing him in the aisle, in front of

its living quarters, from the floor of which Gerald Sandoval, in riding attire, busily scooped hay and manured straw with a pitchfork. Odd, thought Abbott, to be cleaning a stall at this hour, though soon it became apparent to him that, rather than removing the fouled bedding, the photographer, flinging it from the enclosure's center to the far wall, was in fact re-arranging it.

For several seconds he worked tirelessly, his powerful, thrusting movements alternately aweing and horrifying Abbott, as would a large bear meticulously taking apart a fresh kill. He realized what a physically strong and imposing man Gerald was, then, chilled, comprehended his appeal to the psychically damaged or vulnerable: the man's puissance; his resoluteness; his apparent unwavering confidence; his mental and corporeal attitude of earthly superiority.

He tossed aside the pitchfork, got down on his knees above the spot he'd cleared, and swiped at it with his hands. Then he pulled from his pants pocket a small object, which he studiously applied to a task on the floor, obscured to Abbott. A moment later he half stood, then, forcefully grunting, straightened up, raising with him a large slab of hinged floor until it formed a right angle to the rest. With a powerful shove he sent an unearthed door loudly thumping onto the bedding opposite. He adroitly entered the hole he'd opened and bent down, briefly disappearing from the view of Abbott, whose sole thought before seeing the first of two rectangular wood boxes lifted from the enclosure was: How could one of God's creations have emerged so devilishly flawed?

1:35 A.M.   The house looked to Wallace Flabbe to be sending out signals.

On the first floor, lights came on. Went off. Later came on and went off again.

In the darkened master bedroom no sleep could be found. The headboard reading lamps snapped on, one, then the other, casting disturbing shadows on the walls. The bureau light was switched on to remove them, causing the closet's open doorway to suggest from the bed the entrance to a dark cave. The image was cured by the ceiling's light, so harsh, though, that Edmund and Caroline felt examined by it. To temper it, they turned on the orange fluorescent bulb in the fish tank encased by the facing wall. The perpetual circling of the fish was too reminiscent of their thoughts. They fled the room.

On the way to the kitchen they illuminated the corridor, downstairs playroom, dining room, stairway, pantry, living room. Sitting at the circular table, they drank milk, ate cookies, occasionally touched, seldom talked, asked each other with their eyes what if days, weeks, months, years passed, and nothing? They gripped each other's hands in wordless unity against the thought. After darkening the house, they returned to bed.

Soon they were sitting again beneath the bright light of the kitchen. Wallace Flabbe couldn't figure out the interchanging of light and dark in the house. Nor the single bulb burning upstairs where Hannah, in fits and starts, scribbled in her diary the cold winds and harsh storms of pain, guilt, and love she was unable to otherwise give voice to.

2:10 A.M. Just as he heard the step beneath his foot crack, Levy felt it partially give way. There was no rail to grab on to, no way for him to back up before his leg went through. Cursing, he turned toward Renee at the head of the stairs, whose light framed him, halfway toward the pitch-black basement, twisting his lower torso like a screw in his efforts to free it. "I'll come down and help you, dear."

"Don't!"

"What?"

"The whole thing may collapse!"

Levy laid his light on the step above him, then, placing his hands on the sides of the stairwell, tried to push himself up, occasioning a loud rupturing noise.

"Dry rot, dear?"

"Some kind of fucking rot," answered Levy, grasping the step holding the light, which, he recalled, had supported him on the way down. "I don't know wet or dry."

He tugged moderately. The board didn't move. He tried to hoist himself up, but lacked sufficient leverage, so pushed with his free foot against the broken step, promptly disintegrating it. His added weight snapped the step he was holding in two. He grabbed at the well's walls as his flashlight, preceding him into the darkness, shattered on what sounded like a rock floor beneath where Levy stopped, snared at the waist in a splintered hole, his flanks and hands, where they'd scrabbled at the fracturing wood to halt his descent, pierced and bleeding.

"Are you all right, Levy?"

Growling or angry snarling erupted near his feet. Levy suddenly felt as if he were treading in shark-infested waters. "There's something down here, for Christ sake!"

Then Renee heard it. "Don't drop any farther, Levy! It's right beneath you!"

Her light probed to locate the sound's source, but was prevented by the well's planking from illuminating the space left or right of the stairs, and, by Levy, the cellar beyond him. "I can't see anything, Levy! Can you pull yourself up?"

"I'm stuck worse than before!"

The growling intensified, now seeming to have multiple origins. Levy jerked his feet away from whatever they were. Glancing down, he saw two, four, more glowing red eyes than he could count. He considered attempting to hold himself up with one hand while extracting his gun with the other, but even were he to manage it and not fall, he doubted the advisability of firing into a stone floor at moving targets.

"I'm coming to get you, Levy!"

"Christ, no! Stay there!"

She'd already started, though, as was evidenced by the stairs' precarious creak and the light's downward movement. Levy tensed as the tortured wood groaned. Squeaked. Cracked. Gave way. "We're falling, Renee! Grab something!"

Levy hit the floor and rolled, aware of creatures—dozens, it sounded like—scattering all around him, a loud crash to his rear, a human grunt. Squealing wood. Snarling. Mad running. Yapping. Instinctively rising to his feet, Levy hollered, "Renee!"

No answer.

2:15 A.M. The smell of hay and horses created an anticipatory nostalgia in the man's mind for that world he would soon be leaving behind. Not for the community and the vast majority of its citizens, who were as insignificant to him as the fouled straw camouflaging his cache of art and his tools for composing it, but for the remote terrain, which, had he not so rashly snared his first quarry, would have served as his utopia for years to come. That a single impulsive act had undone nearly three years of networking and careful preparation—not to mention renovations to his house, barn, and studio—while he had labored to keep his hunger at bay, meagerly feeding it, night after night, with the same old visible documentation of his prior feasts, affronted his usually meticulous nature.

He disgustedly shoved in the Jeep's rear the second carton of Radford's work, wistfully looking forward to when it could once more be openly displayed around him in a setting permitting him freedom to reminisce on its subjects' minutest details, from an inverted finger to an awestruck eye to a tongue wagging from an unaccustomed orifice. Though boundlessly in love with himself, who, he was certain, had been placed on earth by a miracle greater than conception to span a measurement superior to distance or time, he was more than a little peeved at this exalted being for having briefly conducted itself as a common predator with no motive beyond instantly ensnaring and devouring its victim, thereby effectively terminating his second life.

But she was so delectable, he recalled, shutting and locking the vehicle, then walking to the foyer. And her parents were so unreasonable. And he'd been waiting so long when he found her that the thought of more intellectual maneuvering to have her couldn't stand up to his precipitate passion. Even so, it wasn't as if he had instantaneously ravaged her in the blind, lusting feasts of his youth, in which he'd achieved nothing remotely like the art-inspired satiation that had evolved from that early debauchery. No. From 7:00 a.m., Tuesday, he had been working to heighten his hunger—taking only small nips to keep it at bay—by excruciatingly prolonging it. Now he would indulge it.

But first there was this mess to clean up.

2:20 A.M. Pulling out his gun, Levy circled the darkness with his eyes.

A large shape brushed against his side. He swatted at it, but it was gone. The air smelled old. Foul. Of organic rot. Levy peered toward where he thought the grunt had come from. More shapes breached the blackness. A weight crashed into his shoulder. Levy swung at it, hitting solid, fur-covered flesh. The beast yelped. Ran off. He started forward. "Renee!"

"Over here, Levy!"

Three words told him his world was still intact, even if in disarray. "Where, baby?"

"Here!"

He rushed at the voice slightly left of him, instantly colliding with a bristly body bolting in the opposite direction. While he was fending it off, his side was scratched or bitten. The thing vanished in the same mysterious manner its companions had. A beam of light pierced the black void right of him. "I'm here, Renee!"

"Levy?"

"This way!"

The light found him. He followed it to where she sat half a dozen feet off the ground on the lowest intact step of the dangling staircase. She dropped into his arms. "Can't you just once listen to me, Renee!"

"The fuck-up originated with you, Levy!"

They warmly embraced. Levy thought even hell might be tolerable if she were his fellow occupant. She was all right, she assured him, hadn't even fallen from the disjointed column, so had avoided physically contacting whatever had inhabited the stench of darkness in which they suddenly seemed all alone. "What in God's name were they, Levy!"

"Wild dogs." Levy took her light, remembering the rumors he'd heard of there being more than one pack in these woods. He directed the beam at the opposite wall, illuminating a large circular hole through the foundation. "They left the same way we'll have to."

Renee shivered against him, then drew back, alarmed. "You're bleeding, Levy."

"One of them clawed or bit me. It's not deep."

"Tomorrow you'll have to start a rabies vaccine."

Levy didn't answer, instead staring several feet left of the hole, at where the light had exposed a large pile of scantily flesh-adorned bones and, next to it, a balled clump of fabric.

2:40 A.M. Carrying a large canvas tarp he'd retrieved from the attic, the man entered the master bedroom, angry at having been forced to accelerate his routine, for it was now only a matter of time before the police, as bungling as they were, unearthed his past and connected it to his present.

After spreading the tarp on the rug next to the bed, he pulled a pair of plastic kitchen gloves onto his hands.

Realizing, from experience, how exhausted and disoriented—even panicked—he would be following his final session at the studio, after which he would need to quickly return to and flee from the house, exacerbated his ire and angst. To start over once more, this time alone! The task seemed daunting, particularly as it had been necessitated by his own recklessness. But he'd accomplish it.

Careful not to dampen his jodhpurs, he lifted Claire from the mattress before unceremoniously dropping her onto the tarp. The body landed, thuddingly, at an odd angle. He centered it with his boot. Then he rolled up the canvas, less lengthy than Claire, who protruded from the ends. He squatted down, hoisted her onto his right shoulder, quickly carted her over to the stable, and dumped her on the dung heap in the stallion's stall.

He jumped into the pit, removed from its wood floor his waterproof physician's bag containing his surgeon's saw and scalpels, exited the hole, and tossed Claire into it. After slamming and locking the heavy door, he concealed it with dirty bedding. Then he headed to the tack room for his saddle and camera, confident his wife's remains would not be found for months, if ever.

Ten minutes later, traversing the shadowy, moon-brushed field leading to the woods, neither he nor the horse was aware of the two-legged figure loping several hundred feet to their rear.

3:00 A.M.   In his blind pursuit, Abbott experienced a divinatory vision of himself as a terminated policeman turned oddball bachelor whose sanity people secretly questioned while pointing swirling fingers at their brains. He feared becoming a castaway in an outlandishness from which no exits to normality existed. It struck him that before this occurred and sooner than all his hair fell out, he ought to find a steady girlfriend. A woman sensitive, widely read, with a humorous bent, though serious enough about the world to be interested in doing more than deriding its ironies, tossing one-liners at its barbarities, and scoffing at its underpinning of miracles. Like him she ought to be physically active, a nonsmoker, preferably a vegetarian, in touch with her spiritual side, someone who wouldn't balk at holding him in the middle of the night when he woke shivering from a nightmare of hell derived from his having once encountered a high-ranking visitor from there.

Though his body had stopped registering fatigue from lack of sleep and muscular pain from overwork, his mind couldn't transcend the sight of a man dumping his wife's corpse like a sack of refuse into a hole from which he had earlier extracted cartons containing what could only be a child predator's photographic library and, afterward, a physician's bag—which, when construed with the Portland newspaper accounts of Radford Connor, was to Abbott perhaps the most chilling sight of all. Or had it been the interminable approach of Gerald, shouldering a human-shaped tarpaulin, dangling hair and feet, which only after the bulging cadaver had been tossed on a dung heap did Abbott see weren't attached to Jennifer Follett?

Like thin trickles of sieve-filtered water, moonlight penetrated the coniferous canopy, providing the policeman with the nearly opaque vision of a severe cataract sufferer. On the thin dirt trail, thankfully only sparsely marred by rocks and protuberant roots, he jogged carefully, recklessly increasing his speed only when the steady clip-clopping sound of the rapidly walking or slowly trotting horse preceding him began to fade. He tried to envision himself as the earthbound equivalent of the echo-seeking bats Levy had described to him, yet often stumbled and twice fell, once bruising a knee. The horrible thought beyond words of what would transpire if he lost the stallion allowed him to ignore his bodily pain and to question again his decision at the stable not to apprehend Gerald immediately for Claire's probable murder. Though had he been arrested, Radford Connor likely wouldn't have offered a clue to Jennifer's whereabouts, making it improbable she would ever be found, alive or dead. And given the now obvious depth of the photographer's depravity, a good chance existed she was the latter, even as her kidnapper, with his camera and doctor's bag, rode toward her corpse for motives unfathomable to anyone but him.

At a fork in the path, Abbott suddenly couldn't detect in what direction the stallion's footfalls were receding. He started to the left. Instantly the smell of spruce became stronger, the darkening woods thicker. In seconds, all semblance of light vanished. Then the trail petered out. When he stopped, the policeman couldn't hear the horse at all. Panicked, he turned back. Directly in front of him loomed a tall, four-legged shape. Abbott cried out. The animal—a large buck, he guessed, rather than the big bay he'd briefly imagined—plunged into the blackness.

He quickly relocated the path in the flashlight's beam, sprinted back to the fork, then, several hundred yards up the right trail, stopped and intently listened. An owl's screech, a coyote's mournful yapping, the normal mysterious din of dark woods he hadn't a hope of identifying reached him.

Nothing, though, resembling shod hooves contacting the forest floor.

The ghastly realization that he had gambled a child's life on his ability to successfully shadow a horse through blackened woods struck Abbott. "Please, God," he begged.

Slowly, silently counting, he ran as fast as he could up the path, abruptly halting when he reached one hundred. He extinguished the light. Lay down. Put an ear to the pine-needle-covered dirt. His heart's rabid pounding nearly obliterated the faint, repetitive clomping coming from somewhere ahead of him. Immediately starting after it, Abbott promised God future reparations in the form of good deeds.

3:05 A.M. Renee rapidly exited through the rounded hole, an area of rotted foundation chewed and dug at until it was large enough for most average-size bodies to crawl through easily, but Levy's odd blocky shape, closely following her lithe torso, required painful contortions made even more so because of his injured midsection and hands. "Renee?"

But she left him squirming in the opening, pushing in front of him a cloth book bag containing the Saran-wrapped remains of what was to have been a little girl's lunch and a tooth-gnawed, hardback edition of *Stuart Little*, on the inside cover of which was scrawled "Susan Myercamp." "Baby, wait a minute!"

He extricated himself. "Renee, where are you?"

In the dark section of former backyard, lost to briers and berry bushes, he heard to his left a gagging sound before he spotted her shadowy figure hunched over what she'd expelled, sucking in lungfuls of the pregnant spring air, which, in contrast to the gone stink of that cellar, tasted to Levy like life itself. "It wasn't her, Renee! It wasn't! You hear me!"

With one hand she mutely waved him away as if he were a fly at a picnic. Levy cautiously approached her. "They weren't human—those bones!"

She glanced up, hyperventilating. "You're no goddamn paleontologist, Levy!"

"I recognize a dismembered calf carcass when I see one! So would you if it hadn't been so close to the other—"

"Jesus, Levy!"

"Put it out of your head!"

"My God—I really thought . . . !"

Levy glanced down at the book bag. "I know. Me too, at first."

"I don't want to know about these things! I'm sorry! I just don't!"

"Baby, I tried to tell you—"

"I should be home with Trish!"

"We'll go there now." He put his arms around her, feeling guilty for having allowed her to talk him into bringing her along, professionally elated at the evidence they'd found, personally flattened by what it meant, and emotionally burned out by a profession in which he increasingly compared himself to a janitor called in to mop up a spill when what he really wanted to do was to stop it from happening or to put everything magically back to how it had been.

Renee glared at the waning moon as if it really contained a man's face. "The despicableness! It didn't—the awfulness!—it never hit me until . . ."

Levy hugged her, understanding she was now feeling what he had been since first encountering Gerald Sandoval.

"I suppose now I'll have nightmares for the rest of my life!"

Levy led her over to a willow tree rooted in an oasis of toothwort and columbine amid the roughened brush. They sat down, Levy's back to the trunk and Renee reclining between his legs, their fingers joined in her lap, watching the gentle wind sway of the trees bordering the defeated yard and, above them, the sky, still as a painting but for the blowing clouds scarring it. "From here on"— Renee's hollow, faraway voice seemed to be conversing with a source higher than Levy—"I pray fiery, eternal damnation exists . . ."

Levy yanked up a handful of columbine flowers, flung them one by one into the darkness. "We'll get a search team out here."

Renee wiped cellar grime from her cheek.

"And, based on what we've already found and Ned Bolan's sworn statement, I'll go arrest Gerald."

Fireflies sparked in the facing field, which camouflaged a cooing mourning dove. "She was buried down there, wasn't she, Levy?"

Levy non-responsively poked at his injured side, where his internal and external pain met.

"And the dogs dug up her grave and all they left of her is that book bag!"

"That bag could have been found anyplace it was dropped, Renee!—maybe miles away—and carried back here." Eyeing the dark outline of the hill east of the farm, leading eventually to the Sandovals', Levy considered how his job heightened his distrust of his own relatively charmed existence. When would some event or person come along to shatter it? Preparatory to standing, he tugged the flashlight from his wife's belt and switched it on.

Renee promptly slapped a hand over its end, hissing, "Shhhh!"

Cocking an ear in the direction he'd just been looking, she mouthed, "Do you hear . . . ?"

Levy attempted to.

"That rhythmic . . . ?"

He switched off the light.

They got to their feet, trotted the fifty yards of sky-lit terrain to the house's west corner, squatted down, and listened to a dull, repetitive thud. "Is it . . . ?"

"I'm not sure."

A clear whinny sounded from the crest of the hill. "Christ, Levy! That was a hor—"

"Quiet!"

The ambiguous thumping grew stronger, then slowly began to fade. "It's heading farther west!"

"That doesn't make sense."

"None of it does!"

"Get back down to Bolan's," hissed Levy, "and make that call."

"The problem is, Levy"—Renee abruptly stood, pulling him up with her—"you're holding the only goddamn light!"

Levy perplexedly stared at and beyond her, into the darkness from which the receding footfalls issued.

Responding to his dilemma, Renee confidently squeezed his arm. "I'll just stay behind you!"

"And do whatever I say," agreed Levy, switching on the light. Shading it with his hand, he started off rapidly through the field.

3:25 A.M. In his heightening, barely contained ravenousness, the man leaned forward and expelled in the bay's ear a noise between a pant and a growl, an indecipherable language though the only one capable of even half describing the hunger infecting him, who, by a wonder beyond biological explanation, had been placed on earth solely to feed it.

A blood-curdling shriek from the dark woods they rode into occasioned the stallion, excitedly whinnying, to abruptly halt, then rear.

The man deftly grounded the animal.

"A bobcat, is all," he whispered, firmly stroking the neck of the only confidant to whom he felt free to express the fervor spawned by his darkest thoughts.

Rather than being calmed, the horse restlessly pawed at the soil, provoked, perhaps, less by the hunting cat than by the ardent mouthings of its rider, sprouting in his jodhpurs an erection brought about more from the saddle's rubbing than from his gnawing hunger. Carnality was but one of the many doors through which he passed on his way to sating an appetite beyond depiction. Language could no more describe his unique craving than could science construe an artist's gift. Photographs only enhanced his desire. Mental imagery might make it nearly unbearable. Discipline could keep it at bay only so long, after which it exploded like shrapnel from a bomb. Maybe it started with his mind's eye fixating on the pink virgin flesh beneath a certain child's dime-sized toenail. Or the thought of her fatless, non-bulging breasts. Or of a urine drop descending, like transparent blood, a thigh smooth and white as hand-buffed ivory. From a single such image his hunts evolved, eventually concluding as shockingly as the bobcat's scream, though far more prolonged.

His frenzy when conducting his precise dissections was only elevated by witnessing his subjects' excruciating expressions and agonized cries at his suddenly and inexplicably having betrayed them after he had, until his climactic session, lobbied for their trust, assuring them that, in his care, they would always be safe. Though when at last they exhaled their concluding breaths, each, he was convinced, finally understood how blessed she was for having been chosen by him and how intensely, during the long hours leading to her death, she had been loved and would be anew each time he viewed the artistic masterpiece he had created from her perfect child's body, which, thanks to him, would never be destroyed by maturing.

Fervidly neighing again, the stallion whipped its head left, at the bushes near its tail.

"Where?" quietly demanded the man.

His mount snorted and gazed farther back, toward the dark foliage they'd just exited, where the man heard only the creak of shifting trees and their branches' wind-swaying whisper, though something in there—or beyond—had spooked the bay, whose instincts its rider trusted nearly as much as his own.

The stallion edgily lifted and dropped its feet. The man peered above its rump, over the top of the gently listing conifers, where bats swooped in fly-rich, moon-perforated darkness. He lengthened and lowered his focus, scanning the sparsely foliated, sky-lit rise overlooking the forsaken farm. Through the waist-high brush moved the dark outline of a four-legged animal, or a two-legged one tilted precariously forward. A chill born equally of fear and of anger touched the man. He intently eyed the ghostly shape descending the open embankment until, three-quarters down, it vanished behind a thicket. The man pinched a tick from his neck, squeezed it, then flicked it away.

The stallion shifted its gaze to the black woods to its right, from deep within which came barely audible barking. Nearer the trail, a rodent, probably a porcupine, relentlessly gnawed on a branch. The air had a vibrant, piney smell. The horse inclined its head to the dirt path, bit off a spindly trefoil shoot, twice chomped the weed before spitting it out. The rider reached forward, lightly tapped the bay's nose to quiet it. He mentally envisioned the trailing shape: too ungainly for a deer or a horse, too large for a bobcat, too far south to be a moose. Perhaps a heifer or a large swine, wandered off from one of the hollow farms. Maybe even a bear. Or a creature which, in its night-shrouded movements, closely resembled one of those.

Quietly clicking his tongue, the man backed the stallion off the north side of the trail, several yards into a grove of thinly spaced hemlocks, dismounted, and seized from the forest floor a thick, leafless branch. "Stand quiet!" he hissed, placing his free hand over the bay's muzzle.

3:30 A.M. Myopically peering through the gray-dark saplings toward the ensuing blackness into which he had watched, from the hilltop, the shadow of the stallion disappear, Abbott found himself wishing he were on more intimate terms with God so that he might convince Him to shine His light, visible only to Abbott, where, seconds earlier, following a hideous scream from what Abbott speculated was a very big cat he hoped not to run into, he had twice heard the stallion whinny.

Crouched in the cover of the saplings, the policeman cocked an ear toward the forest edge, which, fifty or so yards ahead, melded with the bottom of the hill. Unable to detect footsteps, a neigh, or a snort, he wondered if the horse could so quickly have gotten enough ahead of him that he had, once more, lost audible contact with it. Or if, for some reason, it had stopped moving. If the latter, why? Could the animal have reached its destination? Or was Gerald down there sitting on it, gazing back up at the illuminated hillside, down which Abbott had just traveled three-quarters of the way and, to reach the forest, would have to go down completely?

The invisible tree trunks beneath the shadowy canopy fronting him were so black they might have been the ocean or a depthless, gravity-free void from which Radford Connor had effused like a toxic fume and then evaporated back into. Though he hadn't been noticeably armed, the photographer might have pulled a pistol from his saddlebags, with which he intended, from the woods' edge, to pick off the descending Abbott. Conversely, he might be well beyond the forest entrance, or already at a concealed haven therein, near to performing God knew what atrocities on the living or dead Jennifer Follett.

His legs hurting him more than from any of the marathons he'd run, Abbott withdrew his service revolver, assured himself it was loaded, returned it to his holster, saturated with the sweat cooling his body in small rivers. The distant bay of dogs he had been half aware of seemed to be drawing nearer. The detective recalled his lifelong failure to win any event he'd ever entered, though, from bowling tournaments to cakewalks to bridge matches to foot races, he had generally performed in them admirably and, often, proficiently. Nonetheless, being the sort of athlete labeled a tireless worker by coaches seeking to positively assess irremediable limitations, he'd never captured the big prize, had not come in first in anything. Even the one woman he had thus far loved had, in the end, assessed his marriage proposal second best to that of a Wharton graduate stepping onto a ladder whose first salaried rung would elevate him above the career vista of a philosophizing small-city policeman.

Abbott speculated that perhaps his always second-banana efforts resulted less from a lack of talent than from a lack of will, and he recalled the story about the little engine that could. While commencing an inclined, serpentine half-jog down the remaining embankment, idly wondering if a gunshot victim hears the discharge of the bullet that slays him, he repeatedly mouthed, "I think I can. I think I can . . ."

Just before reaching a dirt path into the forest, he clumsily hurdled a minor boulder concealed in the grass, scaring up a grouse, leading the startled policeman to dramatically clutch at his heart as if he'd been stricken. Seconds later, exiting the field's relative glare into woods suggesting a room sucked of light, he relaxed some, though past five feet he was blind in every direction but up.

3:35 A.M. Kneeling between a giant oak tree and his wife, his hands forming a cradle for her to step in, Levy, certain that the baying fast approaching them was not from trained hunting hounds, pantingly explained, ". . . only that I'd prefer right now, for a lot of reasons—least of which is those dogs—you were invisible from the ground!" Then, more softly, "If I'm not back by the time the sun starts rising, get yourself down to Bolan's and call in the cavalry."

"That remark concerns more than heartens me, Levy."

Levy forced her to squat. "I mention it only in the event that horse"—he nodded into the darkness ahead and to their right from where, seconds earlier, on the heels of what Levy had recognized as a bobcat's screech, had sounded another neigh, this one much nearer—"leads me to a destination from which, due to distance or circumstances, I'm unable to return by morning."

"And if whoever's on its back or those dogs spot you?"

Levy roughly slipped his hands beneath one of her sneakered feet. "The latter are after that cat, not me, and, regarding the former, I fully intend to be more stealthy than him." He softly kissed her hair. "For my deranged behavior in involving you in this, Renee, I wouldn't blame you for dumping me, though, given my overall record of loyalty and devoted love, I think you'd be making a big mistake."

She squeezed his shoulder.

Levy felt something catch in his throat. "It's probably just some farmer's kid and his girl out for a moonlight ride." Readying to stand, he restrainedly chanted, "One, two, three!"

Renee sprang up with his heft, reaching for the oak's lowest limb, ten feet off the ground. "Shimmy!" mouthed Levy.

She scrabbled at the bark. His injured side feeling over-inflated, as if it would blow out, Levy elevated her. After several seconds, the weight in his hands abated, coincident with Renee gasping, "Got it!"

She sat down on the newly leaved branch, visible solely in

profile to Levy, standing directly beneath her. Able now to be distinguished by their varying barks—half a dozen at least—the dogs came fast from the south. Opposite their approach, from where the horse had neighed, could be heard only the trees. Levy sought to paint a mental picture of what little he could see of the statuesque oak—mostly a gnarled, corpulent trunk indicating it had gotten that way over two centuries—so he could find it later, before, comprehending the pointlessness of trying to remember one big tree in a black forest of them, he decided he had better count his footsteps to the path.

He withdrew his flashlight, turned it on, tempered its glare with two fingers, and pointed it at the ground, whispering, "Don't come down or even shake a branch for anything but my voice or daylight."

"I'm perfectly capable of perching undetected in a tree," Renee sibilantly replied. "You just be careful, do your job, and don't underestimate what's out there!"

Levy strode west a hundred fifty times, halted near a large moss-covered boulder, mentally noted it, then turned north into a stand of pines and hemlocks, in or beyond which, he speculated, was the path the horse must have been traveling.

3:40 A.M. The forest was several degrees cooler than the hillside. The sole breeze blew high in the shadowing limbs of potent-smelling conifers. Gnats sought out Abbott's bare flesh. He heard nothing of the stallion, just the heightening barking—from a hound pack, it sounded like—approaching from the south.

What little he could see of the path seemed wide, with a

well-groomed floor, heading west. Not wanting to use his flashlight unless it became absolutely necessary, Abbott walked fuzzily along the trail, increasingly struck by a sharp, thick odor. Soon he stepped in its source. Horse manure. A huge, steaming pile of it.

The detective nervously darted his eyes at the forward blackness, from which came two soft swishes sandwiched around a gentle slap. The noise repeated itself. Then once more. A sound familiar to him, though he couldn't place it.

He hastily wiped his shoe on the piney ground. Moved cautiously ahead. Halted. Withdrew his revolver. Flicked off the gun's safety. Warily took several more steps. What might have been a sigh or maybe just a zephyr whispered in the trees. A branch snapped somewhere. Abbott once more heard the swish-slap-swish, at the same time realizing he was listening to a large tail swiping at flies. Seeking its owner's location, he wheeled a panicky circle in the path, confronting, halfway around, a rush of air from an invisible object that, a split second later, slammed into his abdomen. He doubled over, unable to breathe. He was hit again, this time higher up, with a bone-crushing thud. Abbott went down, his pistol hurtling into the void.

A human shape raised above his head a club-shaped object whose downward thrust the prostrate policeman calmly understood would kill him.

The cliché about time slowing down occurred to him.

The bobcat's piercing screech, sounding as if the feline was nearly in Abbott's lap, induced a frenzied whinny and the stallion's rearing outline rising directly above him. His attacker darted to avoid or grab the horse. Abbott tried to roll out from under it. Either he managed to or, in landing, the stallion miraculously avoided him. He heard it gallop off. And something—perhaps his assailant—scrabbling in the brush. A snarling, four-legged shape rushed madly across the path. For a fraction of a second, Abbott glimpsed a set of yellow, terrified eyes.

A light flickered somewhere.

An object dropped near Abbott's head.

A person running. One at least. Maybe more. The light vanished. The yap of the dog pack, heatedly pursuing the bobcat. Abbott tried to keep alert, but felt himself abandoned, slipping. Another child's parable came to him: "The fly ran away in fear of the frog, who ran from the cat, who ran from the dog . . ."

3:45 A.M. His hour of restless sleep ended by the firm but gentle bang of a door closing—in his head or beyond, he wasn't sure—Edmund got up and walked down the corridor, into the darkened kitchen, where, prior to seeing it, he almost stepped on a scrawny black-and-white cat he had never before laid eyes on, its fur matted with burrs, drinking milk from a cereal bowl on the floor. "How did you get inside?" Edmund hissed.

The creature skittishly backed off, then returned to its quiet lapping.

"Hello?" whispered Edmund to the room.

No answer.

He flicked on the overhead light, illuminating on the counter an open quart of milk and a package of saltines. He thought about Caroline, in drug-induced sleep in the bedroom. He checked the outside door, which was locked, entered the sun porch and pantry, encountering no one in either, then peered in the living room, where, before the fireplace, Garofalo slept.

At the kitchen table he sat down above the cat, which looked wild and possibly sick, though, something in its pale yellow eyes told Edmund, not dangerous.

While eating, the animal rubbed its body against Edmund's leg. Edmund reached down and plucked several burrs from it. A toilet flushed in the downstairs bathroom, behind the stairs. Shortly after, a door opened, and closed, then a flashlight beam peeked around the stairwell, flicking off when confronted with the lighted kitchen, into which Hannah, barefoot, now walked. "I came down to get something to drink and heard it"—she nodded in her emotionless manner at the cat—"scratching at the door."

Her mid-thigh-length cotton nightgown accentuated the contours of her athletic body in a way that made Edmund uncomfortable. "Do you know who it belongs to?"

"I'd say God alone, by the look of it."

"You've not seen it before?"

Hannah shook her head.

"What if—"

"It's just lost or on hard times, Mr. Follett," Hannah interrupted his unframed question, which had to do with infectious diseases. She walked over to the refrigerator, poured a glass of juice, turned toward the table. "I hope you—it's all right with you."

Edmund half smiled. "It seems quite friendly, actually." He tossed the burrs he'd removed into the wastebasket, then nodded at the chair opposite him. Hannah moved to the table but didn't sit down.

"I want to say . . ."

"What?"

"Tell you about it."

"About the cat?"

Hannah tipped the glass toward her mouth. "Let me . . ."

"Pardon?"

"I think I'd like to drink my juice first."

"Okay."

"My throat's dry," she said in an apparent desire to explain her thirst. "It's one of the side effects of the medicine. It dries my throat."

She sat down, drank more juice. A muscle flickered above her right eye, another at a corner of her mouth. She seemed unaware of or not concerned by her nipples' visibility beneath the thin fabric of her nightie. Edmund couldn't come close to anticipating her thoughts, or to comprehending what her life was like. Looking at her pained him in the way witnessing any living thing caged, fenced in, or out of its element did. "We don't have to talk," he said. "We can just sit here until—for a few minutes—then go back to bed."

Not answering, she gazed into her juice glass.

Edmund picked up an *Architectural Digest*, flicked through it, then placed it back on the table, wondering how he'd ever been so impassioned over the business of designing aesthetically pleasing, functional structures, the actual building of which he turned over to craftsmen. The profession suddenly struck him as irresponsible and terribly isolating. He thought he'd not, in good conscience, be able to return to it. What, though, would he do in the future? Time beyond the present struck him as an impenetrable wall to somehow get over. "It was at least ten," he heard Hannah say, "maybe even fifteen . . ."

Edmund glanced at her.

". . . minutes, I mean, that I was away from the window . . ." She waved at something in the air. Edmund seized the milk container, leaned down, and refilled the almost empty bowl facing the cat, which, purring, massaged its head on his hand. "I should have brought Edmund Jr. here, into the kitchen, so I could see Jen—but I was watching a segment on tele—the *Today* show—in the living roo—I kept thinking a commercial would . . ."

Edmund straightened up, not wanting to hear any more of what might have been. "There's enough guilt, Hannah, for all of u—"

"I'm sorry, Mr. Follett—"

"—to go around."

"—and for how I lied to you . . ."

Edmund touched her forearm. She looked across the table at him, tears, miraculously, dampening her eyes. "You go back up to bed, Hannah," he told her kindly. "I'll put out the cat once it's finish—eaten all it wants."

3:50 A.M. The man careered into a depression, lost his balance, fell face first onto a pine-needle floor, where for several seconds he tremblingly lay, pitying his blind, persecuted self for how the world, which he understood had been created for him to be the axis and master of, had allowed his present plight. His horse had abandoned him, his wife had betrayed him, the police had victimized him. His hunger had completely dissipated, was no longer even a vague gnawing. He was a scared child, his only palpable drive to live, to avoid entering the unknown, and therefore terrifying, state beyond being.

Above the shallow hole, like a scoop taken from the soft soil, he peeked at the thin probing shaft, maybe fifty yards to his left and rear, combing the forest in a slow side-to-side arc before the crunching approach of the invisible thing hunting him. Despairing at the disloyalty of the small-brained organisms upon which he was forced to rely, the man inwardly swore to later shoot and butcher the stallion, not only for running off but for doing so with his saddlebags, containing enough evidence to put him away for life and, more important at the moment, his Davis two-shot derringer.

Seconds following the sound eruption that had shattered them, the woods, beyond the relentless noise of the nearing footsteps, were eerily quiet, assuring the man, at least, that the hounds that he had briefly feared were after him weren't. Who, though, was? It couldn't be the police. Not so soon. Nor without warrants. Then who? Or what? So often in his predatory role at home in the dark, the man suddenly found himself horrified by the trees' shapes, like legs attached to torsos and heads he couldn't see, towering over poor, petrified him, hugging the dirt. "Why am I being put through this?" he mutely railed. "Where is the so-called God or much ballyhooed Devil who will help *me*?"

He slithered blubberingly back into the hole, sightlessly patting it for a potential weapon. Several sticks he deemed too frail to crack open a skull. An ankle-thick pine bough proved to be rotten. When he found one that wasn't, he suddenly realized that to use it effectively he would have to get at arm's length from his prey, who, if carrying a firearm, would shoot him. He dropped the branch and began searching for something that might serve as a projectile, in his heightening panic emitting sounds—squeaks, frenzied sniffles, pathetic whimpers—suggestive of a small, tormented animal. He envisioned his stalker as inhuman, a fanged, flesh-dissecting creature, whose obvious parallels to himself were no more recognizable to the man, who considered fear, dread, pain, despair as relevant sensations only when experienced by him, than were those between his plight and the one he had imposed on his many victims. His silent entreaty was "Help me! Me! *Me*!"

3:55 A.M.   Abbott didn't trust his recall of the explosion of sound and action that had lasted mere seconds before every life in the forest but his had seemingly been sucked into the void. Though he hadn't seen his assailant, it had to have been Gerald, he told himself, but who had arrived with the light, for what purpose, and was he or she chasing the former, or, on the contrary, were they accomplices both of whom had pursued the stallion and would soon return?

Desperately trying again to sit, he was once more flattened by a stabbing sensation, the severity of which suggested an array of dull knives being slowly and fiendishly twisted into his lower chest.

Applying pain-doctored motivation, he inwardly berated himself that in his past training and racing he'd not been totally committed to winning, thus explaining his failure to do so. He'd run for love of the endeavor, its intoxicant effect, its spiritual boost, and because he secretly suspected were he to stop he might seek the same effects in more harmful ways, for

example by drinking himself stuporous each night. Crushing
the competition had never driven him. He'd not before heard,
as every great athlete must, the relentless message repeating
in his head: "Anything less than utter physical and mental
depletion in pursuit of victory will result in total, soul-
crushing defeat!"

His most torturing, though ultimately successful, move to
raise himself preceded by moments the foliage-snapping approach of footsteps from the woods opposite those into
which, minutes earlier, the light beam had vanished.

Abbott frenetically clawed the ground for his gun, gave up,
then quickly yanked out his flashlight to use as a meager
weapon. He theorized he had several broken ribs, a cracked
sternum, likely could stand, maybe walk a little, run not at
all, and defend himself feebly, though not lengthily. His best
bet, he despairingly concluded, was to hide.

The nearing thing broke noisily from the forest onto the
path. Muffling a suffering groan, Abbott pushed himself into
a squat, then tremulously stood, as, on the pine-needle-
covered trail, echoed the dull thud of falling feet. Ker-thunk.
Ker-thunk.

Not a two-legged animal. A shod, four-legged one!

The creature increased its pace. Abbott agonizingly hob-
bled to an aged pine off the path side closest to him, reaching
it just as a trotting quadrupedal shape rounded the curve fifteen feet westward. Sensing or smelling Abbott's presence, it
abruptly halted, then reared.

The stallion. Nothing but a saddle on its back.

Snorting, it pawed the dirt.

Leaning heavily on the tree, Abbott, in his relief, achingly
exhaled, pushing his probing pain deeper. The horse stared

at, then directly approached, him. Not used to and inately wary of large animals, Abbott cowered against the pine trunk. The stallion unhesitantly advanced, breathing rapidly, sweat-glistening, a tremor undulating its withers like wind through high grass. Inches from Abbott it stopped, nostrils palpitating, ears laid back, eyes wide open, pupils dilated. Communicating what?

Fear. Abject terror.

Lost in the same dark as a vicious, screeching hunter and the predators chasing it, the big bay, surmised Abbott, was as petrified as he. Tentatively, he reached out, touched its nose, warmly wet. The horse snickered, lipped his fingers. Abbott stroked its white-diamond-adorned forehead. The horse affectionately rubbed against him. Abbott thought, Tackle your fears head on.

He gingerly stepped away from the tree, approached the animal's left flank. The stallion's rearward-declining muzzle gently nudged his upper abdomen, sending pain coursing into the deepest regions of his brain. Abbott moaned sicklily. His eyes filled with tears. Through clenched teeth he feebly beseeched the horse, "For my inexperience, God-awful hurt, and the rectitude of my intentions, please make allowances."

Understanding of his injuries, desiring in those dark woods the assurance of a warm body on its back, or simply well trained, the bay stood stock-still while Abbott, mimicking what he'd occasionally watched experienced equestrians do, several times failed to raise his left foot to the corresponding stirrup, each miss torturing him worse than its predecessor. Finally, he seized his partially elevated foot near his opposite knee, manually hoisted it the rest of the way to the wooden loop, then, praying the horse wouldn't bolt, inserted it, quickly grabbed the pommel, and, fearing his tormented cry would sound to his mount like the bobcat's scream, hefted himself into the saddle.

The horse throatily whimpered but didn't move.

"Let's go, boy," wheezed Abbott.

No response.

Clicking his tongue, Abbott lightly toed the animal's belly. The bay uninterestedly shook its head.

"Forward," commanded Abbott, without effect.

He let go of the pommel, reached down, and seized the reins dangling from the horse's neck.

The animal immediately turned and moved toward the trail.

"Slow," hissed Abbott, pulling on the left rein.

At a leisurely walk, the bay obediently headed in the direction from which it had just come.

4:00 A.M. The man's frantically searching hand miraculously latched on to a rock shaped like one of the numerous pine-cones he had picked up and discarded, abruptly returning him from the infantile state he'd momentarily been frightened into and prompting him to snort cockily into his sleeved elbow.

Once a varsity pitcher, he recalled the strength and accuracy of his right arm. He foresaw the stoved-in skull of his tracker leaking its brains. As the light swept through the trees east of the depression, he crawled up that side of the embankment as quietly as he could and peered out at the fanning beam, less than twenty-five feet from him. He worried only about standing up too fast or too loudly.

Soon he could make out the upright, blocky shape holding

the light—not a beast, just a human lummox, though of indeterminate identity, and clearly carrying a pistol. As the beam passed over him a final time before its guider walked past him, the man flattened himself, then slowly rose, vaguely aware at the same time of a slight rustling in the trees higher up, beyond his target. Fixating on the back of the head fifteen feet to his front, he cocked his arm, then whipped it forward just as an apparently disembodied female voice yelled, "He's behind you!"

The light-holder simultaneously ducked and wheeled, a moment before the rock smashed into his—or her—shoulder, knocking whoever it was down.

The man charged toward the only creature visible to him in what he suddenly perceived as a forest full of concealed eyes beholding his darkest secrets. Accompanied by a resonant crack, a sharp sting in his right thigh severely hampered his assault, peculiarly so to the man, still trying to run.

The obscured figure, struggling to its feet behind the light now blinding the man, called out, "Halt!"

The man was powerless not to.

He reached down to the fleshy part of his upper leg, inches from his groin, where the rapidly intensifying sting throbbed and his groping fingers became wetly hot. "I've been shot!" he gasped incredulously. "You—Jesus, you! You shot me!"

The light from the risen figure relentlessly held the man's eyes. "Put up your hands!"

"What?"

"Raise 'em up over your goddamn head or I'll put another one in you!"

"Who are you . . . ?"

He heard the pistol cock and saw, several yards to the rear

of the man talking, another primatial shape drop from a branch to the ground. "Please, I haven't done . . ."

"Get your arms away from your body!"

The man instantly turned to vapor a human breath could dissipate. An inward look at himself saddened him, as he was sure it would the world, could it only see the maligned infant he was. He started to cry for humanity's terrible mistreatment of him.

"I'm going to tell you one more time to get your goddamn hands over your head!"

The figure was unmoving. It just stood there, imperceptible behind its white eye probing to the depth of the child's frightened soul.

"You've hurt me! I'm bleeding!"

He saw the second shape, slighter, perhaps the woman who'd cried out, join the first.

"Who are you people? Why have you done this to me?"

"I'm coming over there," said the voice, hauntingly familiar to the man. "The slightest movement from you will result in my shooting your other leg. Or maybe an arm."

The one talking stepped out from behind the light.

"What are you going to do to me?"

"I'm a police officer." The figure walked toward him, slowly revealing his identity to the man, who, in relief and pain, collapsed to his knees. "Gerald Sandoval—or Radford Connor—you're under arrest for the kidnapping of Jennifer Follett. You have the right to remain silent. You have the right to an attorney. If you can't affor—"

"God's sake, Detective Levy, you've harrassed and shot an unarmed person!"

"Are you crying, Gerald?"

From his invocating position, the man feebly raised his hands. "Please hurry and stop my bleeding!"

The detective reached him. He lowered the man's hands in front of him. "Where is she, you piece of shit?"

The vaporous child solidified into the cold rock of its adulthood. Blankly staring, the man swallowed his infant's fear like a pill. "Pardon?"

"Jennifer." Encircling metal snapped his wrists together. "What have you done with her?"

Only dying—the uncertain void beyond living, the inverse of human mastery—intimidated the man.

"We've got a witness who saw you driving down the hollow Tuesday morning from the Dresser place, in the cellar of which, less than a mile from here, we found her book bag!" The policeman laid him on his back to get a better look at the injury. The man heard the smaller figure approaching. "If you possess even a shred of the decency most of humanity, in varying degrees, is born with, tell me—tell the girl's parents so at least they can have some peace—where can we find her?"

The man considered his heightening pain and the crippling nature of his arresting officer's pathetic compassion as positive signs for his survival. "If I should pass out, Detective, I'm allergic to penicillin, have type O-positive blood, and am wearing contact lenses." He moaned agonizedly. "Now, please, sir, hurry and get me to a hospital . . ."

4:10 A.M.   On the canopied swath rupturing the dark woods, the horse's slow, confident gait, in which it deftly avoided potholes and fallen limbs before they possibly could have been visible, suggested it had a good memory. Considering his gnawing pain, made constant by breathing, Abbott was surprised at the relative comfort of the ride's side-to-side swaying. The pine forest's utter blackness was emphasized by their traversing a small clearing—whether made by fire or lumbering, Abbott couldn't tell—where, in the sky's gray light, he briefly glimpsed his shadowy self, tottering atop the bay like an unbalanced sack.

Exiting the conifers, they entered a stand of middle-aged sugar maples, evenly spaced as if humanly arranged, their budded, half-leaved branches filtering like a prism the moon's invading beam. With a screech and a dull thud, a dark, plunging shape struck and seized a smaller bird in the air fronting them, startling the bay into an abrupt swerve, excruciating to Abbott, who wrapped his arms around the stallion's neck so as not to fall, once more made harshly aware of the speed with which lives in that foreign setting were altered or ended.

Echoing more resonantly on the hard-packed earth anchoring the maples than on the needly pine-forest floor, the horse's footfalls, like meditation chants, helped to divert the policeman's thoughts from his pain, his uncertain destination, and its possible concealments. In the bay's heated torso he sensed a similarly warm soul, indentured to a master devoid of one, and wondered what the horse would tell him, if it could talk, about its owner and the dark rides they had shared. More intensely than ever before, he found himself longing for physical proof of God's existence, to see, firsthand, His light, and from then on to feel the heaven-inspired confidence of those possessionless bald youths peddling flowers at airports.

Then he realized he didn't really need to witness His full glare, only a shiver of it, just enough to knock evil back on its heels this one time, salvaging a good life otherwise doomed.

His mind grazed widely and in no apparent pattern over topics on which he held newly clear opinions: the aptness of the phrase "horse sense"; the realization that his ancestral totem was a cat related to the one that had earlier saved his life—if not its actual forebear; that good people tended to pair off not by instinct, as he had always believed, but out of a hope of multiplying their goodness; how the woods at night, in other circumstances, might actually be a peaceful place; his want of riding lessons, of the love of a good woman, and to move beyond the narrow corridor in which he ran and ran and ran . . .

And he envisioned the small girl he knew only through her intimates' words and from a picture he'd first seen only three days before, her face nonetheless permanently etched in his memory as the embodiment of innocence over which, from mankind's inception, good and evil had collided and, in a world where atrocities resulted from hate no more often than from desire—healthy or sick, of the victim or the victimizer— would do so until its cessation.

4:15 A.M. "I mean, he must know—he has to—he's caught, Levy . . ." Beneath Levy's encircling arm, a shiver traversed Renee's shoulders as they stood, backs to Gerald, ten feet behind them. "Why doesn't he . . . ?"

"Might as well ask why a dog licks itself."

Her silent sobs felt to him like accusations over his allowing her, who, by her shout, had perhaps saved his life, not only to have been in the presence of but to administer to and even be stained by the blood of the fiend neither of them would ever forget. "I've never—he can't be human, that's all."

"No other species, I suspect, would claim him."

"But he has nothing to gain—and that poor little girl . . . !"

"The truth is, baby, she's probably past our help."

"You don't say that, Levy!"

"I'm sorry. I'm just try—"

"You wouldn't if it was Trish!"

He kissed her mouth to close it. "You go now—only take your time, don't twist an ankle on your way back to the car or anything. It wouldn't be worth it." He gently wiped her eyes with a finger, then handed her the flashlight and gun. "In case you run into those dogs again."

He kissed her once more before she left, after which he again faced the photographer, flat on his back, his shackled hands to his forehead, grimacing at the pale moon as if challenging its relentless stare, his riding blouse now a blood-soaked tourniquet for his injured thigh, in which the femoral artery clearly was punctured.

"How long, Detective, do you anticipate that good woman will be in returning with medical assistance?"

Levy shrugged. "An hour and a half. Maybe more." He squatted down in the matted brush. "Fifty-fifty, you'll not be alive to see it."

The photographer's normally self-confident voice, now thinner-sounding, betrayed only a touch of panic. "I'm well versed in the effects of human bleeding, Detective, versus the mind's and body's tenacity for living, and I assure you, sir, we are not such easy organisms to kill."

4:20 A.M. The stallion's motive for halting was not initially apparent to Abbott, who for several seconds patiently waited for the animal to urinate or raise its tail and defecate. But it just stood there, softly whickering. The harsh chack! chack! of a brown thrasher, or a mockingbird imitating one, sounded ahead in the dark grove of planted trees, the sky above it touched by earliest morning's barely perceptible light.

Abbott's wary, circular gaze eventually divulged a treeless, brush-foliated swath, wide as the farm road he guessed it formerly had been, running in a straight line through the maples directly to his left and right. Down the latter side, at the limits of his hazy vision, fifteen feet at most, stood the square shape of what looked to be a small building. Abbott's heart's abruptly elevated pounding worsened the harsh pain encasing it. He experienced an irrational desire to interrogate the horse. Dismounting suddenly seemed too torturous to him and what would follow overly fraught by uncertainties with a minimum potential for uplifting resolutions.

He took out, turned on, then directed his flashlight left of him, at a patch of imploded weeds and grass, dotted by small lumps of horse manure in various degrees of crustiness, looking as if they'd been intentionally kicked—perhaps in an attempt to conceal them—out of the mounds they'd once formed. Dropping the reins, Abbott raggedly caught his breath. He slowly played the beam down the swath's opposite side. A thin corridor of the hip-high underbrush running to the building appeared lightly trampled. Abbott abruptly switched off the light, returned it to his belt, two-handedly gripped the pommel, slowly rolled his right leg over the bay's rump, and, in tormenting increments, lowered himself to the ground.

The stallion promptly moved to the left edge of the trail, where, as evidently was its wont, it lowered its head to graze. Abbott pulled out the light, again shone it down the swath's trodden side. He unholstered his pistol. Holding it ready in one hand, he haltingly approached the building, gradually revealed to be a flat-roofed, one-story wood structure with two circular, rusted metal chimneys protruding from its top which Abbott, from his limited knowledge of the maple sugar industry, hypothesized had once vented a pair of large tanks used to boil down sap into syrup.

The building's front, where the swath ended, contained no windows. The only visible entrance—twice the width of a normal door—was nailed shut by half a dozen time-worn two-by-fours. Crawling vines assailed the wood. The roof was a depository for fallen leaves and branches. The edifice looked to have been unused for years. Abbott aimed the light at its base, a six-inch-wide strip merging with the ground, a darker color than the upper structure, and, unlike it, partially moss-encrusted. Abbott lightly kicked the area.

Hard. Unyielding.

He knelt down and felt it. Concrete. Perhaps because of the weight of the tanks when full, the sap house had been built on a poured foundation. Abbott stood. With his pistol butt, he tapped the building's side, hearing, instead of the hollow rap he had expected from the apparently thin planking, a deep, non-reverberating thud. Knocking similarly on the front door, between the parallel attached two-by-fours, he induced the sound again. His skin prickled with newly exuded sweat. Flashing the light along both sides of the structure, from which the thinning brush fanned out toward a surrounding rim of trees, he saw, veering right from the swath's tramped-down way, a corresponding strip of moderately beaten-down foliage. He slowly followed it around to the rear of the building. In the deep grass there, he saw flecks of sawdust and comparatively fresh-looking wood chips like those left by a ripsaw.

No doors or windows appeared on the building's back side. His tapping of it produced the same solid-as-a-heart's-thump-through-a-muscular-chest sound as had his previous attempts. He guided the light up and down the timber-slatted wall, spotting no creases, holes, or cracks. Pressing his ear to the wood, he heard nothing, as if he were listening at a sealed tomb. He gazed up at the roof through the side branches of a maple limb, crooked like a broken finger over it. A half-formed thought caused him to turn curiously and shine the light at the huge tree, fifteen feet behind him, from which the limb sprouted. Beneath the maple sat a medium-sized boulder, its top scarcely three feet from a portion of the over-hanging branch.

Abbott walked over to the rock, draped in berry bushes. The flashlight's beam illuminated around its base more saw-dust and wood chips. The detective's heart relentlessly assaulted his fractured ribs. He tried not to consider the degree of depravity—or just pure evil—one must possess to physically labor to the extent he theorized Radford Connor had in order to accomplish his goals. As the first dawn birds, like an orchestra tuning its instruments, sporadically chirped in the deeper woods behind him, he holstered his gun, pocketed the light, then, relying as little as possible on his upper body, climbed the boulder, onto the limb, and across it to the roof, suffering pain equal to what he had when mounting the horse, though, perhaps from his mental image of it as another fading star in the sky's dissipating blackness, not as long-lasting.

4:25 A.M.   Levy briefly considered physically torturing the photographer, making him writhe until he begged to tell Levy what he wanted to hear. Immediately after, he was shocked at himself for having even entertained the idea, worried that he had exposed in himself a potential, however minute, for the flagitiousness comprising Gerald Sandoval, body and soul.

"Regarding my survival, Detective"—Gerald coughed— "as with most everything else, you are wrong, for which you should be grateful considering that by living I'll save you from a murder charge."

"Have you thought much about the hereafter, sir?"

"You mean like tomorrow or next week?"

"I mean as in the infinite state following death."

"I'm not much for fairy tales, Detective."

"I somehow don't believe that, Mr. Sandoval. I get the idea a monster like you is convinced he's going to live forever, so why pay the other any mind, only suddenly here you are bleeding yourself all over the woods, probably feeling slightly faint, maybe even a little euphoric, hanging on every heart-beat, and, like the little kids you prey on, petrified of what the big man who's about to grab you has in mind."

Gerald moaned. Levy picked up a pinecone and absently tossed it at a sound in the bushes. He gazed down from his haunches at the double tourniquet on Gerald's leg, bright red, moist, and bubbly with effluent blood. "That leak's too big to fix, Mr. Sandoval. You won't live to daylight."

"I don't get that feeling at all."

"Thinking you'll know when the time's come is one of death's misconceptions." Levy tossed another pinecone. "Take my word for it, sir, you're headed down that long chute to forever."

Gerald weakly waved him away.

"You're dying, Gerald, and you can help ease the pain you created in that girl's parents before you do."

"I've no intention—of dying . . . and—as—for a policeman you're a terrible psychologist."

Levy duck-walked up to the photographer's head and stared down into his blank, never-known-to-a-living-soul eyes. "I'm not smart enough to be subtle, Mr. Sandoval, believe me. You, sir, are dying."

"I'm not—I, uh . . . no."

"Oh yes you are."

"No."

"You are, Gerald. Really. You wait and see."

4:30 A.M.   The roof's forest-engendered cargo exhibited no gaps. Abbott slowly circled it, kicking away twigs and rotting leaves, several inches deep in places. Failing to locate an entrance, he began to fear he had reached another dead end. He stopped next to the chimney nearest him, peered inside, and, above what he guessed was a floor or the dark interior of a sap bin, saw, filtering into the piping through apparent holes, slivers of white light. Neglecting to breathe, he hurried over to the other chimney, in which appeared similar light shards and, for a few seconds, sounded a distinct creaking noise. Abbott tugged at the piping.

It didn't move.

He kneeled down and flailed at the earthen debris surrounding the chimney, until he stubbed a finger on an object beneath it. Cursing, he hastily pushed aside the last of the camouflaging leaves to reveal a thick cylindrical dead bolt, much newer than the rusted flashing securing it. Afraid to hesitate or even think, Abbott yanked back the bolt, then pushed against the chimney, hinged to a metal-reinforced wood slab, which, after declining toward the roof, crashed loudly onto it, creating in the sap house ceiling a three-foot-square breach, emanating a dull light and exposing a rope ladder dangling in the void below.

Forgetting completely about his injury or drawing his gun, Abbott stepped onto the ladder's highest rung, then rapidly descended fifteen feet into an underground room, stuffy, though surprisingly cool given that its soundproofed walls were made of unbreathing fiberglass insulation over four-by-twelve beams, and that the ventilated piping from the roof was its sole source of fresh air.

A battery-operated light hung from the ceiling. Photographs of a single female subject and a few pastoral scenes adorned the walls. A minute rocker, a tiny bureau, an even smaller ice chest, atop which sat a number of children's books, furnished the space. A portable toilet, issuing bad smells, sat in one corner of the room opposite a bed on which lay an unmoving, blond-headed little girl, wearing a soiled yellow dress, and tightly gripping a Cabbage Patch doll. Abbott thought he might faint. "You must be—I bet you're Jennifer," he said.

She didn't answer.

"Are you all ri—hurt in any way?"

No response or movement from the child.

"I'm Detec—I came to bring you home."

The little girl, though cowering against the wall, slowly sat up. Her whispered voice was the smallest sound Abbott had ever heard. "How come my mommy and da—"

"I'm going to br—"

"—don't care about me anymore?"

Abbott took a step toward her. "That's not true, Jennifer. Whoever told you that was lying. They sent me to get you."

The girl looked as if she would crawl through the wall. "How do I know they did?"

"I—they—we've all been looking for you, Jennifer."

He moved forward another step. "You don't know how happy I—they'll be to see you."

Her chin fell to her chest. "Some people lie . . ."

"I'm with—I could show you my badge—I'm a police officer." Abbott took out his badge and showed it to her.

The little girl didn't look at it. She stared down at her doll. Abbott sat down on the bed next to her, wrapped an arm around her shoulders, pulled her close.

"It's all right now, Jennifer. I promise—cross my heart—it is. I'm going to take you home to your mommy and daddy and Edmund Jr. and Hannah and Garofalo and . . ."

The little girl started to cry. Then Abbott did.

7:45 A.M.   In the gray dawn, Edmund had gone out looking for the cat that, three hours earlier, had jumped uninvited into his lap; stroking it was the last thing he remembered before waking. After he'd dozed off, Hannah must have come down and put it out, or the cat had departed through Garofalo's hinged exit in the bottom of the back door. Grateful for its gentleness and love, and for bringing him much needed sleep, Edmund hoped that despite its wildness, the animal would adapt to becoming a house pet. He'd been unable to find it, though.

On the woods trail home he considered how each of his footsteps was dramatically affecting countless lives—he wasn't sure how many, though he guessed dozens, maybe hundreds, even thousands—that simply by walking he was, in innumerable minor ways, altering the world, an infinitely vast populated sphere of dirt and water, in all of which he, like the rest of its cyclic, temporary inhabitants, was directly concerned with but a tiny piece and a handful of beings, of which only three—the one he'd joined with his and those he'd helped bring about—was he intimately connected to, making him feel, on one hand, small and irrelevant and, on the other, hugely significant and, in that regard, utterly powerless.

Through the bay window he saw Caroline conversing on the kitchen phone, a simple sight, to him both wrenching and uplifting, bringing to his mind her unbidden, joyous smile, which he most looked to for reassurance of his love for her and of hers for him, a part of her absent now for three days that felt to Edmund like three years. Then he suddenly realized that exultant expression was appearing to him in his memory at the same moment as, magically, it seemed, he was seeing it again. "Wha . . . ?" he mouthed.

Caroline waved and pantomimed something back to him.

"I can't hear what you . . . ?" Edmund's words wouldn't carry. Afraid to give room to thoughts he barely dared hope for, he wasn't sure they were audible at all.

Caroline dropped the phone. Unintelligibly screaming, she ran onto the porch, then, realizing she couldn't exit the house that way, sprinted back through the kitchen, presumably down the corridor, and out the front door, across the lawn, directly into Edmund's arms, at once laughing and thankfully crying.